THE ROMANTIC MOVEMENT

'The novel relies for its vitality and humour on the wit and intelligence of a young author who breaks all the prudent rules, and manages to combine cynicism with cheerfulness . . . It brightens the fictional scene.' – FREDERICK RAPHAEL, *Daily Mail*

'In an age when pop stars look like Phil Collins, it is very good to have such an injection of wanton glamour into literature . . . extremely funny and sad, like all the best art.' – JULIE BURCHILL, *Spectator*

'De Botton is both trenchantly down-to-earth and sensitively intuitive. And he is funny . . . A talent to watch.' – KATHY O'SHAUGHNESSY, *European*

'The pleasure of de Botton's text lies in its meticulous execution; in the wit and stylish irony.' – MICHAEL WRIGHT, *The Times*

ALAIN DE BOTTON was born in Switzerland in 1969, educated at Cambridge and lives in London. He is also the author of *Essays in Love* and *Kiss & Tell*. His work is translated into fourteen languages.

Also by Alain de Botton

ESSAYS IN LOVE

KISS & TELL

THE
ROMANTIC
MOVEMENT

Sex, Shopping and the Novel

Alain de Botton

PICADOR

First published 1994 by Macmillan

This edition published 1995 by Picador
an imprint of Macmillan General Books
25 Eccleston Place, London SW1W 9NF
and Basingstoke

Associated companies throughout the world

ISBN 0 330 33589 8

1 3 5 7 9 8 6 4 2

A CIP catalogue record for this book is available from
the British Library.

Typeset by CentraCet Limited, Cambridge
Printed and bound in Great Britain by
Cox & Wyman Ltd, Reading, Berkshire

For Miel

INTRODUCTION

When people were asked to describe Alice, the word 'dreamer' was never far from their lips. Beneath a layer of civilization and its attendant scepticism, she revealed the wistful, unfocused gaze of a being whose thoughts were forever slipping into an alternative and far less concrete world. Her light green eyes were tinged with traces of melancholy that hinted of loss and inchoate yearning. Confusedly, a little ashamedly even, she could be found searching amidst the worldly clutter for something to imbue her platitudinous existence with meaning. And, perhaps because of the age in which she lived, this desire for self-transcendence [if one may speak so theologically] had come to identify itself with the idea of Love.

Though familiar with the farcical rounds of miscommunication lazily referred to as relationships, Alice had maintained a faith in a passion of inadmissible, almost vulgar, proportions. At the most incongruous moments, hesitating between brands in the aisles of a grocery store, casting an eye through the obituaries on the morning train or licking bitter-sweet stamps on to a set of household bills, she would catch her thoughts drifting childishly yet stubbornly towards a scenario of union with a redemptive Other.

Tired of her capacity for cynicism, tired of seeing only faults in herself and others, she wished to be overwhelmed by her feelings for a fellow human being. She wanted a situation where there would be no choice, no time to sigh and ask, 'But are he and I really that suited anyway?', where analysis and interpretation would be superfluous, where the other would simply be an unquestionable and wholly natural presence.

Shockingly incongruous in a romantic conception of love is the idea one might embark on a relationship not for the richness of another's eyes or the sophistication of their mind but simply to avoid contemplating a diary full of evenings alone. What could be more repellent than to suffer the limitations of others as a desperate alternative to gazing singly at our own? Yet after an exhausting and fruitless search, we may be forgiven [or at least understood] for our decision to share mortgages with a being whose qualities in no way exhaust our imagination, but who is nevertheless the finest specimen to have yet betrayed a sustained interest in us, and whose hunched back, curious politics or high-pitched laugh we find the energy to ignore, retaining a hope of upgrading if a better candidate should subsequently announce themselves.

It sickened Alice to think of love in these pragmatic terms, a question of making do with the misshapen character one had happened to bump into at the swimming baths, a cowardly accommodation with the flawed products of the social world in the name of baser biological and psychological imperatives. Though daily life required nuance, though transcendence was rarely included in the category of the adult, she knew she would never settle for less than the communion of souls so eloquently portrayed by poets and film-makers in the enchanted realm of the aesthetic.

There were other longings: for a sense that life would finally begin, for an end to self-consciousness and crippling reflexivity, for an emotional disposition which would not so regularly catapult her into black moods or periods of ravaging self-hatred. There were material desires too: for a face which would not require a darkened mirror and a sharp intake of breath to contemplate, for the kind of life read about in the pages of fashion monthlies, a radiant, sun-filled life with a glossy house and hand-made clothes, silk blouses from elegant boutiques and holidays by the shores of tropical seas.

To take D. H. Lawrence's definition, she was a Romantic in being 'homesick for somewhere else', another body, another country, another lover – the echo of the adolescent Rimbaud's celebrated '*la vie est ailleurs*'. But from where did this sickness, if one may call such longing for otherness a sickness, arise? She was no fool, she had dipped into the great books and theories, she had learnt that God was dead and Man [that other anachronism] was on his last legs as an embodiment of an answer to Life, she knew one was expected to call stories with happy endings and contented heroines trash fantasy not literature. Yet, perhaps because she retained an appetite for soap operas and songs whose soaring refrains sang of wanting to,

> Hold you, oh yeah, and love you baby,
> I said and love you baby,

she was still waiting [by the phone or otherwise] for salvation to make an appearance.

In a world whose physicality should not, she held, necessarily earn it the title of real, Alice handled clients' accounts in a large advertising agency off Soho Square. She had worked there since graduating from a provincial university a few years before, drifting into the job on the basis of a retrospectively naïve confusion between the pleasure of consuming products and the less gratifying task of engineering such consumption.

She shared a section of an open-plan office with a colleague from the finance department, working under the glare of fluorescent lights and the chill breeze of an air-conditioning unit. At the end of the work day, the Underground carried her back to a flat in Earl's Court which she shared with her friend Suzy. The two women had so far negotiated the hurdles of domesticity without argument, but Alice had recently been returning home with a certain apprehension. The flatmate, a cheerful and practical trainee nurse, had after an age of being single finally fallen in love. He was an eminently sensible boyfriend, a young doctor, intelligent in an unobtrusive way, wry and entertaining, with a taste for macabre anatomy stories.

In the unmentionable, perhaps even unconscious, female hierarchy of beauty, Alice had always considered herself prettier, not dramatically so, but nevertheless endowed with distinct natural advantages. She had in the past comforted Suzy that whatever their paucity, compatible men would in due course announce themselves, that large ankles were no problem and personality was what mattered, reassurance given with the patronizing subtext of someone whose attractions were more securely based and who had a tally of answer-phone messages to prove it.

But whatever the respective dimensions of ankles, it was Alice who now struggled to maintain a smile while Matt and Suzy called one another Babar and Mimi and punctuated their conversations with low, soft giggles whose origins she couldn't understand.

'I always said we'd stay close even if I found someone,' Suzy told her one night, squeezing her hand affectionately.

'You're my best friend in the whole wide world and I'll never forget that.'

Suzy therefore attempted a valiant redrawing of the romantic dyad, inviting her flatmate to restaurants, cinemas and walks by the river. But however heartfelt these proposals, Alice grew unable to accept Suzy's generosity. It was more than she could endure to demonstrate happiness for someone while inwardly destroyed by the absence of analogous feelings. She preferred to spend evenings at home, feigning interest in the fate of war-ravaged lands displayed on the nightly news bulletins, watched from the sofa in the living room, a plate of pale microwaved fish or chicken balanced awkwardly on her knees.

She no longer felt like seeing anyone, or rather, the absence of the One made others seem superfluous. She knew many who categorized themselves as friends, her address book was swollen because she asked people about themselves, took an interest in their lives, remembered their stories and therefore skilfully fulfilled their need for recognition. If the urge to resume contact eluded her, it was perhaps because these friends represented company without for that matter alleviating her own sense of being alone. Loneliness did not cease when she was at a table surrounded by animated faces, it could end only when the level of concern of another human being reached a point beyond the customary pedestrian appraisal. She would have agreed with Proust's conclusion [very un-Aristotelian] that friendship was only a form of cowardice, an escape from the greater responsibilities and challenges of love.

Self-pity rears its head when an objective eye is cast on oneself and a feeling of compassion descends for the person one sees, an attitude implying that: 'If this were someone I didn't know, I'd feel so sorry for them.' It is to be seduced by one's own plight, to grow saddened by one's own sadness. The derogatory associations embedded in the word suggest a historical bias towards over-estimating one's troubles, feeling sorry without good motive. Self-pitiers consider themselves tragic figures if jilted in the course of a banal love affair; they suffer from a mild inflammation of the throat and, wrapped in scarves and surrounded by medicines, shed nose-phlegm as though it were pneumonia.

By temperament, Alice had no time for this. In recent weeks, she nevertheless found herself struggling against an overwhelming desire to burst into tears. It would seize her in the most inopportune situations, in the course of lunches with colleagues or Friday afternoon sales meetings. She felt her eyes swelling and closed them to restrain the tears, but the pressure would force a trace of salty liquid down her cheek, collecting in a pear-shaped droplet at the side of her face.

'Are you all right, my dear?' a kindly looking pharmacist had asked as she returned the change for a prescription Alice had picked up during her lunch-break.

'Yes, of course. I'm fine,' she answered, shutting her purse, flustered at the thought of how visible her distress had grown.

'Take care of yourself, won't you,' the woman replied with a caressing smile as she made her way from the counter.

Alice could make no sense of the despair into which she had fallen. She had always held that happiness should be defined as an absence of pain rather than the presence of pleasure. So why, with a decent job, good health and a roof over her head, did she regularly and so childishly collapse into moist sobs?

She could only complain of feeling distressingly incidental to other human beings, somehow superfluous to the planet and the movements of its inhabitants.

What perhaps lay behind the tears was the sad suspicion that had she one day tripped and slipped off the edge of the globe, no one would have given her absence more than a minute's thought.

REALITY

One weekend at the beginning of March, Alice accepted an invitation to visit her older sister Jane, who lived with her husband on an estate in a run-down part of the inner city. Jane had trained as a lawyer and now ran a community centre for battered women, work she invariably hinted was of far greater value than the marketing of shampoos or household detergents.

The moral structure of the relationship cast Alice in the role of the frivolous, self-absorbed younger sister and Jane in that of the noble and valiant older one, someone who had heroically shrugged off the chance of a comfortable life in the name of helping the under-privileged.

Early on the Saturday afternoon, the two sisters took a walk in a park near the estate. A light rain had begun to fall and added a note of bleakness to the already marked desolation of the scene.

'You look well,' remarked Jane as they opened the gate.

'Do I?' answered Alice. 'Oh, I'm glad, I don't know if I necessarily feel it.'

'Why, what's up?'

'Oh, I don't know, nothing really,' she replied, wary at how her sister might react to the confused welter of her emotions.

'No, go on, I'm listening.'

'Oh, it's silly, it really is, I'm just not feeling very well at the moment.'

8

'Have you seen a doctor?'

'No, it's not that kind of thing.'

'So what is it?'

'It's only in my head as usual.'

'Go on.'

'I just feel sort of tired inside, not physically, but kind of emotionally. I'll look at other people and talk with them, and do lots of objectively interesting things and somehow nothing touches me properly.'

'How do you mean?'

'There seems to be a muffler between me and the world, like a sort of blanket that stops me feeling anything in the way I should. For instance, I was looking at these flowers in a shop the other day, some daffodils actually, and normally I love flowers, but this time I stared at them as if they were objects from outer space. Oh, I don't know what I'm saying. It's probably a really bad example, but nothing feels *real* if you know what I mean.'

There was a pause, then Jane replied: 'I wish things felt a bit *less* real around here. The council's been on my back about funding again. If we let them, the bastards would close the whole place down. It's crazy because we've so much work on at the moment. I've been dealing with a woman whose husband cut off four of her fingers with a saw. Then yesterday, social services brought round a Bangladeshi who speaks no English and whose husband died leaving her with three toddlers. And there's Susan, a thirteen-year-old whose dad's just been put away for molesting her.'

'How awful.'

'I envy you sometimes,' sighed Jane, 'I've had about as much reality as I can take this week.'

*

The history of thought shows there to be an overwhelming temptation to divide the world into two – into a real and a less real world.

Logically speaking, the battles raging over the subject are an absurdity. Everything which exists is for that matter real, but the argument retains interest as a site of ethical rather than epistemic struggle. What is considered real is also what is judged to be of value.

Faced with the disparate froth of the world's phenomena [babies being born, leaves falling off the trees, frogs laying eggs, volcanoes erupting, politicians lying], philosophers provide us with an endless, and of course incompatible, choice of real substances or ideas. For Thales, reality was to be found in water, the most primary and irreducible of elements. For Heraclitus, however, reality was to be found in fire. For Plato, it lay with the rational soul, for Augustine with God, for Hobbes with motion, for Hegel with the Progress of Spirit, for Schopenhauer with Will, for Madame Bovary with Love, for Marx with the struggle of the proletariat towards emancipation . . .

These thinkers naturally realized there to be other things at play in the world, they simply identified their idea as the structuring one, the mainspring to the complex mechanics of human history.

But is Madame Bovary not an anomaly in this list? Perhaps in her status as a philosopher, but her technique of dividing the world in two is most familiar. Like St Augustine before her, she chose to carve things up along the fault-line of Love, though it was now destined for Man, not God.

On the one hand, there was the world of glittering balls, cream-coloured writing paper and meaningful glances, and on the other, the ordinary, workaday existence of the dull

Philosopher	Dates	Ingredient of Reality
Thales	c.636–c.546 BC	Water
Heraclitus	c.535–c.475 BC	Fire
Plato	c.427–c.347 BC	Rational Soul
St Augustine	AD 354–430	Love of God
Hobbes	1588–1679	Motion
Hegel	1770–1831	Progress of Spirit
Schopenhauer	1788–1860	Will
Madame Bovary	1840s–1850s	Love of Man
Marx	1818–1883	Struggle of the Proletariat

Table of Reality

village people, the boredom of domestic life and a husband snoring bovinely in the bed beside her.

Alice was in implicit agreement with Bovary's judgement of the real. She too located the pinnacle of human possibility in the intimacy of two beings, ready to overlook the other triumphs of civilization [egg timers, sky scrapers, home pregnancy tests] to declare herself truly alive only in a state of love. It was a definition far removed from medical science, aliveness here depending not on oxygen circulation or brain activity but on the presence of someone she could share a bath with, curl herself around after making love and talk to using infantile, affectionate language.

It was hard to say when such a prejudice had taken hold. During her adolescence, she had grown aware of a yawning incompleteness which friends or family could not fill, and which gained only temporary reprieve via the mediation of motion pictures or song lyrics.

Since then, the mediocrity of the men she had allowed into her bedroom had done little to alter her values. Even when she heard her sister locate importance in a world where women lost fingers at the hands of mad husbands, she still could not bring herself to admit this was reality. It was certainly a grave problem to lose four fingers and, if one were to ignore the Greeks, a tragedy even. But she would have argued to the end that these fingers, however vital, should not have been considered constituents of the real.

Jane had predictable contempt for this. The issue didn't hang so much on the question of a miserable muffler between oneself and a vase of flowers, on being in love or out of it, but rather on being alive or dead, with a roof over one's head or homeless, battered or healthy. Because money decided such things, life was more real in the East End of London than in the West, a street was more real where gangs of gaunt, acned youths loitered in garage forecourts than where bespectacled men polished the chrome wheel arches of company cars.

Because they would be eating with Jane's husband that night, the two sisters stopped off at the supermarket on the way home. Jane pulled out a trolley and steered it forcefully through the crowd of Saturday shoppers.

'I thought I'd make a hot-pot and some mash,' she remarked. 'Is that all right with you?'

'I'm sorry?' replied Alice.

'Forget it. Listen, just wait here. I'm going to the deli counter for a sec.'

Alice had been distracted by the sight of a couple waiting for a bus on the other side of the large plate-glass window. He was tall and dressed in a thick woollen coat which he had opened up to wrap around his lover. Their breath steaming around them, they formed a cosy bundle against the chill wind gusting down the High Street. He bent down to kiss her neck, she affectionately ruffled his short black hair – and Alice gave out a quiet sigh at the reminder of how she too longed to have someone wrap her in his woollen coat and nibble her neck at arctic bus-stops.

That evening, after the hot-pot, mash and too many glasses of red wine, the dualistic debate over reality articulated itself more fully.

'I don't understand you, I just don't,' said Jane. 'What are you saving yourself for? The Messiah? There's always a problem, isn't there? He's either too intelligent or too stupid, too good looking or not good looking enough, too passionate or too wimpy. Why don't you learn to accept people, warts and all, and get on with what's important in life?'

'Nice to know what's important, my darling,' responded Jane's husband John, leaning back on his chair and lighting a cigarette.

'Come off it, John, you know what I'm saying. I mean, we like one another, we love one another too, but it's not the kind of love constipating Alice, this sort of thing with a capital L, violins and chocolate.'

'Two minutes and we're back to the old caricature. I don't know why I ever bother to share anything with someone who has to dig the knife in whenever she can.'

'That's right, the Othello of the family, stabbing poor innocent . . .'

'Don't get self-righteous.'

'Cool it, dear.'

'I'm cool enough, thanks. I'm simply fed up of how judgemental you seem to be of everything I do.'

'You *are* losing your cool.'

'Maybe I am.'

'Well, there's really no need,' said Jane, 'because I don't think I'm saying anything particularly offensive. I'm just making the very obvious point that, you know, making a relationship work might not be all you imagine it is. It's a tough business, changing nappies and making ends meet, working at it when you're both tired and irritable. There's no glamour in that. Dream on if you think it's like the screen kisses you see in Hollywood movies.'

ART AND LIFE

On the train back home the next day, Alice thought more about kissing: to be precise, she briefly entertained the question of what it meant for her sister and her husband John to kiss each other.

As far as she could tell, it wasn't something they did often. She had rarely seen them exchange signs of physical affection, even before the baby, even before the wedding. A few years back, when she and her sister had been leaving for a month's holiday in America, John had kissed Jane on the lips at the gates of the Heathrow immigration hall. But this was not the kiss of a lover wishing his beloved goodbye for a painfully long time, it resembled a man trying to kiss a woman the way he feels a man should kiss a woman when they are young and in love and she is going away for a month's of holiday with her sister in America. No wonder Jane spoke deprecatingly of Hollywood kisses, no wonder she thought the sort of kiss portrayed in art was fantasy when the kisses she had experienced in life appeared unconnected to the deeper current of emotions she may have felt.

Alice had always held that a good kiss could equal if not rival full love-making in the hands [or lips] of an able partner. She appreciated when a man took time and care with it, when he was challenged to explore the mouth's erotic, technically subtle possibilities. A good kisser needed the skill of a violinist or pianist, needed to know how to control and articulate every muscle of the mouth, needed to know the keyboard, rhythm and tempo, to know when to press hard and when to graze lightly and teasingly, when to open the mouth and when to apply distance. The good kisser had to control salival production and breathing rates, had to know how to sensually alter the positions of the head, to integrate the whole of the face into the kiss, to co-ordinate what was happening around the lips with the fingers' exploration of the ears and the nape of the neck, the temples and eyebrows.

How rare good kisses had been in her experience. The early ones had been perhaps predictably disastrous, either too wet or parched out of adolescent nervousness – but even later, she had found it rare for men to invest them-selves properly in the act. Much of the time, they were concerned with it only as a prelude to undressing her, a polite, obligatory ritual along a far broader and more ambitious design, and once they were together in bed, thought and effort would be unambiguously directed elsewhere.

Hence the reason why Jane's patronizing remark about Hollywood embraces had stuck in her mind. It implied a distinction between two kinds of kisses:

[i] *Real-life* ones, such as could be witnessed between her and John at the Heathrow immigration gate, and
[ii] *Fake, artistic* ones, ambitious sensual efforts known chiefly from Hollywood films, novels or paintings.

But reflecting on the matter in the train home, Alice concluded that if it came to a choice between the kisses Jane and John enjoyed and the ones seen on screen, then the latter somehow deserved to be recognized as the more truthful, more real, though far less practised, of the two.

Aesthetics would have interpreted the issue as part of the familiar debate between Art and Life. Depending on where one stood, either life-kisses were better than art-kisses or art-kisses better than life-kisses. And if, like Jane, one was on Plato's side on the matter, then Life undoubtedly had the upper hand.

Plato was convinced that art could by definition only struggle, and typically failed, to do justice to life. Artists were therefore superfluous in an ideal society because they simply imitated what already existed and hence really didn't need to be reproduced again, however pretty the Rodin or Klimt. What was the point of sketching a bed when there were real beds around? What was the point of filming a kiss when snogging was so commonplace?

Oscar Wilde would have begged to differ. In his legendary if now rather clichéd remark, it was not art that imitated life but life that imitated art. What did Wilde mean by such a puzzling aphorism? That art had the advantage on life, that the kinds of kisses one received from three-dimensional lovers were typically the poor relations of ones witnessed on screen. Wilde's Romantic aesthetic was a judgement on men like Tony, whom Alice had kissed at the Christmas office party, a man whose breath was heavy with onion soup and whose behaviour was akin to an enthusiastic dog greeting its master after a long absence.

Alice returned home from her sister's house shortly after six o'clock on Sunday evening. All the lights were out inside the flat and Suzy's door was open to reveal an unused bed. She walked into her room, set her bag down on the chair and curled up beneath the duvet, staring out through the open curtains at the back of the houses opposite. A woman with long orange gloves was scraping a dish in a kitchen, in the flat above a man was bent over a newspaper in front of a flickering television and above the roof and its medley of disused chimney pots and aerials a crescent of moon flashed intermittently from beneath a muddle of fast-moving clouds.

Alice was startled from her day-dreams by the phone ringing in the hallway, but the line was dead when she reached it. She stayed for a moment in the narrow corridor, leaning against the wall with one foot, her eyes fixed on the naked bulb by the door. She couldn't work out whether she was hungry or tired, wanted to see people or be alone, wanted to read or watch TV. She began walking slowly up the stairs, absorbed in scything a piece of dead skin from around the nail of her index finger. There was a note from Suzy in the kitchen, she wouldn't be back till Monday, there was some lasagne and salad in the fridge, had she had a good weekend?

The lasagne was showing its age, the salad had lost its looks a day or two back. Perhaps she should have some soup. She took out a tin opener from the drawer by the sink and a can from the larder behind the fridge. She heated it until it simmered, then poured the contents into a thick earthenware plate, the red showing up uneasily against the green floral glaze. There was a pile of weekend papers at the end of the table and she glanced through them while she ate.

How lonely to sit in a kitchen and eat a can of tomato soup, when there is no one watching you, no one to alleviate the awful trivial materiality of what is going on, no one to endow the process with any importance or meaning. Dinners for one and tepid soup: there was perhaps a clue here to why at a recent exhibition Alice had so enjoyed the work of pop artists, and what had particularly attracted her to the work of Andy Warhol. It was once more a case of art's ability to enhance life.

Warhol had taken the humble soup can and performed a miraculous operation whereby art not only Platonically imitated an object, but also Wildeanly enhanced it. There had long been something depressing about Campbell's cans, but how much less depressing when one could think that the cans had been seen by another, that some-one had taken care to raise them into objects of value, that they hung on museum walls and possessed iconic stature.

Dismissed for decades as topics for representation, accredited the disdain due to all 'ordinary objects', serious art critics had been forced to look more closely at cans and hamburgers, hairdryers and lipsticks, shower heads and light switches because artists now dealt with them. They had been made to stare beyond their vichyssoise at any number of previously demeaned objects, because it had been decided that these two should be included in the aesthetic realm, along with Madonnas, Venuses and Annunciations of Christ.

A frame around the ordinary prevented the customary neglect of shapes, colours and resonances, suggesting that:

> There is something special going on in here

If Cyril Connolly defined journalism as that which would be considered only once, literature as that which would be looked at again, then Campbell's cans were *journalistic* [mere disposable receptacles for carrying liquid] until Warhol's framing operation elevated them to the *literary* [something to hang on walls for repeated view].

Literary Soup

Could one not have drawn an analogy between what Warhol had done with paint and what a lover might do when he or she praised a long-ignored group of freckles on the beloved's nose or hand? Was it not structurally the same process when a lover whispered, 'Do you know that I've never seen anyone with such adorable wrists/moles/ eyelashes/toenails as you?' and when an artist pointed to the aesthetic qualities of a can of soup or Brillo box?

To marvel at such details was at one level laughable, as laughable as a can of soup on a wall, and yet if one learnt that such trivia stood to be admired because it formed part of a wider and more important whole, the love of a whole person for instance, then a justification might be found. Once a feature was seen as a *detail* of something larger, then it was redeemed from its status as simply trivial – that is, untethered to anything beyond itself.

Sitting alone eating dinner, Alice longed for a day when, because someone cared for her, she too might experience the sense that the small things about her were appreciated, that, without going to the moon or becoming President, elements of her unextraordinary life could take on a certain value, her loneliness could be alleviated by someone who would say, 'It's so sweet the way you . . .' and she could respond likewise. It would be a time when a Sunday evening spent reading the papers with a bowl of soup could avoid its lamentable sadness because there would be some-one [not Warhol perhaps, but someone] there to digest the experience with her.

'I'm such a bitch,' interrupted Alice as these ideas swilled around her head, 'I've got to snap out of this.'

She pushed aside the newspaper and carried the now empty soup plate over to the sink, rinsing it briefly under the cold tap.

'I must be a total narcissist or maybe just completely vain or insane.'

She concluded it must have been the apartment that was making her claustrophobic, and decided to go and see a film. She turned to the listings at the back of the newspaper and saw Jean-Luc Godard's *Breathless* advertised at the Renoir cinema. She rushed to her bedroom downstairs, slipped on another sweater and ran down to the street to find a taxi for Brunswick Square.

The cinema was packed with stylish couples, and as she bought herself a ticket she felt the self-conscious relic of an instinctive fear of visiting a cinema alone.

'What does it matter what other people think anyway?' she monologued, frustrated at the self-centredness implied in her paranoid concerns.

She bought a slice of carrot cake and chose a seat in the aisle of one of the middle rows. The hall went dark, and slowly she forgot herself, floating free of the awkward body which feared the looks of others. She was Jean Seberg standing with the *Herald Tribune* on the Champs-Elysées, she was Belmondo in the American Express office, she was driving down Saint-Germain at night, she was listening to Mozart's clarinet concerto knowing she would die.

When the credits came up, she felt separated from a world she had made her own. She was losing sight of characters and emotions of unusual vividness. She had cried, she had laughed, she had admired Jean Seberg and fancied Belmondo.

A bespectacled couple in black stood up in front of her, and noisily put on their raincoats.

'A good pastiche of Italian neo-realism,' murmured the man.

'Did you think so? More John Ford crossed with Sartre,' suggested the companion.

Alice stayed seated until the name of the distributor and the film stock appeared, somehow hoping thereby to delay the moment when she would have to make the painful transition from film back to life.

She no longer had enough money for a taxi, and so decided to walk to the bus stop at the top of Charing Cross Road. The streets were damp and dark, bathed in orange street light and a smell of greasy food. It prompted a very understandable longing for Paris.

She had spent a year in the French capital before university. It was the first time she had lived away from home, and the experience had infused her with the sort of romantic conception of the city common amongst those not obliged to live there. She had felt spontaneous and confident, had developed a large circle of friends and been chased by admirers who sent bouquets of flowers and delivered lyrical declarations.

She had worked in Montparnasse as an assistant in a travel agency, and because she had been given two afternoons off a week, had managed to equip herself with a thorough knowledge of modern French cinema. Paris had thereby become associated with cinema, as much for the films she had seen there as for the number that had been shot on its streets and boulevards.

Walking down the Tottenham Court Road, she felt a sudden hatred of London for being such an unfilmed city. If she preferred Paris to London, it was because she was approaching the British capital not simply through her everyday experience [after all, one is liable to be equally miserable in the two cities], but through the eyes of the film makers and painters who had been there before her. When she looked at Parisian streets, she saw not only bricks and mortar, she saw bricks and mortar as seen by Manet and Degas, Toulouse-Lautrec and Pissaro, Truffaut and Godard.

The streets of Paris had thereby acquired an *aesthetic*, in a way that those of London had not, an aesthetic defined as the aura attaching itself to the raw material of artistic production. The only aesthetic she could find for London were resonances from murky BBC adaptations of Dickens, or postcard panoramas from early James Bond films [Whistler and Monet had clearly not stuck in her mind].

London had not had enough eyes placed on it and hence could not glow like cities stroked by the brushes, pens and cameras of artists. It lacked the aura of Rome, New York or Prague, the beauty arising out of seeing something someone else has seen before, enabling one to filter one's perceptions through those of another. Alice imagined the great film makers breaking the loneliness of modern metropolises, creating a common image which could unite the scattered perceptions of their terrifyingly amorphous and anonymous populations.

She reached the stop opposite Foyles in time to catch her bus and sat down on a banquette near the ticket collector.

'Nippy night, isn't it?' he remarked conversationally.

'It is, yes,' replied Alice curtly.

Though a few minutes before, she had been thinking of how film makers broke the loneliness of the city, the chance of a chat with a ticket collector now seemed appalling. She was not being socially snobbish, she was being aesthetically snobbish. She was happy to accept bus conductors in films, but was shocked by their raw literalness when they interrupted her day-dreams on the way home.

Her reaction expressed a confused resentment at her own lack of aesthetic. Jean Seberg had played a most ordinary American girl in Paris, yet whereas everything about Seberg's life seemed poetic, everything about Alice's now struck her as banal. She was banal, her friends were banal, her parents, her job, her flat, her city, bus and ticket-collector. What did she mean by this word? That nothing in her life was tethered to anything of value, to a greater cause or story.

Perhaps in another age, God had solved such matters. His would have been the eye in heaven, the sordidness of the world would have been alleviated by the sense that He was watching, and that the banal was hence connected to the illustrious history of good and evil. Though believers were in the Earthly City, their actions nevertheless had relevance to what would happen in the Heavenly. God saw everything, even a journey across London on a rainy, foggy night could be rendered bearable by its witness.

But Alice had never believed, and for her it was art and love that were being asked to shoulder some of the same functions. Much as film allowed her to escape a sense of isolation through the thought that 'I'm not the only one to have experienced this emotion, seen this street, sat in this café . . .' love held out the hope of a being to whom she could whisper, 'You too feel this? How wonderful. It's exactly what I thought when . . .' – the contents of one soul finding tender analogy with those of another.

STORY ENVY

If she woke up early on weekends, Alice was in the habit of driving her VW to a nearby bakery to pick up fresh bread. The following Saturday, she had trouble sleeping much past eight o'clock and so decided to surprise Suzy and Matt by preparing breakfast.

She parked on the High Street, picked up some still warm croissants, then dropped off a pile of dry cleaning in a shop a few yards away. When she returned to her car, she noticed an envelope placed under one of the windscreen wipers. Relieved to see it was not another parking ticket, she slipped it into her shopping bag and loaded the car.

She returned home to find the two lovers still asleep, and so made herself a cup of coffee while listening to a current affairs programme on the radio. A minute later, recalling the envelope, she fetched her bag and opened the following letter:

Dear Stranger,

Forgive these words, but for weeks now I have had an uncontrollable urge to write to you. I see you coming in to buy bread and am made speechless. I find your smile irresistible, I ask myself when I will ever find the courage to speak to you. I know nothing about you, apart from the fact that you have a nice red car and a lovely smile. You mustn't think I'm simply a shop assistant. In fact, I'm a great lover of music, a composer. If you want, I could cook you some dinner one night, though it would be microwaved (probably) and vegetarian (definitely). I hope to see you again soon – even if only as a customer. Your visits and your smile make the mornings seem worthwhile (honestly, the rhyme was accidental).

Oh, Christ! thought Alice, summing up an impression of the shop assistant in question, a young man whose face was cruelly ravaged by acne and who had come to her attention chiefly on account of somewhat furtive and anxious behaviour.

'Who's the lucky girl with mail this morning?'

'Hi, Suzy. How are you?'

'I'm fine, sweetie. And you?' replied Suzy, giving Alice a kiss on the cheek.

'I just got this really odd letter.'

'Odd letter?' exclaimed Matt, emerging theatrically bleary-eyed from the bedroom. 'Wouldn't touch one of those at this hour. Would you, Suzy?'

'Well, go on. Tell us who it's from.'

'Ah! She brought croissants,' said Matt, brightening at the sight of the bag of goodies. 'Alice, you're fantastic. Look at this, one for each of us. Oh, and jam too.'

'Shush, Matt,' said Suzy, 'I want to hear about this letter.'

'I wish there was something exciting to say,' replied Alice. 'It's just a sort of love letter . . .'

'Just a sort of love letter! Never known anyone to be so blasé about one of those,' said Matt.

'. . . from this guy at the bakery.'

'Guy at the bakery?' puzzled Suzy.

'Yeah, this young man who sells bread, he's written me a love letter. He says he likes my smile and wants to cook me a vegetarian meal at home sometime.'

'Oh, well, that could be nice,' said Suzy, used to looking on the bright side of every situation.

'Don't fancy vegetarian myself,' reflected Matt. 'I was quite keen on those nut cutlets for a while, but you've got to keep a balanced diet. Still, a vegetarian baker with a fondness for your smile – sounds fishy to me.'

'He's a jerk anyway,' said Alice. 'I mean, what a nerve to write a letter like that.'

'Oh, don't say that,' piped Suzy, 'baking is a really interesting job. I once knew a baker. He had a wonderful way with rolls.'

'Way with rolls?' queried Matt.

'Well anyway, I'm not interested, so that's that and let's eat,' said Alice. 'I'm throwing this letter in the bin.'

Given sufficient optimism or imagination, one could of course have hoped for a very different outcome to such a missive, a story even, at least of the airport novel variety. A young baker falls in love with a slightly older and more sophisticated woman. The road to happiness is littered with conflicts, there are class and age lines to cross, the woman's friends and milieu object to the baker, her father tries to shoot him, the baker's mother is Oedipally threatened and refuses to iron her son's shirt for a vital dinner date in a West End restaurant, he is a vegetarian, she loves steak tartare, he listens to bizarre Indian string instruments, she prefers Mozart. And yet the strengh of their passion [opportunity for furious, flour-covered love-making] overcomes the obstacles and triumphs in a joyful resolution somewhere around page 350.

Instead, the letter found itself in the bottom of a kitchen bin and the story ended its possibilities there [though Suzy continued to suggest that the most disparate people sometimes got along, supporting her argument by explaining that she hadn't liked Matt when they had first met on the wards of University College Hospital, Matt undermining this thesis by relating how she had been flustered enough to blush and collide with a swing door].

Alice knew only dissonance in her stories. A common issue of desire was always at stake, there was simply a conflict as to who wanted to give what to whom.

In January, Tony, the man responsible for the Christmas party kiss, had proposed dinner and a weekend in Torquay. Alice appreciated the compliment and liked his company, but honesty called for a just-good-friends speech to prevent developments. She had at the same time acquired a crushlet on a man responsible for fixing her department's photocopier and printer. It led to frequent calls down to maintenance on the pretext that one of the machines had a problem with its toner cartridge. But a few weeks into this narrative, the handsome mechanic Simon casually announced that his friend Tom and he would be going out to dinner to celebrate their second anniversary that night – and maintenance promptly never heard of toner problems from the third floor again.

No wonder Alice admired the great love stories, with their enviable sense of necessity and inevitability. Her attraction was not naïvely based on the assumption that stories were happy, but rather that they had sense to them. Every scene was there to make a point, even a boring scene was there to say something about boredom. Aristotle defined the difference between horror and tragedy as plot. With a master narrative, however grim things might appear, one could at least be certain that they were not just a tale told by an idiot, full of sound and fury signifying nothing.

The heroines of romantic fiction were presented with jealous husbands, dark lovers, difficult locations and obstacles tough enough to make life interesting without rendering it hopeless. The gun mentioned in the first act would, at whatever cost, duly go off in the fourth.

As Alice prepared to drift through yet another month of her middle twenties, a distinction could be made between two sorts of time:

🕐 **Meaningful Time:** such as stories were full of, time that revealed character and was sequentially linked by words like *thereby*, *in order that* and *because of*.

🕐 **Clock Time:** Simply the movement of the hands across a dial, a chronological development devoid of a story's reassuringly tight classical structure, built out of the impregnable model of:

$$\text{Need/desire} \rightarrow \text{Conflict} \rightarrow \text{Resolution}$$

Alice's needs and desires amounted at best to a formless, rambling epic, where things happened for apparently no reason, desires never led to conflicts, conflicts happened without desires, resolutions were but temporary plasters on unstable wounds and the whole thing lasted for years without so much as the respite of an advertising break.

In her personal history, the knots had rarely been granted freedom of expression. She had loved her father but had never had a proper relationship with him, busy as he had been running an international chain of department stores while lacking any rapport with children. Her mother was thought of as sophisticated and charming in the social circles in which she moved, but Alice had known her only as a spoilt, childish and [had she not been so vindictive] slightly pitiable character. Her parents' obsession with their own lives had conferred on Alice the sense that her problems did not warrant display. History had forced her into the camp of the nail-biters rather than the screamers, her life an inner not an outer drama.

It was perhaps no coincidence that she had always been fascinated by the story of Ariadne's thread. The ancient Greek myth recounted the arrival of Theseus in Crete, where he was to be imprisoned and meet his end in the labyrinth-shaped palace of the fierce Minotaur. But before being put away, Theseus was glimpsed by the hot-blooded Ariadne, one of the daughters of King Minos, who fell in love with the handsome youth and resolved to rescue him from his cruel fate. Risking her own safety, she slipped the young man a ball of string which he might use to trace his way back out of the labyrinth. Love being tightly linked to gratitude, when Theseus managed to kill the beast and escape the maze, he reciprocated the princess's feelings and fled Crete with beloved Ariadne in tow.

Alice was touched by what she took to be the symbolism of the story; the need for a thread with which to trace our journey, and the connection between this thread and love: that it was the lover's gift that would offer a chance of orientation.

What she had no doubt forgotten – her knowledge of Greek mythology was not precise – was the story's rather crueller ending, which in its different versions included such unhappy outcomes as Theseus abandoning Ariadne soon after they left Crete, the two lovers being separated by accident, and Ariadne being taken away to the land of the Gods by a jealous Dionysos.

CYNICISM

The following week, Suzy invited her friend Joanna for dinner. Joanna was a tall beautician who took pride in painting her long nails mauve, battling hypocrisy and being frank with people, the last of which typically involved finishing a conversation by offending someone, then defending herself with the question, 'Well, if I'm not going to tell them, then who the hell will?'

The three women were seated around the kitchen table drinking wine and eating salad.

'So tell me, how's your love life?' Joanna turned to Alice and asked.

'Oh, fine.'

'I love this girl, she's always so polite! "Oh, fine," she says. It's like I was asking about the weather.'

'Sorry, what should I be saying?'

'I don't know, tell me who you're grinding with, tell me about who's making it happen for you, that sort of thing. Are you still together with that, that what's his name . . .?'

'Tony. No, that finished a while back, didn't it?' intercepted Suzy, anxious at the tone of the conversation.

'Hey! The girl's got her own mouth, let her talk,' protested Joanna.

'Yes, well it did end, she's right. You know, we weren't suited and so, yes, I decided it would be best if . . .'

'You know what they say, all's fair in love and war,' reflected Joanna and paused as if something profound had been said. There was a silence while she lit a cigarette, inhaled deeply, then remarked. 'You know what? I'm going to give you a real treat. I'm going to set you up with someone special. I know this guy, this friend of my brother. You'd love him. He does weight-training, he's a computer engineer, very sexy and charming. I think he could solve all your problems.'

'Very funny,' replied Alice.

'Funny? I thought you'd jump at the chance.'

'Oh, sure.'

'Well, why not?'

'Because I'm fine on my own.'

'You may be fine, I'm just saying you'd probably be a lot finer with this guy between your sheets.'

'That's not for you to judge.'

'Well, I'm sorry. I just thought you had a little vacancy in the bedroom department.'

'It doesn't bother me. I mean, if I'm with someone, then that's nice, and if I'm not, then that can also be nice.'

'So who's the one going around like it's about to be the end of the world?'

'I don't know.'

'Listen, baby, believe me, your life may be nice and all that, but everyone needs a change of scene sometimes. Are you keener on the smooth or the furry?'

'I beg your pardon?'

'Do you like chests smooth or with hair on?'

'I don't know, I don't care. It depends what the person's like.'

'So sensible! Listen, let me give him your phone number, then you two can make up your minds, feel the vibrations and see. All right?'

'Not all right.'

'Why not?'

'Because, quite frankly, Joanna, I don't *need* anyone.'

'OK, don't get excited. Christ, people can be so sensitive!'

'And maybe you could get just a little less insensitive.'

'I was just saying that I knew this guy who seemed sort of interesting and given the fact that you don't . . .'

'What's wrong, Alice? Sweetie, what's the matter?' asked Suzy who noticed Alice's eyes swelling with tears.

'Nothing, I'm sorry,' she answered, rising suddenly from the table. 'I think I must be tired. I need to lie down for a while.'

Her departure induced a tense silence. Suzy stared at Alice's half-finished plate, her napkin thrown hastily aside.

'Hey, don't blame me,' preempted Joanna. 'I was just suggesting. She's moping around clearly unhappy and I thought she had to get out and meet someone. I tell you, this friend of mine, he's great. And anyway, if I'm not going to tell her, then who the hell will?'

Whatever the merits of so-called honesty [separated from rudeness by only the finest of lines], Joanna had a point. Though Alice longed for love, she had with time grown ever more reluctant to admit the fact to herself and others. Whereas her single state had previously been a matter for jokes and light teasing, its longevity had gradually endowed it with unmentionable gravity.

The romantic problem was driven underground, but its repercussions were felt elsewhere. Having in the past been of optimistic temperament, Alice's friends now found her arguing for a decline in every sphere of life: her predictions for the global economy and output, for the future of male/female relationships and the family, for civilized values and educational standards, for the cleanliness of cities and the price of shoes, for the weather and the destruction of wildlife all took on the most morbid colours. She would deliver profound judgements along the lines that 'Life's meaningless anyway. Men and women will never understand each other. The whole thing's a sick joke from beginning to end.'

It was surprising how simple a transition could be from the thought: 'I'm unhappy', to the rather larger thought: 'Existence on earth is a futile exercise'; how the vulgarity of the complaint 'No one loves me' might find itself sublimated into the elegant aphorism 'Love is an illusion'. The interest lay not so much in whether existence and love were or were not futile [how could any individual possibly claim to know?], but in the way that the catalytic element could be disguised, leaving nothing but a most general, unself-referential maxim.

Illustrious examples of the phenomenon abound. Take the case of the philosopher Arthur Schopenhauer, who had a legendary hatred for his mother and a most gloomy, Hamletian disposition. When he was seventeen, his father died and his mother uprooted her family from their native Hamburg to Weimar. There she turned into a happy widow, leading a highly social life, throwing parties, having affairs, buying expensive dresses and spending money in the way people who don't make it will. She became a snob for everything cultural and began a salon which Goethe was said to have visited. She even successfully published novels, and developed a literary reputation which far outstripped that of her son [his major book, *The World as Will and Idea*, was turned down by three publishers and earned him nothing]. Now anyone can be unlucky with their mother, but it takes a particular kind of mind to universalize from this experience and start integrating into their philosophy of life ideas that women are 'childish, silly and short-sighted, in a word big children, their whole lives long', or that 'only a male intellect clouded by the sexual drive could call the stunted, narrow shouldered, broad-hipped and short-legged sex the fair sex', or that 'neither for music, nor poetry, nor the plastic arts do they possess any real feeling or receptivity'.

The interest lies in the way that in all the thousands of pages he wrote Schopenhauer avoided talking of the one thing that really bothered him, the one woman who bothered him, as opposed to the women who he insulted as a race, namely the mother who threw parties and squandered money in the way people who don't make it will.

Or take the unfortunate duc de La Rochefoucauld – the author of pessimistic maxims on life declaring that however bad things might look, they were in truth a whole lot worse. But the maxims shed some of their universal authority when one looks at the life of a man who experienced an almost unbroken succession of disasters; who took the politically reckless decision to side at court with the faction of Anne of Austria because he was in love with her maid of honour, who paid a price for it by being banished for two years by Richelieu, who later received no thanks for his loyalty from Mazarin and Anne when she became regent, a man who was on the wrong side in every battle of the Fronde, whose castle was razed to the ground, who was blinded for a time by an explosion, who never fulfilled his hopes for a brilliant military or political career, and whose quest for love remained for the most part unrequited.

*

Several weeks after Joanna's visit, a large stiff envelope dropped through the front door.

'It's for you. Open it,' said Suzy, sliding it over the breakfast table towards Alice.

'I told you, I only get bills. I'll read it tonight.'

But it was no bill, it was an invitation sent by a woman Alice had known at school years before but had not heard from since.

'What is it?' asked Suzy.

'Oh nothing, I can't go.'

'Let's have a look. God, it sounds great. Dinner, dancing. Brilliant.'

'Is it?'

'Of course it is. What are you going to wear?'

'Grow up, Suzy.'

'It's an important question.'

'I'm not going. I've got a lot of work on at the moment. Moreover, I don't have anything to say to anyone. I can't understand why people socialize. I mean, they go out for dinner, and it's all just some ridiculous hollow ritual. One person asks, "So how are you?" then the other one burbles on for ten minutes and you have to sit there and politely listen – then you get asked, "And how are you?" and you can then burble on for a while. And then that's it.'

'It's not always like that, sometimes you can have good conversations.'

'Yeah, normally with some angel who wants to get you into bed and will never call you again.'

Because experience had taught Alice she only ever enjoyed things she wasn't looking forward to, she struggled to look forward to nothing. It was the notorious connection between thinking pessimistically and thereby hoping to avoid the failure one had envisaged. If she thought the worst, then the worst would not happen. The price she had to pay for anything that went right was a constant and tiring obsession with everything that might go wrong.

Therefore, when she came into Suzy's room on the night of the party and complained her dress made a dustbin bag look aesthetic and she would be back in time to catch the ten o'clock news, this was not meant as an evaluation of either her dress or time of return. She merely thought that if she first called her dress a dustbin bag and then the evening short lived, they might somehow turn out to be neither.

PARTIES

The party was held in a converted warehouse set on the Thames in Rotherhithe, decorated in a blend of industrial and baroque furnishings. The equivalent of the great balls of the past, the evening's exclusivity was based not primarily on money or class but the intimidation of style. Large chandeliers hung down from ceilings painted with reproductions of Italian masterpieces, above the dance floor was painted a section of the Sistine chapel bathed in a rotating medley of colours. Velvet drapes lined the walls of the dining-room, small dimly lit alcoves ran along a ceiling gallery where guests drank out of blue fluted glasses and recognized each other with exaggeratedly affectionate gestures.

Alice left her coat in the lobby and walked up the large exposed staircase, folding and refolding her ticket. She found her assigned table and saw that her fellow guests [none of whom she knew] had yet to arrive, so she stood behind her chair, admiring a huge bouquet of bright plastic flowers set in the centre of the table.

'Now you're thinking, "Shit, I should have stayed home, I know no one, I'm looking awful, how will I ever get through this, etc."? Right?' asked a man standing at the far end of the table.

'Actually, I was just wondering why we'd be needing three sets of knives and forks,' replied Alice curtly.

'Ah, I'm sorry. I guessed wrong. Perhaps I'm the one

thinking, "Shit, I should have stayed home, I'm looking awful, and how am I ever going to get through this"?'

'Is that what you're thinking?'

'I don't know actually. I was a minute ago, but you can never tell how things will turn out. I wonder, do you think I should have worn a shirt and tie?' asked the man, dressed in a charcoal-grey polo neck beneath a dark suit.

'I don't know.'

'Yeah well, I never know what to wear to these things. Do you ever get that? Not knowing what to wear, or rather having something you want to wear but not knowing if anyone else will be wearing that kind of thing, so you end up putting on what you think others are going to wear and getting it wrong while still not wearing what you want?'

'I suppose it's happened to me a few times,' answered Alice, a faint smile involuntarily appearing on her face.

'While there's time, why don't I swap the seating plan and come and sit next to you? I don't think anyone will notice, do you?' asked the man with a mischievous but endearing expression.

'Why would you want to do that?' asked Alice.

'Because I'm sitting next to Melanie on one side and Jennifer on the other and I think I hate them both already.'

'That's rather closed-minded of you. Maybe you'd find they were really nice.'

'I don't know, I have some bad associations with those names. I had an arthritic and insane great aunt called Melanie and my dentist is a Jennifer and does her best to make my life miserable.'

'And what if I enjoyed sitting next to Robert on one side and Jeff on the other?'

'Surely it's better the devil you know,' replied the man devilishly and started rearranging the cards, so that in an instant, Alice found her dinner-guest destiny altered and a man called Eric [for that was the name on the new card] beside her.

Gradually the other guests arrived, seated themselves unknowingly in their new locations, and the meal began. There seemed to be an energy and impatience to Eric which put Alice in the defensive role, answering rather than asking, responding rather than initiating. She felt herself attacked by the rapid succession of his questions: What was her job? How old was she? Where did she live? Had she ever been in love?

'I beg your pardon?'

'I asked if you'd ever been in love.'

'Why would I tell you that?'

'Ah! You'd prefer to go back to the weather. I'm so sorry. I wonder when we'll next get groundfrost. I hear in Scotland there's black ice on roads and fog in mountain valleys. Oh, and a chance of light snow on higher ground.'

'Am I boring you?'

'Not at all.'

'So, what makes you think I even believe in love?'

'I have the honour of a cynic beside me.'

'Just a realist.'

'And I'd always thought every woman's goal was to find the man of her life.'

'What chauvinist rubbish. Some do, but not every one. It's not my goal at all. I'm just interested in independence. I want to learn how to spend time not seeing anyone and be unaffected by it. Not that I have a problem now. I'm quite good on my own, actually. I know people who can't be alone at all. Take my flatmate Suzy. She'd rather be with anyone but herself, she'd go out with the first bloke she met simply not to have to spend an evening alone. I mean, she's nice and her boyfriend is all right too, it's just I wouldn't want to end up like her, in some cosy little situation where she's not really facing up to things.'

'You've got a beautiful necklace,' interrupted Eric, and reached over to touch it lightly between thumb and index finger.

'It belonged to my grandmother,' replied Alice, her voice faltering slightly.

'It's so rare to find a necklace as elegant as this.'

'Thank you.'

Alice was instinctively suspicious of men like Eric, he had a brusque charm which put her on her guard, it seemed he might be treating the whole evening as a joke. But though she doubted his sincerity, she didn't doubt his attraction. There was an engaging sexuality about his simplest movements, in the way his fingers crushed open a roll of crusty bread or the skilful rapidity with which he piled vegetables on to his fork.

Eric worked as a banker dealing with commodities and futures, but recounted a less than typical career. Initially he had trained as a doctor and had worked in Kenya delivering babies before leaving medicine for more commercial pursuits. He had started a successful record label with a friend, had then been involved in a chain of clothes shops and had only recently moved to banking.

'The thing about commodities is that the sums involved are enormous,' explained Eric. 'They're so enormous, you forget it's real money you're dealing with, it's sort of all very intangible. That's what I liked about clothes shops. In banking, you can make or lose ten million in a few seconds and hardly notice it, but in a shop, you'll get some crazy customer coming in to scream at you for half an hour because their miserable ten pound T-shirt has shrunk in the wash. It sort of puts things into perspective. Are you listening?'

'Yes, yes, of course I am,' replied Alice, realizing she'd been staring at him without absorbing a thing he'd said.

'You're blushing,' said Eric.

'No, I'm not.'

'You are.'

'Really? It's kind of hot in here.'

The dessert came, a chocolate cake arranged in the centre of the plate with a raspberry coulis surrounding it.

'How come you've got about ten strawberries, and I haven't got any?' asked Eric, looking at Alice's cake. 'Can I take one?' he asked, but had it on his fork before she had a chance to answer.

He had a way of charming which seemed to absolve him of risk. He played according to the Latin model of seduction, in which he was open with his desire, making rejection at once more possible but less shameful – this flamboyance in contrast to the approach of pale-faced Northern seducers [Werther *et al*] who would spend lifetimes clumsily and abstractly whispering their love and silently commit suicide if the point was missed.

But if Eric was so ready to admit his intentions, it made sense to acknowledge their effect.

'OK, I know what you're thinking,' he preempted. 'You're having a good time, you're laughing, but what's bothering you is you don't know whether or not you can trust me. You're thinking, "Is this guy genuine or is he some kind of a creep? Is this all just a joke or is there something serious behind it?" You don't quite know how to act. If it's all a joke, then you want nothing to do with it, but one side of you thinks it might not be, and hence you should stick around. It's the permanent female problem, whether or not to trust a man when he's seducing. You may like a man without trusting him, but one thing you want to avoid is getting hurt again.'

We shouldn't think Alice excessively vain, but there was something enticing about a man who told her how she felt and got it more or less right. It would have taken more cynicism than she could muster to ignore someone who looked her straight in the eye and declared that though he hadn't known her for long, he knew she was a woman of unusual sensitivity.

'You're probably incredibly suspicious of people like me,' said Eric.

'Why?'

'Because you're someone who's suffered.'

'Not more than most.'

'You have. It's just you make light of your problems, probably because no one has ever allowed you to take them seriously. You feel a lot of things others don't, you feel things deeply, and that's why you've been forced to develop a protective shell. A lot of your energy is taken up with that, you can see the tension in the way you hold your shoulders.'

'What's wrong with my shoulders?'

'Nothing, it's just that your posture says a lot about you. Has no one ever remarked on that?'

'No.'

'Well, people aren't very observant, are they?'

The enduring appeal of horoscopes and personal prophecies betrays how our desire to be understood typically overrides doubts as to how accurately such understanding can have been reached. Eric knew how quickly one could engender trust on the simple basis of telling people one understood them. So keen were others to believe they were in fact knowable, they would be inclined to melt at the first authoritative account of themselves, be it from a well-shaped mouth or paragraph on Gemini.

'It's so noisy here. Let's forget about dancing,' said Eric. 'Shall we go off and have a drink somewhere quieter?'

'Those places would have all shut by now.'

'Perhaps we could go back and have a chat at my place?'

'What?'

'I said maybe we could go back to my place.'

'I'm not sure actually,' replied Alice, who very much wanted to accept but didn't want to seem like one of those women who agreed to such offers.

'There's a problem with my key,' she declared. 'We've got a funny lock that needs to be opened in the right way. I told my flatmate that if she came back first, then she should put the second lock on, but that if I came back first, then I should leave the light on in the hallway, rather than first put the lock on the door, and then ring. Well anyway, what I'm trying to say is that I think it's a bit difficult.'

The issue of how to cede to seduction is tortuous: too soon and one may appear unworthy, too slow and one may lose the interest of the partner. Should Alice have accepted the offer of a chat at Eric's place at the cost of implying a dangerous lack of self-respect, or politely have said good-night at the risk of never seeing him again?

Prudery and laxity may share a common anxiety. A person could agree to make love at once for fear that delay would irrevocably lose the partner's interest, or they could never make love for fear the fact would lead to instant abandonment.

By nature, Alice was inclined to react according to the first fear, intolerant of romantic inflation, the process by which the seduced flirtatiously gamble on continued demand in the face of curtailed supply.

Though governments profess to hate it, and many lovers too, for a correctly functioning amorous economy it may sometimes be useful to have inflation, it may help [perversely no doubt] to have one lover say, 'No, look I'm sorry, I have a headache/boyfriend/girlfriend/indigestion and therefore let's call it a night,' and the other pining that the course of true love never did run smooth. It may benefit the situation if one person is left feeling, 'I'm insufficient, the other's price is too high.' It is then the seducer takes to buying chocolate truffles, sighing deeply and writing poetry to the effect that 'Had we but world enough, and time, this coyness, lady, were no crime . . .'

'Look, I completely understand,' answered Eric, 'I don't want to put any pressure on you. It was just an idea. I thought it might be nice to talk in quieter surroundings, but what the hell. I mean it's late, and you don't know me well. I respect you for your decision. I hope we'll be able to meet some time, perhaps go and see the Italian film you were telling me about.'

'Sure, that would be nice.'

Alice left the party shortly after one in the morning, and because her flat was in his direction, Eric offered to save her a taxi by driving her home.

But by the time they reached the area where he lived, it suddenly occurred to Alice that if he really understood how difficult it was for her to agree to his offer and if he had so politely respected her decision to decline it, then there was really no reason why she couldn't safely change her mind and let him know that a metaphoric chat might after all be just the thing to round off the evening.

VIRGIN BIRTHS

Eric turned out to be a most skilled lover, gentle, consider-
ate and full of imagination. He knew how to put Alice at
ease, and at the same time release her desire in unexpected
ways. Their love-making alternated between a tender play-
fulness and stretches of uninhibited intensity. Questions
which had plagued her up to the first kiss were now laid to
one side and made room for unreflective delight.

To go to bed with another is in some way to collide with
the memories and habits of all those they have ever slept
with. Our way of making love embodies the mnemonic of
our sexual history, a kiss is an enriched model of past
kisses, our behaviour in the bedroom filled with traces of
past bedrooms in which we have slept.

While Alice and Eric made love, there was a meeting of
two sexual histories at play. Eric had picked up from
Christina the way he was now licking Alice's ears, from
Robert, Alice had learnt a way of dancing the tongue
delicately around the lips, Rebecca had taught Eric how
to caress the other's teeth with his tongue, reaching deep
into the mouth to run along their unexposed side. Hans
had been an enthusiastic professor of nose-kissing, but
it seemed from Alice's tentative lick that this wouldn't
be to Eric's taste. She had been enraptured by the way
Chris had puckered her neck, and, by the odd process by
which one performs on the other what one in fact enjoys

oneself, Alice was now busily performing the action on Eric.

Though a sexual history may have been desirable from a purely mechanical point of view, it revealed a pyschological complexity. To have a sexual history did not only imply one had made love to a succession of people, it also suggested one had either rejected or been rejected by these same bedroom companions. A more melancholy way of looking at the history of sexual technique was to read it as a history of disappointment.

There was hence a curious tension in the proceedings: on the one hand, the lovers appeared to be reinventing the world through their passion; on the other, their gestures carried evidence of a past from which they had had to keep travelling.

The energy of Alice's love making symbolized a revolt against such history, she wanted to forget other kisses and nights which had begun like this, energetic and intense, before ending in recriminations, he declaring he couldn't commit, she disgusted by the look of his vacant face behind the morning paper.

How great the longing seems to be that 'there should have been nothing or no one before I arrived here,' a relic of the [virgin] Berkeleyan fantasy that 'perhaps I invented a world, perhaps the world was born along with me, and I am its creator'. Nietzsche famously complained that the most common oversight of philosophers was to ignore the historical dimension of subjects, and even outside the academy, there are countless cruel examples of revolutionaries who have wished to start the world at the year zero. A deep ambivalence seems to reside in the approach to history – on the one hand, a desire to preserve everything [encyclopedism], on the other, the desire to start everything anew [revolution].

It was not difficult to guess at which extreme Alice fell in her attitudes to love. Though she had often been disappointed, she maintained an idealism which was the antithesis of the historical approach: a romantic revolutionary, she wished to believe that the man she slept with might somehow prove to be the end of her sexual history, might prove to be the answer of her lifetime.

They collapsed exhausted on the bed, and after fetching a drink from the kitchen, Eric curled up under the duvet beside her, mumbled what sounded like a grateful, 'Thank you,' and rapidly slipped into the world of dreams.

Alice always had difficulty cutting the anchor of consciousness in such circumstances, in a strange room, on a different bed with a foreign body breathing beside her. She played and replayed the evening in her mind, trying to understand how she had ended up here, how she had seemed both in control and yet curiously out of it. A puritan instinct asked if she hadn't perhaps done something wrong, that some terrible retribution might be meted out to her for the pleasure she had enjoyed. The issue of trust shot across her mind, only to be annulled by a hand that fell into her lap.

In his sleep, Eric's arm had migrated in search of her, and the presence of this lonely arm, separated from the rest of his sleeping self, suddenly filled Alice with unexpected affection for her bedroom companion.

She took his hand and looked at his face in its state of childlike repose, wondering, 'Who is this person I have found?' She tried to infer a future from the evidence of a past etched on to his face. How would he react to a woman who loved him? What did he find ridiculous? Who did he dislike? What were his politics? How would he behave to a child crying? To a betrayal? To a feeling of inferiority?

Impressions, as ever, were liable to be based upon insufficient evidence. We leave a party and are asked by a friend what a fellow guest was like. To be honest, we would have to say, 'How can I possibly know? I only talked to them for two hours.' If we have lived with someone for a hundred and twenty years, and are asked for an opinion, to be true to the complexity of the other's character, we would have to answer, 'I'm only just getting to know them.' Instead, within two minutes of meeting someone, an impression is formed: *I like them/I don't like them* – the reaction a primitive relic of biological necessity; the cave man, upon seeing another of the race, having to decide at once if this was to be friend or foe.

Perhaps because she had been waiting so long, or because he really did look adorable asleep beside her and had been gentle and kind, or simply because it was pleasant to stay up deep into the night and entertain such notions, Alice found herself thinking that the man sharing her bed might yet prove the embodiment of a host of surprisingly intense desires she had till then almost forgotten she had.

IN LOVE WITH LOVE

Alice awoke to find Eric's lips tracing a path down her neck
and along her shoulders, filling her with spontaneous well-
being at the thought of where and with whom she was
starting her Sunday morning. A huge smile opened in the
centre of her face as she turned to face the purveyor of her
happiness.

'Hi,' she said.

'Hi.'

'Did you sleep well?'

'Like a baby,' said Eric, and reached over to plant a kiss
on her forehead. 'And you?'

'Fine.'

'Takes a little getting used to, doesn't it?'

'You could say that.'

A silence followed, the lovers retreating into an embrace
to escape it.

'It's so nice being here with you,' murmured Alice.

'Ehhhmmm,' answered Eric breathing in the smell of her
skin. 'What do you think we should do today?'

'I don't have any plans.'

'I'm in luck. Let's do anything.'

'What?'

'Let's do anything you want. Let's have a day of complete
indulgence. We could go anywhere, do anything, be
anyone.'

'You're mad.'

'No, go on, tell me what you want to do. We could go and have breakfast somewhere, we could take a boat down the river and eat ice-creams in Greenwich. Or we could walk up to the top of St Paul's or go to Kew Gardens. We could have lunch in a Chinese restaurant in Soho, or have a picnic in Hyde Park. We could go to the movies, watch six films in a row and eat twelve buckets of popcorn. We could rent a hot-air balloon and fly to Brighton. We could take Concorde, have lunch in New York and be back in time for dinner in London. Anything you want.'

'Well, let's start with a shower,' suggested Alice more prosaically, 'and take it from there.'

After driving by her flat to pick up fresh clothes, Eric and Alice brunched in a French bistro near Hammersmith. They ordered eggs, toast, coffee, orange juice, and sat side by side reading the Sunday papers on a velour-covered bench, breaking off occasionally to hold each other's hands or caress the other's knee. It was one of those mild, idyllic spring days novels tell us are made for lovers, and Alice and Eric did their best to live up to meteorological and other expectations.

But what did Alice know of her companion on the bench beside her? Her knowledge was brief in the extreme, it included such apparently random details as that:

—he was being flown to Frankfurt the next day for a business conference
—he had told a funny joke about a couple of Belgians and a parachute
—he had said, 'I value honesty above all'
—he liked to caress each knuckle of her hand
—he had deep blue eyes full of expressiveness and energy
—he had said his medical experience had taught him each day had to be enjoyed as if it were the last.

These pieces of information were at one level commonplace, but the judgement passed on their owner depended on the way they were connected. Given sufficient desire, given a generous interpreter, they might appear as the tips of wonderful icebergs. They could prove evidence that Eric was:

—successful in his job
—funny
—self-aware and frank
—gentle and erotic
—handsome and wise.

It would have been crudely premature to speak of Alice falling in love with Eric. After all, she had spent only an evening and a night with him, and he was only halfway through the second egg of their first brunch of the initial morning after. Nevertheless, her feelings seemed so ready to outstrip the available evidence that before speaking of love we may have to speak of a different phenomenon, to which Alice had always been prone, and which was perhaps a central feature of the first days she spent with Eric.

After brunch, they drove to an exhibition in Whitechapel, then caught the tail-end of the Sunday market on Brick Lane before taking a boat upstream to Westminster, from where they walked over to Battersea Park. Eric pointed out the Chinese Pagoda by the bank, impressing Alice by talking of the wise Chinese philosopher Confucius, whom he called Confaustus – not that Alice noticed, intent as she was on savouring the pleasure of walking arm in arm with a wise and handsome man by the great River Thames on a sunny spring day.

If Alice couldn't possibly [maturely speaking] have been

falling in love with Eric, then she was perhaps falling in love with love.

What was this curious, syntactically repetitive emotion?

It expressed a certain reflexivity about the amorous state, it meant deriving more pleasure from one's own emotional enthusiasm than from the object of affection which had elicited it.

Rather than simply holding that X was wonderful, the in-love-with-love lover would first think, Isn't it wonderful to have found someone as wonderful as X? When Eric stopped to tie up his shoe lace on the middle of Battersea Bridge, Alice thought not just, Doesn't he look adorable tying up his shoe?, but also, Isn't it a dream to have at last met someone who I find ties up their shoes in an adorable way?

In diagrammatic terms, the object of desire [labelled C] was at this stage something of a side-show next to desire [B] itself.

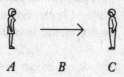

The object C stopped tying up his shoe lace and, because evening had begun to fall, suggested he drive Alice home.

'It's been a fantastic day,' she said as she opened the door to his bottle-green car.

'I'm glad. Pity about Concorde though.'

'Ah, that's for next weekend.'

'I'll save up all week for it.'

Back home, Alice hastily threw her bag on to the bed and clapped her hands twice in rapid succession, betraying a sort of excitement one should [after the age of twelve] at all costs prevent another from witnessing.

To understand her joy would mean understanding how the previous barren months had gradually led to a destructive suspicion of her own lack of desire. She had given up asking what was wrong with men, and had instead begun asking, 'What is wrong with *me* for finding so much wrong with them?' Magazine articles had suggested gruesome explanations – she was afraid to 'let go', she had perhaps been abused as a child, or might unconsciously have been more attracted to women. When a man like Tony had made advances at the Christmas party, she had thought him most unsuitable, but had quashed the idea that he might not have been right with the injunction, 'It isn't right to keep thinking people aren't right.' She had kissed her seducer to escape the fear of what might have been wrong with her for not wishing to do so.

Alice could now clap her hands because Eric had rendered this counter-intuitive approach superfluous. There was overwhelming relief in finally being able to think [though not yet say], 'You know, I think it could really work with someone like you.'

When Suzy reached home later that evening, the risks of over-exaggeration were therefore predictably prevalent.

'He's wonderful, you'd love him. He's good looking and clever, and very gentle too. I felt so comfortable around him. We didn't really talk much, but that didn't matter. It was like we understood one another intuitively. It was so moving to wake up beside him, his scrumptious little angel face smiling there. Oh, it was great!'

Alice lost herself in her own rhetoric: phrases like 'scrumptious little angel' tripped readily off her tongue; for so long deprived, she happily savoured the richness of a newly available amorous dictionary.

INDETERMINACY

A fascinating fragment of Eric's portrait as it was sketched for Suzy that night lay in Alice's claim that the two lovers 'understood one another intuitively', information preceded by an admission of a paucity of verbal communication.

To the sceptic or those enamoured of dialogue, a claim of intuitive understanding may appear worthy of suspicion if not ridicule, something invented to make up for a lack of audible evidence then falsely raised to a status superior to words themselves. The privileging of silence may be judged a mere subterfuge, an excuse for inarticulacy or worse.

But Alice's conversational poverty did not prevent and may even have enhanced her sense of how much Eric and she had in common, things that would naturally prove incapable of exchange via the lumpiness of language.

When Eric had been kissing her neck and shoulders, Alice was described as overwhelmed by a sense of 'spontaneous well-being'. Though a cursory description of what was travelling through her consciousness, its inadequacy goes beyond that of the author. Inadequacy was the inevitable result of words when faced with the sensations of love. Love lay beyond language; it could certainly attempt to sketch its contours, but like a map which indicated the qualities of a terrain, its efforts could never more than poorly approximate the sensations themselves.

Alice had nevertheless spoken to Eric in bed that first

It's so nice being here with you

morning. She had said to him, '*It's so nice being here with you.*'

No wonder she hated words. All those sensations to find that what emerged from her clumsy, ill-shaped mouth was the sentence, 'It's so nice being here with you.' For God's sake! What was wrong with language? Words were like a giant sieve at the top of which she would pour all the richness of her morning-after happiness, only for the unfortunate Eric to be left with the knowledge that she was finding it all very nice.

But indeterminacy turned out not to limit itself to words.

Burdened by the weight of romantic expectation, Alice and Eric agreed to leave fluid the nature of their commitment to each other. They would see one another when it was convenient, when it felt natural and would be prey to no extraneous compulsion.

When they spoke of the issue on the Tuesday after their first weekend, the phone conversation was littered with the contemporary dialect of non-involvement.

'I think it's important not to get too heavy too soon, do you know what I mean?' said Eric.

'Heavy? Sure, I understand. You're right, there's nothing worse than that. We should just see how it goes, take one day at a time.'

'It's really important to keep your own space.'

'Of course. You want to have a life outside a relationship.'

'Right.'

'Oh, by the way, do you want to come out to a film tonight?' proposed Alice. 'There's a Wenders season on at the National.'

'Er, listen, I don't think I can. I'm pretty busy at the moment.'

'Oh, that's fine, I was just wondering. Well, perhaps we can do something later in the week?'

'It's probably best if I call you at the weekend you know, because there's a lot going on and stuff.'

'Sure, sure.'

'I'll call you though.'

'Great, so we'll speak soon.'

'Yep, 'bye then.'

Alice told herself and her friends she was entering into a 'mature relationship'. It was hard to say quite what she meant by this, but the definition reflected a prejudice that a man who refuses an invitation to the cinema and calls for space is somehow more mature than a lover who finds it cruel to spend more than an instant out of sight of the beloved.

Despite a lack of regularity, the liaison acquired all the trappings of a romantic scenario. Letters were exchanged, phone calls ran late into the night, Alice would come home to find bouquets on her doorstep with cards attached on which was written, *You are my flower, love, Eric*.

It was early enough for the 'love' indicated not to suffer analysis. When they went out for dinner, the conversation rarely strayed from topics covered in quality daily newspapers. There seemed to be no need to trawl through the past, for Alice to catalogue her disappointments or ask Eric about a history that might have made her jealous. The lovers' wish for harmony meant the question of whether they in fact had anything in common remained somewhat irrelevant to the project.

In a sense, they had ceased to listen to each other. When Eric told Alice [with little awareness of the precedent of the sentence], 'I really don't know what someone as intelligent and sensitive as you sees in some dull, lousy banker like me,' Alice took this as evidence not of how dull and lousy he was but of precisely the opposing qualities.

She had placed a snapshot of him on her desk and now regularly glanced at it during the office day, drawing out of her lover's face all the evidence for her feelings. She recalled the surfaces of his skin, the little irregularities she had explored at night – the freckle to one side of the mouth, the trace of a scar by his left ear. She would look lovingly at his impish expression and boyish laugh, and feel her stomach tighten with longing.

In a phenomenon observable not simply in the first stages of love, desire hence flourished in a situation of minimal detail, the imagination suitably exercised to compensate for the blanks.

Whenever film companies summon their courage and accountants to make a version of *Anna Karenina*, *Emma* or *Wuthering Heights*, they must brace themselves for the charge that they have betrayed the reader's imagination with their choice of actress. The charm of literary characters depends on a complex interplay between suggestion and indeterminacy. Critics point out that Tolstoy never specified throughout the course of *Anna Karenina* what his heroine actually looked like, but this was perhaps no oversight on the great master's part. It is the prerogative of books, freed as they are from the tyranny of the image and hence at some level of reality, to leave things to the reader's imagination. What need did Tolstoy have to tell us exactly what Anna looked like? If the writer thought his heroine beautiful and simply wanted the reader to feel the same way, then it was best to say she was beautiful and let readers get on with the rest – they were far better placed to know what set them salivating in this area.

A form of poetic association collects around well-chosen details. When Rimbaud wrote his famous sentence, *'Heureux, comme avec une femme,'* he captured something of the state of love with minimal description. The phrase teeters on the verge of the banal, only to be rescued by its universality, by the idea that anyone who has been *'heureux avec une femme'* [or *avec un homme*] will arrive at the reading with their own stack of sepia memories – for some it will evoke breakfasts in bed, others will recall walking through the Marais on a Sunday afternoon, ambling hand in hand down the Bahnhofstrasse or necking in Nihonbashi.

But if Rimbaud had written, *'heureux comme avec une femme portant un tailleur Saint-Laurent, avec un cappuccino, une édition du* Figaro *et une table au Café Flore donnant sur le boulevard Saint-Germain*', most of the world's population would suddenly have felt the foreignness of the line. Only those who had spent time in Paris, liked women who wore tailored suits, frequented Sartre's favourite café, read the serious French right-wing daily and had a taste for coffee would have been able to sigh nostalgically and say, 'How I remember those days . . .'

At the time Alice met Eric, her advertising agency was handling the account of a resort chain called Break-away Hotels. In a lengthy meeting, the client had briefed the agency that they wished to endow their business with an image of luxury, youth and romance. The creative team had smoked three hundred cigarettes over the problem and in the end suggested a black and white picture of a couple kissing in a hotel room, with a short message below it: *Quite Simply Paradise*.

What exactly a hotel room, with its usual assortment of room-service menus, televisions, mini-bars and bathrobes, had to do with paradise was left discreetly unmentioned. Though everyone might have had an image of the place, though it would in many cases have included something approximating the kiss depicted, and though there were no doubt guests who had on occasion embraced passionately and derived inordinate enjoyment from their stay [and might even have jokingly referred to it as 'just heavenly'], it was somewhat far fetched to limit the definition of paradise to a particular chain of concrete roadside hotels in the north-west of England.

But saved from the need to explain themselves fully, both the advertised hotel and the desired lover could serve as triggers for the fertile imagination. Much as the viewer of the advertisement was unburdened by a potentially inhibiting knowledge of the colour of the bedspread or water pressure of the shower, so too Alice had yet to see Eric through the variety of moods or range of time necessary to map the contours of another's character. The image she had was vague enough to contain her desires without specifying any of her disappointments.

MEDIATION

In the first week of May, a restaurant opened on the waterfront in Chelsea and created a sensation. The Melteme at once became the talk of the town, or rather the talk of a small and privileged section of the city that shaped another small and privileged section of the city's belief that it spoke for and represented the whole. The wheel of fashion had come to a halt at its doors, and pronounced with all the force of a religious injunction that it would henceforth be the centre of meaningful dining, until new culinary faiths emerged, followers defected and Jerusalem would lose its holy status.

Alice mentioned the restaurant a few times in the disdainful spirit of someone who didn't expect to eat there and could therefore be mean about those who did. She couldn't have suspected that Eric would leave a message on her answering machine one Friday morning, telling her he had booked a table there at eight thirty – or the extent to which this surprise would alter her original judgement on the place.

The philosophy of the Melteme was to leave things open to the eye of the diner. The kitchen was exposed behind a large glass pane where chefs were seen at work, an overturn of the traditional ideal whereby the kitchen's existence was denied. The decoration followed this see-through approach, for the ventilation, electric cables and piping ran along the outside of the walls and ceilings. Halogen bulbs descended from above in long tangled coils like bizarre tentacles of a giant Hydra.

Much as the architecture had avoided cornices and plaster mouldings, so the cooking had reduced itself to fundamentals. There were no culinary equivalents of false ceilings, namely the sauces that blurred distinctions between ingredients and disguised gradations and disruptions of flavour. Sauces were built on compromise, ingredients should be made to stand on their own. The food revealed its structure, it had the boldness of a palette of primary colours.

The starters included a salad of dark green lettuce leaves over which were shaved pungent slices of Parmesan, the whole bathed in a golden, rich olive oil, and presented on a large earthenware plate. There were slabs of rare-cooked tuna beside char-grilled vegetables, the dark and always complex aubergine side by side with an assertive red pepper. The restaurant dared to stick to traditional foods, yet was so skilled as to almost reinvent them: the large golden french fry seemed in its perfection to be the embodiment of the Platonic form. Desserts were equally lacking in timidity, including as a highlight a mound of deep chocolate off-set against slivers of the lushest mango and papaya.

Restaurants may capture the imagination in a way impossible for other commercial enterprises appealing to other and less vital appetites. They may assume the status of erotic experiences, and the Melteme had generated near-hysteria. Tables could only be booked far in advance, celebrities fought and bribed their way inside, pop stars and businessmen, politicians and artists were to be seen there at all times, and every fashionable magazine and newspaper was running a story on what was decreed the dining sensation of the decade.

Having only recently been eating tinned soup alone and somewhat unused to entering hallowed dining establishments, Alice's pleasure at finding herself on a Friday night with Eric at one of the Melteme's coveted corner tables was predictably intense.

'Isn't it just fantastic?' she exclaimed.

'Yeah, it's fun,' replied Eric, in a tone indicating this was perhaps not the first time he was dining with a woman in a restaurant which had been decreed the dining sensation of a decade.

'What are you going to get, then?' asked Alice.

'Oh, I think I'll go for the crab, and then the duck.'

'I just can't decide, there's so much, I want to take everything.'

She eventually settled on a more dietically reasonable approach, ordering a salmon carpaccio and a sea bass, both of which had been described as modern culinary classics by reviewers.

If, out of the many dinners Eric and Alice spent together, attention is focused on this one, it was perhaps because of the peculiarity of the pleasure Alice derived from it, and what this suggested of the nature and origins of her desires.

When her first course arrived, Alice remarked to Eric how delicious it looked, then leant over and kissed him on the cheek.

'What did I do so right?' asked Eric ironically.

'Oh, just a bit of everything,' she replied, and lifted her fork to take a first mouthful.

'Yum, it's absolutely delicious,' she reported a second later.

Because Alice told Eric how wonderful her salmon carpaccio was and how elegant she found the restaurant, one might imagine her pleasure to have arisen directly from the food and surroundings. But watching her eat the first course, it was peculiar to note how her enthusiasm had become a distant subsidiary of the thought [rather than the fact] that she was eating a well-reviewed dish in a restaurant talked of all over town which had only that week hosted a dozen of the top personalities from the worlds of film, fashion and music.

The distinction was a reminder of two models of desire; on the one hand, the **autonomous** decision that 'I like this restaurant because the food tastes good to *me*,' and on the other, the **imitative** thought that 'This restaurant must be good because *everyone I know thinks it so.*'

In the former case, a direct line linked desire to the object.

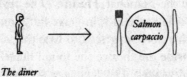

The diner

In the latter example, desire was first filtered through intermediary channels, the review pages of the newspapers or the mouths of the celebrated.

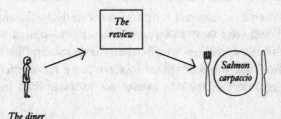

The diner

> Diners will at once feel at home in the charm and elegance of the Melteme restaurant, decorated by the famed Andalusian decorator José de la Fuenta, also responsible for the Croque Monsieur in Mayfair. Enjoy delicious sea-food, great river views and a chance to sample over twenty different varieties of fish and lobster. The chef is French, and the atmosphere conducive to romantic and sophisticated dining. Prices are reasonable too, around £25 per head without wines, of which there is a wide and tempting selection. The carpaccio (£6.95) is already fast taking on the status of a classic, said to be a favourite among the elegant stars of the fashion and music world who frequent the Melteme. Also recommended are the polenta, the red snapper with peppers and the lightly grilled tuna. Clearly the place to be. A winner.

Of the two models, Alice had always been prone to following the latter, the model of imitative rather than autonomous desire, whereby her longings for a certain dress, pair of shoes, restaurant and indeed lover were typically generated by the words and images of others.

She had the previous week seen Samuel Beckett's *Waiting for Godot* at the National Theatre. The reviews had been ecstatic, people spoke of it in grave but glowing terms and Alice had therefore suggested to Eric that she buy tickets. But once inside the theatre she found herself scarcely able to stifle her yawns. The language seemed contrived and drawn out, the pauses so long between each line as to break any continuity. There was simply nothing in the world of the two tramps she could relate to, it seemed a world of poverty, sadness and absurdity from which she wished to flee.

When Eric dropped his programme midway through the first half, she bent down to pick it up and smiled at him with an expression which could have meant, 'Isn't this awful?' but was ambiguous to allow room for alternatives. In the interval, she was careful not to speak first, lest her judgement jar with that of Eric and the three banking friends whom he had invited to come with them.

'This has got to be the single greatest piece of theatre the twentieth century has produced,' Eric declared after silently pouring a tonic into his gin in a corner of the crowded bar, a statement carrying all the authority of the main review in the arts page of *The Times*, 'and this is certainly the best production that's been on in London for the last fifteen years.'

Eric's opinion, though bold, seemed exactly in line with that of his banking friends, and therefore, because everyone was nodding and proclaiming it the greatest piece of theatre since some other play she also recalled yawning through, Alice could do little, when finally asked for her thoughts, but concur with the enthusiasms thus far displayed.

Moreover, when the second act came around, she was not only less bored, she actually began to enjoy the performance. When she emerged, she declared with little conscious bad faith that Beckett was indeed a most impressive and moving playwright whose work she would be interested in exploring further.

If Alice's responses shock, it may be because the last four hundred years of philosophy, politics and art has spent its time praising autonomy – the free are those who can spontaneously direct their desire, follow their own heart, and not be swayed by public opinion, by fear of the crowd or by what the wheel of fashion decides is in or out. The denunciation follows that of the world as a theatre, the *teatrum mundi* with 'all the men and women merely players'. The desires of the world's 'players' [typically the desire for fame, money or political power] are socially based and hence somehow fraudulent. An actor whispering fine words will only be echoing sentiments originating in a figure off-stage – much as Alice could sit in a restaurant and praise the salmon carpaccio with an enthusiasm which had in origin been forged by the appetite and pen of another.

Alice at least had enough distance to admit at the end of her first course at the Melteme how happy she was to be eating in a place so obviously '*where it was at*'.

What did it mean to want to be 'where *it* was at'?

To want to be where *others* had decided *it* was.

It was a longing to be part of a centre, a centre of value to which all eyes were turned and which could hence have indubitable importance. In previous ages, when people had wanted to be where it was at, they had been able to turn their eyes to Rome, Mecca or Jerusalem, to the monarchy or nation. These were common centres of value, which a broad range of people had decided were worthy and decorated and treasured accordingly. But with a decline in the great ideologies had come a certain confusion as to the centre of things – no longer was there one indubitably fashionable place to dine in a capital, but a choice of hundreds of restaurants and private individuals, all vying to capture the precarious centre.

For a brief period, the restaurant had laid a successful claim to the roving heart of the universe, but even when one had fought to get a table and been seated in the hallowed establishment, there was a certain paradox to the quest.

Guests looked at each other across the crowded and bustling dining-room in a frantic search for those whose value had been socially confirmed. The people at table 14 imagined those at table 15 were witty in a way they weren't, had read something they'd missed, cavorted with friends more interesting than theirs. But those seated at 15 looked over their shoulders at 16 with much the same anxieties, 16 looked at 17, 17 at 18 and so on.

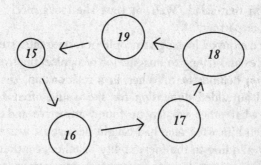

There was of course no 'centre' to the restaurant: its 'centredness' couldn't be pinned down to any one place, to the gigantic lobster tanks in the middle of the hall or the attractively positioned tables by the windows [which Eric had unfortunately been unable to obtain]. The Melteme achieved its success by the artfully contrived impression of a centre, by being able to embody a lure while remaining an empty referent.

'Everyone is seriously well dressed, don't you think?' asked Alice, looking around the room during the second course.

'I suppose so,' answered Eric, showing more interest in his duck.

'Look at that couple over there. His face looks familiar. Is he on TV or something?'

'Don't know.'

'I think he is. He's on that show where people get interviewed in the shower. The blonde he's with is stunning, she's so beautiful it makes you want to give up. I wonder if she's a model? I've never seen such a figure. I'm sure she hasn't eaten anything all week in order to get through that salad. Well, at least she looks nicely bored with her partner.'

Alice enjoyed looking at people in restaurants, studying the faces and trying to imagine [or recognize] the lives that went on behind them. When in a relationship, the game gained an added dimension for she would often ask her lover what other women he found attractive and would then tell him what men had caught her eye. It was a game gently alluding to the inevitability of others continuing to attract or at least draw one's attention, however in love one claimed to be.

Yet Alice had an intuitive sense that it wasn't possible to play this game with Eric, for the game was premissed on a crucial detail – that the attractions confessed would be available for discussion because they weren't serious. *I will allow you to talk of those you find attractive because I am secure enough to think the attraction unthreatening*.

However, Eric's obvious charms and his fluid approach to relationships left Alice without a sufficient margin to joke about infidelity. But we shouldn't pity her unreservedly, for what had in part attracted her to Eric was this very sense that he was attractive to other women. Her feelings for him shared structural similarities with her enthusiasm for the restaurant, for in both cases the sense that others valued and coveted them added a decisive ingredient to her desire.

When Eric had been choosing a tie to wear for dinner

earlier that evening, he had called Alice over to his cupboard to help with the choice.

'I've just got so many ties,' he'd said, 'I get given them all as presents.'

'Oh, I feel so sorry for you,' Alice had answered, 'all those hundreds of women who've given up hard-earned money to buy you ties! And all you can do is complain.'

The passing reference to hundreds of women wasn't coincidental. Alice genuinely believed Eric had known many women – and the thought, though it had its jealous component, was at another level curiously pleasant.

Love had for her always been linked to admiration. 'I can't love a man if I don't admire him,' she would say. And admiration implicitly meant that not only had she to admire him, but others should do so too. The poverty of her own self could be avoided by a man whose shoes came from Italy and suits from Savile Row – but who had nevertheless chosen her from a large group of fellow admirers. That others desired him, but that he nevertheless desired her confirmed a precarious sense of her own value.

A man with a hundred love-ties was hence more valuable than a man with only a single tie, Eric predictably resisting the temptation to disabuse her of such notions – for many of the ties hanging in his cupboard had as much to do with promotions received at business conferences as with passionate gifts of the heart.

When she returned home that night, Alice mentioned to Suzy how attractive Eric had been looking, which led on to a broader consideration of men and their physical appearance.

Suzy had long claimed to suffer from the Quasimodo complex.

'Show me a hunchback or guy with one hand missing or a cripple or something, and I'll find that so sexy,' she explained.

'God! How could you? I mean, I feel sorry for these people, but I just couldn't go out with them.'

'Why? It's much more interesting to go out with people who aren't obviously attractive.'

'Is it? Why?'

'Well, because then you're the only one to know what it is you find sexy and wonderful about them. And anyway, when you love someone, what does it matter what other people think?' asked Suzy, whose current boyfriend Matt, though not missing a hand or vertebra, was perhaps several inches too short and pounds too heavy.

'I just don't understand you. I couldn't go out with someone who wasn't very presentable. You remember that guy Chris, who was after me a while ago, I mean, he was really sweet but so awkward, so uncomfortable with himself. I couldn't stand to be with someone like that, I'd always be self-conscious, sort of having to make excuses for him.'

Suzy had enviable confidence in her ability to declare things good or bad without the support of others, to call a small local Polish restaurant the best in London though no critics were saying so or to love a man though the world was conferring on him no great honour or attention.

Alice, readier to collapse under the weight of social opinions, ensured that the price to pay for a man who others admired was an inability to pass catty but nevertheless trusting judgement on the peculiarities of bored blondes seated in the corners of fashionable restaurants.

SEX, SHOPPING
AND THE NOVEL

Her other sin was that she loved to go shopping.

'You know the place in Camden I was telling you about?' Alice asked Eric the following morning.

'How could I forget it?' he replied, deep in the financial pages of the weekend paper.

'Well, it says in this magazine they've got a sale on there this whole month.'

'God is merciful.'

'I've been looking for a cardigan for ages, and I think they've got just the right one.'

'Which one?'

'The one she's wearing,' she explained showing him a picture of a model. 'What do you think?'

'Hum.'

'It has to be more than "hum", it costs a fortune.'

'Sorry. How can I put it to you? This cardigan represents the triumph of Western civilization's attempt to produce the perfect woollen garment. It is the apogee of design, the flower of the fashion industry, the *Mona Lisa* of cardigans . . .'

'All right, in that case will you drive me up there today?'

Eric agreed, but Camden turned out not to be their only destination. The shop in question did not stock the right sized cardigan, though it did have a pair of very special sandals which it seemed a pity to miss now they'd gone so far north. Then, because it happened to be on their way back, they stopped off in Notting Hill, which had a fantastic selection of fashionably ripe Indian buttons. Then, because they were already in Notting Hill, it seemed silly not to go down towards High Street Kensington, which only naturally led to South Kensington, from where it was only a few steps to the King's Road, which was not in the end that far from a quick tour through the West End, Bond Street and Covent Garden.

The journey left Alice in the possession not only of the aforementioned and long-desired cardigan, but also a pair of shoes, earrings, three pairs of tights, assorted items of make-up and a flask of perfume. To her delight, Eric turned out to be a most shoppable partner, betraying none of the customary male impatience with the ritual and insisting he pay for a cardigan which would have chiselled a large dent in her bank account. The credit cards worked effortlessly, attendants were obsequious, taxis were found to ferry them across the capital. They lunched in a small café near Hanover Square, then returned to Eric's apartment in Onslow Gardens, where they began making passionate love on the sofa amidst bags from half a dozen of London's fashionable boutiques.

The publication of *Madame Bovary* in serial form in the *Revue de Paris* in 1856 gives Gustave Flaubert a claim to be the author of the world's first sex and shopping novel, or at least the first novel to make the connections between these two activities so explicit and so psychologically intertwined. Though Emma shocked her contemporary audience chiefly by her adultery, her downfall had as much to do with her addiction to shopping for the latest fashions and thereby involving herself with a crushing burden of debt. Spending money was for Bovary a libidinous exercise carrying all the risks of a ride in a shuttered cab, and possessed of many of the same pleasures.

Did Flaubert approve of sex and shopping? Could one argue that his '*Bovary, c'est moi*' was indicative not just of sympathy with the romantic temperament, but also of a deeper understanding of the lure of consumption?

It is perhaps significant that commercial and sexual orgasm led Bovary to ruin at precisely the moment when industrial capitalism was undergoing what historians now refer to as a consumer revolution, and when the wave of nineteenth-century puritanism belied certain progressive gains for the freedom of women. The attempts to have the novel banned might hence be understood as a moralistic attempt to curtail not simply sex, but primarily shopping. Once the arguments against copulation without reproduction began to lose their religious power of intimidation, the arguments against consumption without need gained an added fervour [only eleven years separate the publication of *Madame Bovary* from that of Marx's *Capital* in 1867]. There is an all too obvious link between a moral attack on shopping without need and a moral attack on copulation without reproduction – in both cases, it is pleasure which has been censored, more particularly, feminine pleasure, typically by men with top hats and bushy beards.

The dominant vehicle of Alice's desire appeared to be the large number of magazines she read every month. They had a luxuriance to them which books could not rival, the crispness and cleanliness of their pages coated in a sheen like that of a well-polished apple. She often joked about wanting to 'disappear into a magazine', and articulated a confused ethical vision of wishing to 'magazinify her world'.

What these magazines had in common was a sense of clarity absent from daily life, a world of perfect beings standing against mossy stone walls modelling the autumn collections or seated in Milan cafés dressed in cotton designs for spring. Beautiful men held beautiful women in pouting, provocative poses, models gazed wistfully out to sea dressed in the lightest of fabrics, giant lipsticks and lush red dresses featured alongside high-powered sports cars and tropical fruits.

The magazine was an instrument of longing, but appeared moral in offering solutions to the human condition. Though it claimed to wish to satisfy its readers, the magazine had only performed its commercial – as opposed to literary – task when it left them miserable at the absence of a hundred items which would have to be bought.

The magazine *had* to make Alice unhappy. It couldn't tell her that what she was wearing would be fine for another year, that appearance didn't matter so much anyway, that it didn't count who you knew or what colour your bedroom was. The clothes section had to leave her lamenting the garments missing from her own wardrobe, the holiday section had to remind her of the many corners of the world which were sunnier than her own, the section entitled 'lifestyle' had to humiliate her with the implicit message that she probably had no life and it certainly had no style.

Madame Bovary read romantic novels, Alice, a modern dreamer, read magazines, but there were important structural links between the two activities. In both cases, the novel and magazine functioned as a [shop-] window on to another and more enchanted world, stimulating desire by being practitioners of a particularly evolved and deceptive form of 'realism'.

Though clearly based on fantasy, nineteenth-century romantic novels made strenuous efforts to introduce verisimilitude in setting and extraneous details, thereby differentiating themselves from traditional escapist genres. The novel grew meticulous at describing houses and landscapes, social mores and facial appearances, the longing created being all the more intense because all the more plausible. Though plot lines were often unusual [much swooning by moonlight and sudden inheritance of vast fortunes], the narrative techniques gave readers enough detail to suppose that such things really went on in the big city or isolated village to which they'd never travelled. Because he or she had been told the colour of the horse, the number of freckles on a hand or the reflection of sunlight on the rusty revolver, the reader might prove more forgiving if the horse carried the heroine away to a remote Scottish castle, the honest virgin with a freckled hand received an offer of marriage from a wealthy and impossibly good-natured landowner and the rusty revolver went off and shot a jealous rival to the course of true love.

The magazine followed this flirtation with the possible by its caricature of dirty realism; there were articles on what nail polish to use when scuba diving off Mauritius, tips for recreating Giverny in a south London back garden, how to cook dishes interesting enough that one might wish to eat them, but just complicated enough to prove impractical.

Alice's love of such literature was not a coincidental part of her psychological make-up. It reflected a deeper question of identity: unsure of who she was or wanted to be, she was naturally prone to adopt suggestions from elsewhere. Her quest to find a cardigan represented an attempt to fit her own confusion into a pre-existing style, modelling herself against an image provided by another. It was a form of elegant and expensive caricature, the reduction of a potential infinity of traits to a few central strokes which could anchor her to a socially recognized form.

The fashions displayed resided in an ever shifting schizophrenic order of truth or falsehood operating on the dualist basis of 'in' and 'out'. The metaphor was important – fashion was a house, something one could come into or be excluded from. That particular month, lightly flared sleeves, low necklines and soft fabrics were decreed the sole authentic options. Buttons with intricate Indian patterns received discreet praise from the right quarters, as did long hair tied in a bun with a large pin. Jewellery was declared out, women wearing men's watches in, long dresses were out, denim dresses in, cashmere was out, silk in, blusher was out, toner in, purple was back, orange a crime. Designers were struggling to assert the importance of layering, the survival of the species appeared to rest on long loose shirts or tunics worn correctly over leggings.

Conclusions on such matters were not arrived at centrally, irrigated instead by a thousand capillaries of the giant organism *taste*: a shifting, unpredictable monster whose homunculi included the young, the famous, the rich, the creative and the beautiful in a permanently unstable cocktail. Unstable because these conclusions relied not on the particular qualities of an object, but on the place of that object within a wider chain of goods. Without itself altering, a now elegant cardigan could be superseded in the market place by designs which would show it up as reactionary or false. Did a particular cardigan evoke the glamour of the twenties, or [the greatest sin] lay bare the attempt of a contemporary designer to recapture an already overexposed conception of the glamorous twenties?

WASH CYCLES

Depending on her state of mind, Alice's outlook on life [if one may talk so grandly] alternated between two schools: that of the *staircase* and that of the *tumble-dryer*.

When she was in a staircase mood, what happened to her was taken as evidence that life was moving slowly but inexorably upwards towards a state of happiness and repose at the top of a metaphoric landing. She of course understood there would be horizontal stretches, but held that despite periods of anguish, self-hatred or boredom, the essential direction remained vertical. When she compared herself to the child she'd been, or the moody adolescent or university student, she felt herself successfully clearing the obstacles which the past had placed before her, developing self-confidence and an understanding of others.

Eric's arrival had naturally counted as a great upward lift.

Here at last was someone who made her happy, around whom she felt comfortable, and who had saved her from the melancholy round of parties and evenings in front of the television. Their relationship seemed free of the obvious turmoils of past liaisons, there was a commonsense stability about him which she admired. Eric seemed to know what he wanted and felt, he was older than her [in his early thirties, she in her twenties], he had weighty opinions on politics and economics, he seemed sure of the world and his place within it.

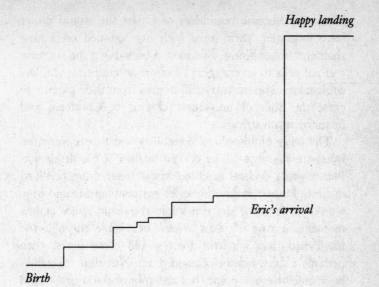

Happy landing

Eric's arrival

Birth

There was nevertheless a certain defensiveness about Alice's staircase mood; she behaved like someone who after years of trying to grow rich finally makes ten million and can't help stressing the point.

A *nouveau content*, she had in sadder days acquired the friendship of a number of comfort friends, women to whom she had been drawn on account of a common unhappiness inflicted at the hands of men. Belinda and Margaret were two such companions from the Dark Ages. The three of them had spent many an evening in Belinda's Clapham kitchen, exchanging anecdotes and laughter over cups of coffee and too many biscuits.

But Alice felt she had now hoisted herself off their step and made excuses not to see them, letting the answering machine pick up the phone rather than risk a conversation.

They had become reminders of a past she would rather have forgotten, their links with her founded on a now shameful unhappiness. She looked back down the staircase and fell prey to an exaggerated effort at independence, like adolescents who overplay differences from their parents to erase the guilt of previously cloying to emotional and financial apron strings.

The other philosophical possibility was that represented by the *tumble-dryer*. The crucial feature of the dryer was that it was a cyclical machine whose inner drum revolved in time. Put a certain number of garments inside and they would settle along the rim while the drum spun; at one moment, a pair of jeans would be visible through the toughened-glass window, then would come socks, then perhaps a shirt, a dishcloth and so on. Not all items would be visible at every point, but the spin of the drum would force them to make an appearance at regular intervals. If the jeans stood for happiness, the socks for elation, the shirt for boredom, and the dishcloth for screaming misery, then the drying process stood to be compared with the living process, where what came around once would inevitably come around again, suggesting there were repetitive givens in a human life, that existence was a cyclical affair.

Alice had been with Eric a little over a month now, a time which had coincided with the onset of spring. London looked its best, a charming muddle of villages with trees all in blossom and quaint crooked houses set against a pale blue sky. Alice felt her life had finally begun, and that the earthly happiness she had long craved was within her grasp. Outside her emotional life, the office was growing more challenging, and there were rumours she might be promoted on account of the excellent work she had done on a wool softener campaign.

The past weekend had been particularly pleasurable. She and Eric had spent Friday night at the Melteme, on Saturday they had shopped for her cardigan and assorted goods, in the evening they'd been out for a drink with an old friend of Eric's who had come in from New York, and had then gone dancing in a club off Piccadilly. On Sunday morning, Alice had suggested a trip to a museum near Tower Bridge, they had lunched on the terrace of a nearby pub, then, because it was a balmy day, walked back to Parliament Square following the path of the river whenever they could.

Shortly after she and Eric had returned to his flat, a deafening peal of thunder tore through the sky. Dark clouds had been blowing in rapidly from the west, massing themselves over the capital, and now released themselves with the pent-up vengeance of the English climate when five days have passed without rain.

'It's unbelievable!' exclaimed Alice looking out of the living-room window on to Onslow Square which looked like the interior of a high-pressure shower. 'This is a monsoon.'

'They've been predicting it all week,' said Eric.

'Have they? I never believe it when they do. Do you ever get that? I always think when it's nice, it'll always be nice.'

The climate begged to differ. Because an inclination of 23.5° meant the sun was directly over the Tropic of Cancer [23.5° N] on June the twenty-second, London summers were warm enough to sunbathe and Eric could play tennis in the evenings and breakfast on his small rear patio. But because the sun arrived directly over the Tropic of Capricorn [23.5° S] on December the twenty-second, the winters were without leaves on the trees, the nights were dark and taxis impossible to find in the rush-hour drizzle.

'Wouldn't it be nice to live somewhere where it was always warm?' continued Alice in a reflective mood. 'You know, you'd only have to have one set of clothes, and you wouldn't have to pay any heating bills, and you'd be in such a good mood all the time . . .'

'You, in a good mood all the time?'

'Why not?'

'You'd still be yourself?'

'Yes, but myself in a good sunny mood.'

'Weather doesn't change anyone like that.'

'It changes me.'

'I forgot you were a biological exception.'

'Spare the sarcasm. Scientists have proved it.'

Ever since she had spent a year in Mexico as a child, Alice had been much attached to the equatorial regions of the earth. Between latitudes 15° and 30°, meteorologists tell us, warm air blows throughout the year, giving high rainfall but a most stable climate. Temperature variation is minimal, the air staying almost constant at 20°–30° C, rendering the division of seasons almost imperceptible.

But in the North Temperate Zone, in which Alice and Eric's story unfolded, the subtropical and subpolar air masses were in violent collision, a succession of cyclones and depressions swinging eastwards and bringing with them belts of moist maritime air. The result was a constant meteorological struggle, warm fronts struggling against cold fronts and forming unstable alliances in occluded fronts, a conflict which, on the day Alice watched the rain fall looked something like this:

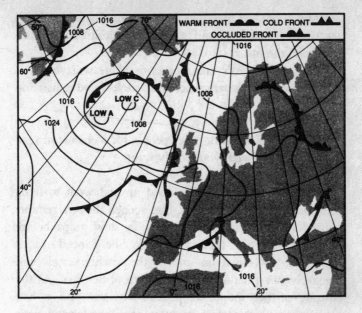

Eric lost interest in the rain, and went to turn on the television in a far corner of the living-room. A financial programme was in progress, examining the activities of a ball-bearing firm in the north of England. Alice joined him on the edge of the sofa a moment later, wrapping an arm around him and giving a loving look at his intense, concerned expression while he gazed at the screen.

'What do you want?' he asked brusquely without turning to face her.

'Nothing,' she replied.

'Why are you looking at me, then?'

'No reason, you just looked really sweet, so absorbed in the TV.'

'Yeah, well shush, these are people we're going to be doing business with, so be quiet.'

'How about if I give you a silent, non-disturbing kiss?' asked Alice cheekily, and slid beneath him to peck him briefly on the lips.

'Alice, for Christ's sake, leave me alone will you? I'm trying to watch a programme, and I can't if you're hassling me.'

'I'm sorry.'

'Well just think about other people for a change instead of always doing what you bloody want.'

'I said I was sorry.'

Eric didn't answer, Alice stood up and went to fetch some water from the kitchen. She opened the refrigerator, poured herself a glass and drank in slow gulps before throwing most of it back in the sink. She glanced over at the clock, sat down on one of the kitchen stools and pensively ran a hand down the length of her face. At the latitude of her mouth, approximately one and a half centimetres north-east of its outer edge, she located signs of imminent dermatological disaster. Quite how or when it had begun, she couldn't tell, but in the course of the day [or did its origins stretch further back?] a sebaceous gland had become clogged and now, in protest at this enforced confinement, planned to swell into a vengeful pimple. The whole area surrounding the epicentre had taken on a different quality, the skin tauter and harder in preparation for the volcanic eruption of the morning. Or worse perhaps, the pimple would be incapable of explosion, imploding instead, taking days to disappear and threatening future gestation.

While one side of her contemplated the facial damage, another noted with clinical detachment that Eric's rebuff was the first time he had shown anything but politeness towards her, politeness not in the stiff handshake sense of the word, but in the sense of hiding irritations from and with her. The 'Leave me alone' symbolized the *me*'s first assertion, a *me* which had till then practised subservience in the name of helping Alice with her coat or letting her walk first through revolving doors.

She couldn't analyse why but, sitting on the stool in Eric's darkened kitchen, she felt a sudden and dramatic loss of self-confidence. Whereas only a few moments before she had had faith in her power to survive in the adult world, to play the requisite parts and not trip up, everything now rapidly disintegrated into a spiral of self-accusation and loathing. Her confidence had always been a precarious structure nurtured by confirming events – if she had wanted something and succeeded in obtaining it or if she had liked someone and he had liked her, then she could begin to build up faith in herself and others. But this belief was like a leaking tyre which constantly needed replenishment, and when it proved impossible, she sank rapidly into a state where all the previous optimism seemed an arrogant sham and this, the rain, her true state, the hand God had dealt her and with which she should never have tampered.

'Shall we order a pizza for dinner?' called Eric from the next room. 'I can't be bothered to cook or go out.'

He was lying across the sofa, a hand scratching inside his trousers.

'Do you have to do that?' asked Alice.

'Do what?'

'That.'

'If I'm itchy, yeah, why not?'

'Very pleasant.'

'Or do you want to get a Chinese instead? We could always nip out for a curry of course. What do you think?'

It seemed most inappropriate given the question, but Alice suddenly longed to say to Eric, 'Just hold me.' More than any pizza, curry or noodle soup [and a lot less rationally], she wished to start crying without explanation for this lachrymation other than 'Because I'm sad.' A feeling of complete fragility had descended, leaving her unable to co-ordinate her responses with the demands of the world. She wished to be given room to fall apart, to be held quietly in someone's arms until she could put the pieces back together again.

'Er, look, listen, I can't, I mean I don't really want any supper.'

'What?'

She couldn't summon the energy to verbalize her feelings, without saying anything, she wished he could simply look at her and whisper, 'I know, I know.'

Instead, he remarked, 'Why are you making a face like Bambi's mother just bit the dust? I only asked you what you wanted to eat.'

'I'm sorry.'

'There's nothing to be sorry about. The face quite suits you, actually.'

'Listen, I think I should go home. I have some work to finish for tomorrow. OK?'

'Fine with me, Bambi.'

In bed an hour later, Alice thought bitterly of how she was split into a bewildering range of moods, akin to a number of TV channels, which a petulant demon was forever flitting between on a remote control.

On Channel One	She was confident, at home in her body, creative, curious, funny and at ease with others.
On Channel Two	She felt overwhelmed by a cluster of unspecified fears which left her biting her nails, drained of energy and closed off from others.
On Channel Three	A physical state where her body felt as heavy as 'a lump of grey, cold porridge'.
On Channel Four	The grass was greener on the other side and her life markedly inferior to that of almost anyone she knew.

When she thought of 'finding herself', what she meant more than anything was to find *one* self, one channel which could confer a modicum of stability and repose, an end to this infernal tumble-drying.

VALUE SYSTEMS

There were the first signs that night that Alice's idealized lover was not a mirror image of her romantic aspirations. He was not necessarily unworthy of fantasy, simply independent of her projections.

Yet if the time Alice and Eric spent together now began to reveal tensions based on dissonance, then around what were these conflicts centred?

Attempting to read disparities between people without the usual linear framework, one might study character as manifested in subsidiary details which could nevertheless reveal surprisingly coherent, if conflicting, systems of value.

[i] Interior Design

The month before meeting Alice, Eric had finished having his flat redecorated by an architect in a Japanese minimalist style. He had decided to fulfil a dream he had had ever since opening a book on Eastern interiors a decade or so before, and his job had recently given him the financial possibility to put his ideas into practice.

The cupboards and lights had been recessed, the floors laid down with strips of bleached Japanese oak, the mouldings and skirtings planed off and instead of curtains simple white venetian blinds hung flush with the outer rim of the

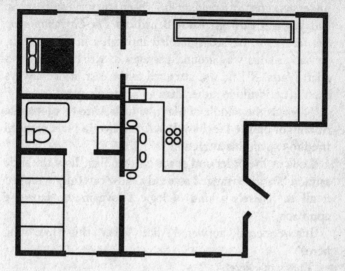

window frames. The fittings were entirely without orna-
mentation, the door handles were a chrome Bauhaus
design, the kitchen was built out of the heavy-duty stainless
steel units found in canteens and restaurants. The bathroom was tiled in white with a cedarwood tub in the centre
and a washbasin to one side carved from a block of Carrara
marble on a base of Yorkshire sandstone blocks. In the
bedroom, the floor was assembled out of tatami mats, on to
which a futon could be rolled at night and hidden in a
cupboard during the day. The walls were painted white
and decorated with occasional pieces of contemporary
American art, black and steel cubes and oxidized copper
coils.

Eric had spent a year in Japan with his bank, learning
about currency markets, but taking time at weekends to

explore the culture. He couldn't have claimed a deep understanding, his reading had been cursory at best: he had yawned through Ruth Benedict's *The Chrysanthemum and the Sword*, he had stumbled through a little Mishima, he had felt his way around passages of Krishnamurti and Alan Watts. If Eric was attracted to the east, it had always been in an intuitive rather than an academic way.

Towards the middle of May, he took Alice to a Japanese restaurant on the Finchley Road, and over a plate of sushi tried to explain his attraction.

'Look at the order and space on this dish, how the little salmon bits are arranged so neatly, how carefully wrapped it all is. There's a kind of logic I love in the Japanese approach.'

'It's wonderful,' answered Alice. 'What's this white thing here?'

'That's mackerel.'

'And this pink stuff in the middle?'

'That's ginger. And what you'll see is great about a meal like this is that you can eat a whole plate and feel completely clean and light afterwards, not like a Western meal where everything is in a mess and you feel so heavy.'

When speaking of the East, Eric kept returning to a few key words: *lightness*, *order*, *logic*, *cleanliness*, *space*. He found such qualities in the pieces of sushi he ate, in the black lacquer boxes in which the food was presented, in the freshness of the chopstick wood, in the calm atmosphere of the restaurant. He had observed similar elements in the temples of Kyoto, in the calligraphy of the Zen masters and in the few haiku poems he had attempted.

While a waitress in kimono poured them tea, he went on:

'The world is so crowded and complicated, what I love

about the Eastern aesthetic is that it seems to have space, and a kind of rationality. I did my flat up in this way because I wanted to come home from the chaos of the office and find myself in an oasis. The idea of things being open plan is so there's no room for dust, dirt or junk to collect: things have to be kept tidy. I wanted a house where nothing would be superfluous. I used to go sailing as a child, and the thing you learn about racing boats is that everything on them is there for a purpose, because there's no room for waste or useless cargo.'

Eric's interest in interior design spread down to the smallest accessories. He spent time shopping for the perfect alarm clock, corkscrew or calculator, he paid minute attention to the everyday items of his bathroom, kitchen and bedroom, to the choice of radiators, light switches, knives and towel rails.

How could one interpret this desire [expressed in modern dialect] to accessorize? Perhaps as an attempt to control everything about a given environment, so Eric could know that from the paper-clip holder to the wine stopper, from the light bulb to the extractor fan, he was living in a space in which nothing had been left to chance. In most houses, drawers revealed objects which were hideously redundant, which were built with no aesthetic in mind, which had no value other than the sentimental. But this would have meant elements in Eric's life which were wholly unplanned, in his house yet dangerously other.

The arrangement of furniture may be taken as a mental mirror of the one who arranged it, a non-verbal, non-active repository of character. When psychoanalysis moved into the treatment of children, it soon confronted the problem of using a 'talking cure' with those whose mastery of language was far from perfect. Theorists like Klein, Anna

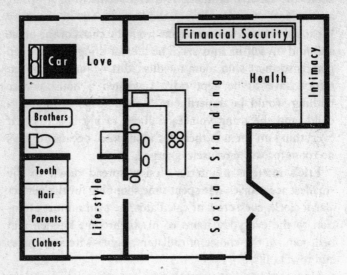

Freud and Winnicott soon realized that children could as well represent their inner world through non-verbal means, primarily by the use of toys and other objects. Unable to verbalize their problems, with a wooden stick or ball of wool a child might *act out* a conflict for the analyst to see. Similarly [though Eric would vehemently have opposed such an interpretation of his aesthetic], one could have argued that his tastes represented a form of acting out of his inner self.

Because he thought functionally of his life, he wished for it to be as well arranged as his apartment – where his social, financial, romantic and sexual pursuits could all assume coherence and harmony.

Though his existence seemed apparently well ordered, there was an argument for thinking he in fact had a much greater fear of, and hence sense of, disorder than others. A cobweb, a basket of dirty laundry, a broken window or plate affected him more than one might have expected in a man used to turmoil in his professional life. If Alice left a pile of newspapers in a mess on his floor, he could be guaranteed to flare up and deliver a viciously sarcastic remark.

'What does it matter if I leave the TV guide like that?' responded Alice one Sunday morning.

'It matters because I can't stand to see all this paper strewn everywhere.'

'But I was going to clear it up when we got back tonight.'

'You mean you were going to leave the whole place in a mess for the entire day?'

'Well, I was going to, but you make it sound like it's something you'd be sent to the Nuremberg Trials for, so I guess I won't.'

He was similarly frustrated if the phone cord was left with more than three coils in it, if the television remote control wasn't returned to its home above the set or if the books on his shelf were replaced without coordination [he had chosen a bibliographical method where volumes fitted in descending order according to size – *Treasures of the Louvre* placed next to *Great Wimbledon Moments* because their dimensions happened to assure a visually harmonious line].

Eric had grown up in a family whose outward façade of bourgeois respectability had hidden less palatable fissures. His father had worked as a lawyer but had been ignominiously fired for mysterious reasons when Eric was young. He had then been involved in a succession of disastrous business ventures which involved buying up land in Ireland, and plunged the family deeply into debt. His mother, a severe but intensely disciplined and resourceful woman, had struggled to keep up appearances and used a modest sum of money she had inherited to put her sons through public school. His father had begun to drink, and was prone to violent rages whose intensity his mother concealed as much from herself and her sons as from the neighbours in the genteel Notting Hill crescent in which they lived.

Eric had become a man who as far as possible wished to control the uncertainties of place, people and profession. He had started off in medicine because he had been attracted to its security and prestige, but had grown impatient with its salary structure. Wishing to insulate himself from long-term financial exposure, he had embarked on what had turned out to be a highly successful career in banking. One side of him was still a gambler, a risk taker, but only in an environment where the major elements of his life were on the right shelf.

There was on the other hand nothing minimal about Alice's bedroom, apart perhaps from its size. It was crammed full of every conceivable object and decorated in the gaudiest colours. To the side of the bed ran a large bookshelf stacked with battered paperbacks, the classics beside the garishly coloured not so classic, beside it sat a small black-and-white television with a looped aerial, above which was suspended a large cork pinboard with a bright collage of photographs. There were shots of mini-Alice and her family by the seaside, of her old house, of her dog Gatsby, there were friends and past boyfriends, aunts and grandmothers. Beside the pinboard was a chest of drawers decked with make up, hairbrushes, sprays, keys, a cylindrical yellow earthenware bowl she had bought in Bordeaux and an old Victorian mirror from Whitechapel market. Next came her desk, on which sat an old typewriter whose letters 'r' and 'y' didn't work, but on which she occasionally hammered out correspondence. In the drawers was stuffed mail she had received over the years, and fifteen volumes of her diaries into which she had been pouring her thoughts for half a decade. On the opposite wall sat an imposing wardrobe full of testaments to the changing history of fashion. Beside the bed were two piles of magazines, on top of which sat a radio and a confusion of cassettes.

When Eric first spent the night in Alice's room, he nicknamed it the junk yard, a label he thought so apt it became his regular term for it. He particularly objected to the cushions and furry animals on top of Alice's bed. More specifically, he developed a hatred for a pink furry heart-shaped cushion on which was written *I love Rome*. Whenever he slept in her room, he would throw the cushion into the bin at the other end of the room, or else place it on the top of the bookshelf beyond her reach.

'You little shit, why can't you leave my cushion alone?' asked Alice after this particular trick had been played yet again.

'Because it's the most offensive, ugly, disgusting, awful thing I've ever seen and I refuse to share my bed with it.'

'Well, you'll have to choose. It's either me *and* Rome-cushion or nothing.'

Alice wouldn't have claimed for a moment that the cushion was an attractive or in any way aesthetic object, but she nevertheless cherished it and had provided it with a home for the last ten years. Because she held to an *affective* rather than a *functional* view of interior design, an object's value was not for her primarily determined by how well it performed its task, but rather by what subsidiary associations had come to gather around it.

The heart-shaped cushion had been a present from

Alice's father, given during the last trip she and her parents had taken together before they divorced, a trip down one side of Italy of which she retained fond memories. There were certainly many more elegantly crafted cushions than this, cushions of a finer material and less vulgar dimensions, but none of them would have carried within their seams the particular history and affective charge possessed by this one, an embodiment of unusual happiness on a last family holiday many years before.

[ii] Sentimentality

Alice and Eric had recently eaten dinner in a small Spanish restaurant near her house, and there had fallen into a discussion over a rabbit Eric was planning to eat for his main course.

'Oh, Eric, don't. Can't you order something else?' pleaded Alice.

'You're being ridiculous, this rabbit looks delicious, cooked in white wine, with a selection of fresh vegetables . . . Yum.'

'I hate the idea of rabbits being eaten,' said Alice, who had in her childhood been very fond of an uncooked hazel-coloured version called Patch.

'You're such a vegetarian mystic.'

'Can I take your order?' asked the waiter.

'Yes, I think we're ready,' answered Eric assertively.

Fifteen minutes later, a rabbit arrived on a large steaming plate, and its famished recipient picked up his knife and fork and began eating with gusto.

'Ooooh, poor little baby-rabbit getting eaten by the big

bad wolf,' teased Eric, 'look at the big bad wolf with his claws chewing the lovely succulent rabbit meat.'

'Stop it, you bastard, I really don't see why you had to go and order just this rabbit when there were a hundred million other things on the menu.'

'Listen, Alice, I don't know why you're getting so excited over some bloody rabbit. You eat meat like anyone else, and the only reason I can see why you're getting so worked up over a rabbit is because it happens to have a slightly cuter face than a cow or sheep, and I've never seen you get qualms about munching into them. You've got a great moral code! Darwin should have thought of that one: survival of the cutest.'

Eric continued to tease her on the issue, and casually asked her the next day, 'So, Vegan, are we off to build any more boxes for rabbits today?'

Alice was perhaps hypocritical [why worry about a rabbit but not an ugly old sheep?], yet Eric's annoyance with her sentimentality was too persistent not to attract a degree of suspicion. He was unsentimental not just for logical reasons [if sheep why not rabbit?], but also because situations beloved of the sentimental stirred something in him. He rarely resisted being sarcastic about those who took a moist-eyed view of the sick, the helpless, one-legged cripples, lame ducks, unhappy lovers, weepy children and arthritic grannies, his sarcasm hinting at an embarrassment at the appalling frailty they represented.

If he teased Alice for crying every time she saw *Love Story* [and she had seen it perhaps ten times], it was because he shunned a sadness of which her tears were a symbolic reminder. It was no wonder he was often brusque when she tried to tell him she was low or feeling 'as fat as an elephant'. His remarks to the effect that of course she was fine and beautiful and could they please move on to another subject had as its message, '*Of course you're OK. You must feel OK – I couldn't take it if you weren't . . .*'

Children were an embodiment of weakness, so Alice and Eric's contrasting attitudes to them were significant: Alice loved them, Eric would say, 'If I had kids, I just couldn't wait till they were grown up: I hate it when they're at that goo-goo gaga stage.' When they went to see Jane's son Tim, Eric asked the four-year-old some simple questions, but because Tim sensed a disapproving tone, he lost confidence, mumbled and looked sheepishly away – and would have burst into tears had his mother not at that moment picked him up.

Whereas it bothered Eric to decode a child's hesitant mumbles, Alice had no qualms making up for the child's faults with her own understanding, filling in the gaps he or she couldn't yet close. Though adult in all the obvious ways, Eric's reaction was curiously childish in expecting of others what children expect of their parents – namely infallibility. He was unable to use his own strength to make up for the weaknesses of others, unable to adopt the role of forgiving parent to the faults of those around him.

One weekend, Alice and Eric were invited for lunch with friends who lived in a village near Oxford, and because Eric had to be back in London sooner than Alice, they agreed to take two cars. Alice wasn't sure of the way, and asked Eric if she could follow behind him. He was used to driving his BMW in the fast lane of the motorway, and was therefore irritated when he noticed how slowly he would have to go for Alice's VW Beetle to keep up with him. At junctions, he would see her in his rear-view mirror looking cautiously both ways before advancing. 'What an old granny,' he muttered to himself. At a roundabout near Reading, the Beetle stalled and Alice lost sight of Eric and the correct exit to take. When he noticed she was no longer following him, he cursed her again, but didn't return to the roundabout. He knew she had the address, directions and a map, and would therefore eventually find her destination. He preferred to speed on rather than play parent to Alice's automotive weakness.

It was logical if Eric did the opposite of feel *sentimental* [i.e. feel sorry for the weak], and respected instead those who had overcome obstacles with dignity and force of character. An unsentimental person, Eric was poised between denigrating the weak and admiring the strong.

[iii] Nudity

On the first night they spent together, and only a few hours after he had addressed his first word to her, Eric hoisted Alice on to the dining table and slipped off her underwear. For Alice, the process from seductive glance to penetration normally lasted anything from a weekend to a few months, so that she was herself surprised at the strength of her desire and the rapidity of proceedings. However much one side of her might have wanted to resist, she had found herself unwilling to bow to the relics of inherited morality dictating what a good girl should do. What the hell! she thought, and abandoned herself to the moment. She let Eric energetically undo her dress and unclip her bra. She let herself be carried naked, first on to the sofa and then into the bedroom, while Eric cheerfully shed his own clothes and scattered them across the apartment.

After they had made love, Eric climbed out of bed to get water from the kitchen, and returned carrying a large bottle and a couple of glasses. He was an incongruous sight, standing stark naked beside the chest of drawers, carefully pouring the water like a waiter in an elegant restaurant.

'Don't you want a dressing-gown?' asked Alice.

'No, it ruins all the post-coital erotics,' grinned Eric.

'I thought post-coital meant there were no more erotics.'

'Ah, that's the traditional view, but . . .' answered Eric suggestively.

From the first night, it was obvious how comfortable Eric felt with his own body. In a most unreflective and immediate way, he took pleasure in his physical form and was therefore happy to suppose others would do likewise, rendering the use of a dressing-gown or towel superfluous. He rarely saw a need to draw the curtains to deny the neighbours a view of a deep French kiss, and was ever ready to strip naked for a swim if a river, jacuzzi or swimming-pool presented itself.

Alice admired Eric's physical candour, a candour which – moments of passion aside – she found herself unable to match. Her first impulse was to reach for a dressing-gown or T-shirt, to dim the lights and avoid the verdict of full-length mirrors. A body was not something to parade unnecessarily around the apartment, unless it was a question of love-making, an occasion carrying with it assurances that the male would be sufficiently aroused for his critical faculties to be forgivingly distracted.

Eric teased Alice about this. 'I don't understand why you're telling me to shut my eyes when you're going to be naked next to me in about half a second,' he told her when she insisted he look away while she got undressed before bed. 'I can't see why you won't let me see you walking across the room when I know exactly what you look like.'

For Alice to show herself naked was to reveal an area of potential shame ['You call those breasts?' 'Are you sure those feet don't belong to a duck?' she would ask herself in self-hating moods]. When the make up was removed and the clothes lay in a heap on the floor, she felt stripped of her defences, and in a vulnerable state looked for reassurance from her lover that he would not laugh or use the physical evidence against her. She experienced her body as a liability, a weakness, something she was at the mercy of others to be generous toward. However irrational, she couldn't help but feel a reserve when naked, a need to convince herself she could trust the man she was with – mixed with a lingering, near irresistible urge to bolt into the bathroom.

'You idiot, give me my things back,' she pleaded with Eric the morning he decided to play a practical joke on her and hid her clothes in a secret recessed cupboard. 'You've got one minute, and then I'm calling the police.'

'Fine, here's the phone, they'll agree with me, you look much better undressed than dressed,' he answered.

'Don't be so nasty Eric, I'm going to get *really* angry if you don't do what I tell you,' warned Alice, standing in the middle of the living-room, an impatient Eve after a fig-leaf.

'Relax.'

'Relax. It's all very funny to you, isn't it? Well it's very annoying for me, OK. So please, just give me back my clothes.'

'All right, my honey, they're in that cupboard by the kitchen – just don't get so hassled.'

[iv] Emotional Nudity

However much Eric may have prided himself on his physical ease, he reserved crippling coyness for another form of nudity – but in an area so different that for a long time Alice failed to link it to her own pursuit of a fig leaf. Eric may have been happy to gambol naked through rivers and forests, but what made him run for a symbolic dressing-gown with immeasurably greater urgency was the mere threat of emotional nudity.

What makes emotional nudity harder to detect is its lack of clear definition. To be physically naked is a visual fact – and therefore prudes in this area can be easily hounded and their clothes hidden by contemporary pleasure moralists with their emphasis on physical ease. But because the self is enclosed in the body, emotional coyness can take longer to identify and unclothe, though there may in this area be as many if not more prudes.

Emotional nudity hinges on the revelation of one's weakness and insufficiency to another human being, a dependence on them which strips us of a capacity to impress in any way other than through the sheer fact of our existence. We can no longer lie or bluster, boast or hide ourselves behind fine words – as Montaigne said of the moment of death, when emotionally naked, we must speak plain French [or whatever language happens to be naturally our own].

I strip myself emotionally when I confess *need* – that I would be lost without you, that I am not necessarily the independent person I have tried to appear, but am a far less admirable weakling with little clue of life's course or meaning. When I cry and tell you things I trust you will keep for yourself, that would destroy me if others were to learn of them, when I give up the game of gazing seductively at parties and admit it's you I care about, I am stripping myself of a carefully sculpted illusion of invulnerability. I become as defenceless and trusting as the person in the circus trick, strapped to a board into which another is throwing knives to within inches of my skin, knives I have myself freely given. I allow you to see me humiliated, unsure of myself, vacillating, drained of self-confidence, hating myself and hence unable to convince you [should I need to] to do otherwise. I am weak when I have shown you my panicked face at three in the morning, anxious before existence, free of the blustering, optimistic philosophies I had proclaimed over dinner. I learn to accept the enormous risk that though I am not the confident pin-up of everyday life, though you have at hand an exhaustive catalogue of my fears and phobias, you may nevertheless love me.

And what therefore is emotional clothing? It consists of a whole wardrobe designed to preserve from another's sight the soft interior, the symbolic genital vulnerability, the great and secret '*I need you*'. To be clothed is to refuse to place oneself in the hands of another whom one cannot control, one who may by definition hurt or drive us crazy by not answering a call or flirting with the legs opposite.

Eric rarely entered a relationship without making sure he had a full wardrobe of double-lined suits, aiming to construct a life where love would not be the chief pillar, where he would not be forced to cede the autonomous foundations of his happiness.

One could divide architects in this area into the romantic and the sensible. Sensible architects have learnt the basic rule that the weight of a building must be spread out across many supports [the more the better], so in case of an accident, the weight may shift from a damaged part to a succession of intact links.

Eric spread his weight widely; his pillars included keeping up with several female friends [reducing the consequence of structural collapse on account of a single rejection], socializing with a sufficiently large set to survive falling out with a particular group and earning enough money to spread the risk of a given deal falling foul.

Alice was a different and far less wise architect altogether, for she tended to place all her needs on one pillar and hoped against hope that it would take the weight.

Though currently such a pillar, Eric was remarkably reluctant to acknowledge himself in this supporting role. There was a certain un-self-referentiality about him, a hesitancy in accepting his position in the relationship, in asking, 'What do *I* feel?' 'What are *we* doing in this together?' 'What will *we* be doing next weekend?'

His reluctance was not based on a neglect of Alice's qualities, it was simply the attitude to these qualities which marked him out as an emotional prude – his reluctance to admit he would have had trouble living without them.

Alice had initially accepted this as part of the rules – during the first weeks, it wasn't expected that couples discuss what they meant to one another, for fear the feeling was not mutual. References to the future were curtailed in case one party could not envisage one.

After two lovers have shared a bed for the first time, the mention of another meeting in days or weeks to come is normally interpreted as deeply significant. There is rarely anything casual in the way a lover says, 'So maybe we'll go to that play on my birthday,' when the birthday in question lies two weeks away. The proposal represents a subtle but distinct signal that the couple will survive till then at least. As a relationship progresses, one expects the projected time-frame to increase, to the point when one may with some assurance say, 'Why don't we start saving up to go skiing at the end of next year?' or even, 'How about a cruise when we retire?'

Yet the time-frame Eric displayed was stunted in the extreme: it rarely extended beyond the week. Though Alice hoped that the future would soon appear more settled, he simply discovered ever more ingenious ways to side-step the danger of chronological self-referentiality.

Even the declarations were coded. The couple had recently gone to see a bad American film, the story of a Texan couple whom circumstances separate but for whom love triumphs over the odds. The lead male actor [named Billy in the film] bore a striking resemblance to Eric, which both Alice and he had mentioned on coming out of the cinema. Eric felt close to Alice that night and on the way back to the car wrapped his arms around her. He wanted to tell her how beautiful she looked, and how he cared for her, but instead of doing so in the accent of his class and nation, he chose to do so through the voice of the lead male actor of the film.

'My honey pie, you're the sweetest little thing I've ever seen in my whole goddamn life,' said Eric in Billy's Texan drawl.

'Oh, it's nice of you to say so,' replied Alice in her usual accent, taking his hand and stroking it gently.

'You know, you're the best thing this side of the Mississippi,' added Billy/Eric poetically.

'Am I? Then who's the woman I should be jealous of on the other side of the Mississippi?'

Eric was similarly used to disguising emotional needs under the more acceptable level of the physical. If he wished to gain Alice's attention, he was more comfortable declaring he had a cold, bad flu or devastating back ache than admitting the real pain which might have lain behind this somatizing.

Illness would mean putting on a woollen cap, wrapping himself in overcoats and lying in bed announcing his imminent demise.

'Nurse Alice, help the patient, can you be an angel and get me some vitamin C?' he would call out from his deathbed.

He could escape the risks entailed in the lover/loved scenario by casting himself and Alice in the roles of patient and nurse; a primitive need to be cuddled and adored could be satisfied by calling out for more nose drops and cough syrup.

In June, Eric flew to Frankfurt to secure valuable business for his bank, but returned to London bitterly disappointed after the deal went to a German firm instead. At dinner that night, he was mostly silent and picked morosely at the meal Alice had prepared. He went to sit down on the sofa, and because he looked so miserable and dejected, she stretched herself beside him and took his head in her hands.

'Well, you're still my hero, whether you come back with your bounty of Deutschmarks or not,' she said to him, brushing back his hair and looking at him tenderly.

'For God's sake, Alice, don't bloody patronize me, OK,' he replied, the natural reaction in a man who lived under the punishing, lonely belief that he deserved love solely for his successes.

[v] Generosity

Eric had always been a notably generous person. Even in the days when he had had little money, he had been the first to offer the drinks or pick up bills in restaurants. When his friends had birthdays, he took care to send them flowers and gifts, he supported a range of charities and at work supplemented his secretary's salary with a share of his own. When Alice and he went shopping, he was often ready to pay, aware of how much more he earned.

After a weekend with friends in Dorset, Alice returned

with a present for Eric, a local cheese wrapped in aluminium foil.

'They make it in this tiny farmhouse with only a couple of cows, I don't even know the name, but you'll love it,' said Alice.

'How sweet. No one's ever given me a cheese before,' replied Eric, touched as much by the dairy product as by the care that had gone into packing and carrying it back to London.

Though indeed delicious, this symbol of Alice's affections was nevertheless experienced as a burden far heavier than the material cheese itself – the burden of being in debt to her for the care and love the gift embodied. Its presence in Eric's refrigerator symbolized all the effort that Alice had made for *him*; she had gone to a farmhouse, handed over money, wrapped the cheese and put it in her bag, and all the time it had been him she had had in mind. What a delight! What a weight!

It was therefore no surprise if Eric shifted the burden of gratitude and surprised Alice the next day by buying her a beautiful ring they had both seen and liked in a shop near Oxford Street.

'I can't believe it,' exclaimed Alice as she opened the box, and rushed to give Eric a kiss. 'It's so generous of you.'

Eric had been financially generous – the ring wasn't cheap, and yet the action had perhaps been less emotionally generous, a miserly attempt to lighten the debt engendered by Alice's five-pound cheese. He had wished to be the greater gift giver, as much because he enjoyed giving as because he hated to experience the lack of autonomy involved in filling a position of gratitude.

Though debts are condemned in the financial world, the

world of friendship and love may perversely depend on well-managed debts. What is good fiscal policy may be bad amorous policy – for part of love is to fall into debt and yet tolerate the uncertainty arising from owing someone something, trusting them with the ensuing power, the choice it gives them of how and when to claim their dues.

Though Eric paid his bills on time, it was a pity for Alice that he couldn't exercise an equivalent emotional maturity by forgetting to pay her back so promptly.

KNOWING ANOTHER

In the first week of August, after Alice had been going out with Eric for over five months, she received a phone call from a girlfriend who now lived in Holland and whom she had first known in a summer camp in Massachusetts many years before.

'So tell me the gossip. Who is he?' asked Monica.

'He's called Eric, and he's a banker.'

'How long has it been?'

'Oh, God, quite a few months, six I think.'

'Sexy?'

'Yeah, I guess.'

'What's he like?'

'What's he like?'

'Yeah, you know.'

'I don't know really.'

'How do you mean you don't know? You're the one going out with him.'

'Well, he's . . . I don't really know how to explain, he's . . . he's just kind of odd,' said Alice, and laughed because the word *odd* had slipped out quite without her having planned it.

'Odd?' asked Monica. 'You always went out with such normal guys, what's come over you?'

And yet thinking about the word on the way home that day, Alice realized that with the accuracy of all parapraxes, it perhaps reflected the truth of her feelings better than other and more polite words. Eric was not openly odd: he didn't think himself Napoleon or wear a shower cap in bed; but the sum of his behaviour nevertheless came over as odd because Alice could fit it into no predictable category.

The pattern of our behaviour towards others is guided largely by an unconscious notion of their likely reponses to us. We project a mental map of the other's traits, using this to orientate ourselves in choosing what to say or do to them. It is a model operating on the basis of: *If I do or say x, then s/he will do y* . . . Enriched beyond a certain complexity, this model is what allows us to make the more or less tentative claim that we *know* someone. Alice remembered a billboard aphorism she had once seen by the American artist Jenny Holzer. It read quite simply:

> SPIT ALL OVER SOMEONE
> WITH A MOUTHFUL OF
> MILK IF YOU WANT TO
> FIND OUT ABOUT
> THEIR PERSONALITY FAST

Without actually going so far as to spit milk at someone, Alice would sometimes amuse herself by passing an imaginary milk test on people: what would the man reading the sports pages on the train opposite her do? How would this government minister react? What would be the response from the taxi driver or flower shop assistant? It was an absurd imaginary test that would nevertheless quickly reveal the particularities of a character, the potential for irritability, for humour, for vulnerability. And Alice found in thinking of this test that there were always people whose responses she could comfortably predict, and others who left her completely blank.

There was for instance no doubt that Alice could claim to *know* [in the sense of predict] the behaviour and character of her work colleague Xandra. Xandra was a thirty-five-year-old accountant who sat in the desk opposite, dressed in yellow and burgundy jackets, and had a behaviour map whose contours could be plotted to comic perfection.

Xandra may at origin have been a psychologically complex person, but the practical outcome of her history had the regularity of clockwork. It was her monistic theme that others were fated to lead a better life than her and that it was a duty to alert others [over endless cups of coffee] to her monstrous disappointments. If Alice told her about a pleasant weekend she had spent, Xandra's first response was sure not to be, 'How nice for you,' but rather, 'Why don't I ever get to spend nice weekends?' If someone was promoted, she would remark, 'They're just doing it to spite me.' If a good-looking man walked through the office, within one to three minutes [Alice had amused herself timing this], Xandra would begin a speech complaining in some way of the inferiority of her own boyfriend, an overweight electrician whose dramatic lack of qualities made the sane wonder why Xandra stayed with him. Even buying an imaginatively filled sandwich from the deli downstairs provoked the comment, 'Why can't I ever choose such exciting fillings?'

No one could have been further from her affections than this despicable colleague, yet Alice had to admit that interaction with her had an element to it that life with Eric unfortunately did not. She simply didn't *know* Eric in the way she *knew* Xandra, her behaviour with him could count on none of the set responses Xandra produced. He was still more or less a mystery to her, someone whose sudden piques of anger, bursts of generosity, emotional blind spots and great insights followed the contours of none of Alice's known psychological models.

She would sometimes join Eric and find the conversation stilted and awkward: 'It's like we're strangers tonight,' she would say.

'Is it?'

'Yeah, I felt we were really comfortable last night, and tonight it's like we just met.'

'Well, these things happen, don't they? Is there any of that pasta left in the fridge?' [Eric had a remarkable ability to make his own shortcomings seem like the work of others: Alice felt an idiot for bringing the matter up, Eric settled happily into the remains of some lasagne.]

Nor could Alice predict when Eric would lose his temper. If she was anxious, she was in the habit of taking the sleeve of her jumper and burying her face in it. She was in the midst of performing this particular tic on a drive to Hampstead when Eric braked the car suddenly and bellowed at her: 'Don't fucking do that!'

'Do what?' asked Alice alarmed.

'With your hand, that, with the jumper,' he blurted, hardly able to formulate his annoyance.

'I'm sorry, OK, my God, what's so bad about that?'

'It just drives me crazy, that's all.'

But before she could definitively label him a cantankerous bastard who flew off the handle at the slightest provocation, he would surprise her by reacting calmly to situations where others typically lost their nerve. When she was sent to visit clients in Peterborough, Eric lent her his credit card, only for her to leave it behind or have it stolen in the course of making a phone call in King's Cross Station. Traumatized at the thought of what would ensue when she told him his Visa card had gone missing in the midst of a busy train station, Alice reached a point where she was so fearful of his reaction, she decided to settle the issue by announcing gravely to him: 'We have to stop going out.'

'What? Why?'

'Because I've done something so terrible, I simply can't be forgiven, and it's better if we just end everything now. So I'll just take my stuff from the bedroom and call a taxi, and we'll just stay out of one another's way for a while, and perhaps then . . .'

'What are you talking about? What are you saying? What's up?'

'Oh, shit,' said Alice and bit her lip.

'What?'

'I can't tell you.'

'You've got to tell me.'

'I can't.'

'Don't be silly, what is it?'

'I've lost your credit card.'

'Is that all? My goodness, you really scared me.'

'You mean you don't mind?'

'No, it's no problem, we'll just call up the card people and they'll cancel it and send me a new one on Monday. There couldn't be anything easier. Alice, don't look so worried, it's fine, it really is, I mean it, I don't mind about some silly old credit card, it's good you didn't lose anything more valuable. Come on, let's just forget the whole thing, it isn't worth talking about for another second.'

Eric's elusive behaviour frustrated Alice's need for certainty, she was constantly drawing maps, then having to review them in response to geological shifts in his nature. Evidence of love was her willingness or energy to apply the best interpretation to this confusion. If he was irritable, it was only because he was overworked, if he was uncommunicative, it was only because he was tired or hungry. At one point, she defined Eric as 'someone who surprises himself by his own niceness, and then feels the danger associated with surrender, so has to temper this with meanness'. And after he had again been unreasonably irritable, she would tell herself, 'Don't take it personally, this is someone who is basically kind, but afflicted by an as yet unclear psychological trauma that makes him get angry with others when he's really frustrated with himself.'

For a long time, she understood his lack of emotional communication under the mental compartment labelled 'shyness'. This was the dominant interpretation of rather brusque behaviour after love-making, or an off-hand way of ending phone conversations. Added to this was the thought, 'He's very English,' – a vague cluster of ideas derived from the store of national folk wisdom which tells us English people overcook vegetables and don't like to speak of their emotions. On top of this, she formed another theory after a meal with his parents, in which the silent and austere way in which they had directed the meal had caused her to think: 'He can't help it, it's his family background.'

Alice therefore understood his lack of dialogue, a section of his behaviour that was troubling her, by placing it under three implicit headings:

1) Shyness
2) Englishness
3) Parental influence.

But no sooner had she gotten used to accepting these traits than they would go away for a weekend to a friend's house outside London, and a whole other side to Eric would emerge: very communicative with friends, gentle, helpful, apparently very un-English against a background of others. So the lack of communication would be explained otherwise, the result of:

1) Overwork
2) Urban life
3) [*more alarmingly*] Her own inability to bring out his latent warmth.

It seemed as though Eric had a resistance to being wholly loved or hated. He had antennae for times when Alice questioned the relationship, but none for her feelings any way before that. If this was a conscious phenomenon, there was an element of brinkmanship to the way he would ignore her for days, only to pull back or apologize just when she wished to confront him.

She was forced to realize how little she knew of the man she loved, what a mystery his behaviour still was. Eric had never seemed less complex than on the first night they'd met. On that first meeting, she had seemed to 'know' him in a way she could no longer claim. He was like an object that seemed whole from a distance, but had fragmented into a million pieces on closer inspection. She wondered how so many apparently irreconcilable elements could co-exist, and felt weary at the effort this unpredictability entailed, its lack of stability entailing only perpetual questioning and interpretation.

PREDICTABILITY

Before we need to know whether someone is good or bad, we crave an assurance that whatever the answer, they'll stick to being one or the other. Of course it would be better if they were good people, people who asked us questions and remembered our birthdays, but if they were to be bad, clearly evil, perhaps a little perverse, then we could as easily learn to keep clear of them, dismissing them with a remark that it takes all sorts to fill the world, happy not to have to share a bunkbed with them.

It isn't easy to realize someone can be nice to their secretary but beastly with their spouse, intelligent at maths but stupid at emotions, great with soufflés but disappointing with lamb. If we appease our social guilt via affiliation to a wildlife group, we don't like hearing Hitler loved children and animals. If we consider ourselves sensitive for crying during *Snow White*, it isn't nice to be told Idi Amin considered it his favourite film. If we like German literature, it's disturbing to learn that commanders liberating Auschwitz found copies of Goethe in the SS officers' mess. Isn't it more pleasant to consider oneself off the hook as a potential mass murderer simply because one is stirred by passages of *Dichtung und Warheit*?

Leafing through yet another biography of poor Flaubert, one finds the famous author described by his biographer as a 'strange animal', who was 'bristling with contradictions':

His loathing for the bourgeois was all the stronger because he felt himself to be bourgeois to the bone, with his love of order, comfort and hierarchy. He condemned all governments but couldn't stand the excesses of the rabble when they dared to defy them . . . The sworn enemy of priests, he was attracted by religious problems. Obsessed with feminine charm, he refused to become attached to any woman. A revolutionary in art, he was conservative in daily life. Hungering for friendship, he lived most of the time apart from his fellow men . . .*

That M. Troyat chose to call these things *contradictions* has something of the mock innocence of nuns bursting in on an orgy and pretending to be shocked when human nature isn't quite what they had expected. It implies attachment to the possibility of a *non*-contradictory character, a world where those obsessed with feminine charm would automatically find themselves involved with the object of their obsession, where everyone attracted to religious problems would naturally want to take tea with priests, where those who hungered for friendship would at once join a bridge club.

Flaubert seemed instead to have had a mind [in the philosopher Amelie Rorty's phrase] like a 'system of double-entry bookkeeping', one where incompatible elements ran in parallel train-tracks beside one another.

Biographers may be accused of a certain temperamental intolerance as regards train-tracks, attempting to ingeniously explain away the contradictions of their subjects. The revolutionary who loved fine dining was only doing so in the name of the class struggle: 'Trotsky's taste for venison and rare-cooked sirloin was only a subtle attempt to offend the vegetarian lobby and hence hasten the demise

* Henri Troyat, *Flaubert*, translated by Jean Pinkham, Viking, 1993

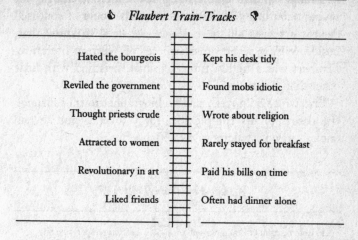

Flaubert Train-Tracks

Hated the bourgeois	Kept his desk tidy
Reviled the government	Found mobs idiotic
Thought priests crude	Wrote about religion
Attracted to women	Rarely stayed for breakfast
Revolutionary in art	Paid his bills on time
Liked friends	Often had dinner alone

of the capitalist state . . .' The idealistic philosopher whose writings worshipped children while failing to provide for his own offspring did so for consistent motives: 'Rousseau's apparent cruelty to his own children was at heart a well-meaning attempt to prepare them for the rigours of society . . .'

When contradictions threaten to gravely undermine biographies, they may be rescued by the use of the word 'genius'. Flaubert was contradictory, but that's the price for being able to write *L'Éducation Sentimentale*. Picasso was nasty to his wives, but painted important pictures – complex perhaps, but could one really expect less from the twentieth century's greatest artist? Genius is for the intelligent what 'madness' is for the dim witted, an extreme state in which everything becomes possible, and the normal rules miraculously don't apply.

But outside the world of biographies, contradictions seem less anomalous. Far from earning Flaubert the title of a 'strange animal' for wishing two different things, for saying one thing and doing another, his welter of confused desires gives us all the evidence we need to know that, beside writing several masterpieces of Western literature, Flaubert was a highly typical animal, bristling with little other than normality.

Eric wrote no novels, had no biographer to trail through the debris of his complexities [only lovers], but he had enough inconsistencies to rival Flaubert.

☙ *Eric Train-Tracks* ❧

Admired the calm of Zen philosophy	Lost his temper regularly
Enthusiastic about good organization	Often late calling
Gave money to mental charities	Didn't suffer fools gladly
Loving one day	Indifferent the next
Capable of empathy	Then selfish in the extreme
Insightful about relationships	Blind in his own case

The contradictions were rendered all the more unassailable because Eric was so ready to admit to them. He could quite cheerfully tell Alice, 'I know I'm a nutcase, I never claimed anything else.'

There is a frustratingly candid way of behaving which one could call Cretan, named after the '"*All Cretans are liars,*" *said the Cretan*' paradox. The Cretan personality is ambiguously placed within their own pronouncements, and allows an interlocutor to have no sure footing of what is truth and what falsehood. What Eric said at one moment contradicted what he said or did at another: his warning that Cretans were liars was rendered void by the news that he too was a Cretan. Far from being unaware of his contradictions, Eric was more aware of them than most. In so far as he was ill tempered, he was the Cretan kind of choleric who admits they are choleric ['I know I'm a choleric,' says the choleric] – and hence renders their offence less susceptible to criticism. It left Alice asking: 'If he really was an ill-tempered bastard, would he be talking like this?' She was prey to the belief that being aware of a fault was almost tantamount to not having it; 'Surely the point about being a true bastard is that you don't understand you're a bastard. If Eric realizes the danger, how can he actually be one?'

There are people who are so simply and unselfconsciously evil, they present no challenge to the understanding from a conceptual [as opposed to moral] point of view. Then there are those who can't be so easily dismissed because they are themselves partly aware of the things others find distasteful in them, they are their own self-critics and hence escape the full force of external attacks.

Eric could behave obscurely for days, then suddenly declare to Alice, 'I'm being impossible at the moment, I know. Believe me, I understand what you're going through. Don't start seeing me as someone who isn't interested in you or anything. It's just a phase I'm in.'

His contradictions threatened to undermine her understanding of logic. How could a man both love her *and* be cold towards her? She often tried to neutralize the contradiction by removing one factor from the equation – perhaps he didn't love her, or else perhaps he wasn't really cold toward her, simply tired or shy.

Yet he never allowed her the stability of such conclusions, for no sooner did she begin to reconcile herself to one or the other than he would disprove in the act of confession the trait of which she thought him guilty. He denied the legitimacy of ambivalence towards him: he seemed to understand ambivalence better or before she did, leaving her with complaint but no original grounds for it.

'I don't blame you for getting annoyed,' he would tell her candidly. 'Believe me, I wouldn't live with a guy like myself if I had any choice in the matter.'

In one of his lesser-known experiments, the great Russian psychologist Pavlov discovered that a dog could be driven to a state of neurosis, trembling, urinating and defecating, if the signals it had been trained to respond to were sufficiently confused. If a bell which had come to be associated with food suddenly became the herald of an empty plate, the dog could, after a few examples of this, be reconditioned to accept a state of food-less affairs. But if the bell sometimes produced food and sometimes did not, if there was total irregularity in the proceedings, the creature would no longer know what to think: confused by the mysterious connection between the food and its non-appearance, between bells that sometimes meant one thing and sometimes another [though always the opposite of what one expected] the dog would slowly slide into a form of canine insanity.

LOVE PERMANENCE

The psychoanalyst Donald Winnicott famously suggested that only a finite period of time separated the moment when a baby was left by its mother and the moment when the baby gave up on the mother's continued existence and hence possible return:

The feeling of the mother's existence lasts x minutes. If the mother is away more than x minutes, then the imago fades, and along with this the baby's capacity to use the symbol of the union ceases. The baby is distressed, but this distress is soon mended because the mother returns in $x + y$ minutes. In $x + y$ minutes the baby has not become altered. But in $x + y + z$ minutes the baby has become traumatized. In $x + y + z$ minutes the mother's return does not mend the baby's altered state. Trauma implies that the baby has experienced a break in life's continuity . . .*

Winnicott's insight was that the image of the mother within the child was highly precarious, and might suffer irreparable damage with time – a mother's ten-month trip overseas would seem like a death to her son or daughter, however many presents might appear from faraway lands. Adults would by contrast have achieved a more robust faith in the survival of others beyond their immediate surroundings. Someone's mother could depart for a year to Australia, but her image and memory would be capable of surviving the time and distance, even if she neglected to

* D. W. Winnicott, *Playing and Reality*, Routledge 1991

send back the promised postcards. She would not be killed in the imagination simply because she was absent – out of sight would no longer be out of mind.

Winnicott emphasized that this *image-constancy*, the factor which assured a sense of continuity of objects beyond the visual field, was a developmental feature rather than a given. It was something we learnt rather than inherited, something founded gradually on a sense of faith – a faith that because until now mother had returned every time, she and her substitutes in adult life [lovers and friends] would continue to do likewise.

Adding to this thesis, the psychologist Jean Piaget discovered that children below a certain age had no idea that objects removed from their visual field continued to exist elsewhere. One could wave a toy bear in front of a baby below eight to ten months, then hide this bear beneath a cushion, and the child would have no interest in looking for it, simply accepting it had gone forever. The baby would mourn the bear's symbolic death rather than shake off its tears and pursue it. But beyond this period, Piaget suggested the child would have developed a sufficient sense of what he called object permanence to go hunting for the bear, tracking it down under the cushion out of an acquired faith in its continued existence.

To push Winnicott and Piaget's theory to analogy with Alice and Eric might have been far fetched, but there was at issue a common idea of permanence, not *object-permanence*, but rather *love-permanence*. What did this love-permanence imply? A certain faith in the other's love which could endure beyond immediate proof or sign of the lover's interest, faith that though in Milan or Vienna for the weekend, the partner was not in the process of sharing a cappuccino or Sachertorte with a rival sweetheart, faith that a silence was simply a silence and not an intimation of love's demise.

Alice's sense that Eric loved her often necessitated an element of faith akin to the baby's belief in the absent mother, something to be held on to despite lack of immediate visual or tactile evidence. Whole dinners they shared in which she had the impression he was not really quite there, that the most important part of him was at the office or somewhere worse, tethered to a crisis on the foreign exchange or another's fluttering eyelids. She would take his hand and ask, 'Is everything all right?' and he would answer, 'Of course,' as though to ask had been taboo. His speech would grow empty of affect, she would feel his uninterest in the current location, he would talk without focus on the personal status of his interlocutor. He would say, 'I'd really like to see you at the weekend,' yet deliver the message in such a way that its meaning was in effect, 'Perhaps staying home would be better' – the difference signalled by the merest inflexion on the *really*, the voice dropping slightly on the *you*.

Then would come more tender times, on the way back home in a taxi, he would put an arm around Alice and kiss the top of her head. In the symbolic sense, he had come home. And yet the interval between time x, when he had left the conversation, when his speech had become empty, and time y, when he had kissed the top of her head, had been a time of anxiety. Alice had known how to master this, she hadn't forgotten him as Winnicott's baby might, and yet she had felt a trace of the primitive pain of the abandoned infant, asking herself wretchedly: 'Is it something I did?'

Love has the capacity to transform otherwise sober-minded individuals into paranoiacs, obsessed by calamitous, millennial thoughts – *S/he doesn't love me any more, s/he's bored, I'm sure s/he's calling the whole thing off as soon as it's decent to do so . . .* Paranoia may be the most natural response to the feeling of love, to fully valuing another and hence growing aware of the ever present potential for their loss. But for those already drawn to scenarios of disaster, love can only aggravate a raw wound.

Alice worried about everything: she worried that a pipe was leaking gas in her building, that the strange noise after take-off meant an engine had caught fire, that a small mole on her back was cancerous, that she was losing her memory and her friends.

The origins of these worries were hard to trace. They clearly had nothing to do with the object of worry themselves: the worry was in a Freudian sense only a *symptom*. Perhaps, to return to Winnicott, it had something to do with her experiences as a child. Perhaps her mother had returned after $x + y + z$ time had elapsed. Her mother was indeed very unreliable. She would call Alice from Miami where she lived with her third husband and tell her how much she adored her and looked forward to seeing her on her next trip to Europe. She would then fly into London, stay in a suite at a glamorous hotel, and make an appointment with Alice for which she would be an hour late, arriving with the apology that she had after all decided to fit in a pedicure and that the dear girl had taken longer than expected.

At university, Alice had spent several months in a passionate relationship with a bearded marine biologist, who had turned to her one sunny May morning and explained, 'Listen, I just don't think I have this boyfriend-girlfriend feeling with you any more.' The appalling grammatical structure of the sentence aside, the message couldn't have come as a greater shock. Only the previous day, they had been rowing on the river, he had joked to her that they had compatible skin types and had played with her feet and caressed her knee. How in that case could he suddenly have decided, in the space of little more than twenty four hours, that the so-called boyfriend-girlfriend feeling had deserted him? There must have been an appalling discrepancy between her feelings when she had given him her hand and his when he had held it.

The experience had helped shatter some of twenty-year-old Alice's illusions. She had become aware of the possible insincerity of actions: the way a man might kiss and hold her hand, but his thoughts could be elsewhere entirely, an almost immoral gap existing between surface expression and underlying intention.

A problem of trust had opened up, it becoming harder for her to believe in the sincerity of others, every betrayal she had suffered adding to the thesis that human beings were essentially treacherous and had to be kept at a safe distance. If she now showed signs of paranoia, if she needed to be held at more than normal intervals, it was in part to repair the damage past experiences had inflicted.

One could have likened the scenario of love-permanence to a suspension bridge, in which the reassurances of love were symbolized by supporting pylons, and the times in the cold by the metres of cabling strung between them. A kiss on the head, an affectionate glance, could count as a pillar, a silent meal, a phone call unanswered, could stand for the cable in between.

It was strange to think of the differing degrees of reassurance people might require, the differing lengths of cable involved in relationships. Some, in which both partners were warm, open or simply needy, the pillars would be placed very close to one another, there would be constant signs of affection and little slack between each pillar.

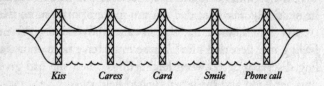

In others, huge distances might stretch without support.

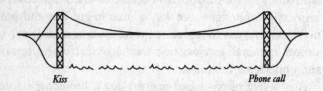

The length a cable could be strung would depend on the temperament and history of the lover. Someone who thought themselves inherently loveable would need little reassurance, and could hence carry a cable for hundreds of metres without another's pylon. *I love you* would be required much less frequently because *I love myself* would make up for any shortfall. *Why shouldn't you love me?* would be the basic attitude of the self-lover when in love, *Why shouldn't you feel about me what I feel about myself?*

But in Alice's case, the pillars needed to be kept much closer together, because her basic disposition was always: *How can you possibly love me?* The point was not that Alice didn't trust Eric, but rather that she didn't see *herself* as someone who could command the allegiance of another's affections for a sustained period. She didn't trust herself to attract far more than she may have doubted Eric's capacity to stay attracted.

Trust could be defined as a way of interpreting absence

reasonably. But with Alice, a wink or an odd laugh could set off a catalogue of fears – 'What did he mean by that? Was he laughing at me?' There was of course something rather selfish or at least self-centred in this, paranoid people believing in a world in which others would always be giving off covert signs *for their benefit* [even the man in the post office was winking at *them*].

Yet Eric did frequently leave the relationship genuinely ambiguous. Attached to his freedom, he had the habit of introducing Alice in public as someone only incidentally connected to him. He behaved in company as though they had just met on a train that afternoon. 'Am I really such a burden you can't even admit we're together?' she would ask. And Eric would invariably answer that they were not married, and therefore had every right to be separate.

They had recently been dining in a restaurant in the West End with some friends of Eric from work. Alice was seated at the opposite end of the table, but heard him involved in a conversation about bras with a brunette who was very much bursting out of hers:

'So do you like the under-wired type?' asked Eric.

'Well, I think they're so fifties and I like them for that, but you know, over a certain size, I don't really think you need them. I mean if you've got small breasts, then they're great, because they kind of push forward your cleavage and make you look like you've got balloons. But in my case, it's just a bit overwhelming.'

'If you say so yourself,' flirted Eric.

'Don't be nasty now, it's true, I mean, I've got big breasts, and I might as well admit it, I don't care, it's just something in my genes.'

'It's no sin, right.'

'Absolutely, it's just a fact of nature.'

By now, the rest of the table had either ceased talking or was listening to the conversation with one ear – and Alice was left pushing a piece of salad around her plate and wondering why she ever bothered.

To excuse Eric somewhat, the development and expansion of paranoia was fuelled by Alice's reluctance to communicate her fears, the legitimacy of whose expression she questioned.

Eric's bank was planning an important conference in September at the end of which a large dinner was to be held. Alice was alone in his flat when his secretary happened to call and leave a message on the answering-machine giving details of the event and adding that he should bring his partner along with him.

Alice was too discreet to mention the message to Eric, but at some level hoped and expected he would eventually ask her to join him – a request which never materialized.

'What do I care? It's not like I'm his chattel, and there's *MASH* on TV that night, so it's fine,' she told herself. 'I can have a pleasant evening in. I don't want to go to some boring conference dinner anyway.'

But in the week before the evening in question, she couldn't prevent the gestation of certain thoughts. Does he think I'm going to embarrass him in front of his colleagues and bosses? Is he taking someone else?

Yet these fears were prevented from finding expression by other reservations: What right have I got to worry I haven't been invited? Why am I being so selfish? Why do I deserve to go to this dinner anyway?

A conflict brewed between a very strong disappointment on the one hand and on the other a very strong sense that she had no grounds for complaint.

On the appointed evening, Eric called her before leaving for the party and told her cheerfully that he had spent ten minutes trying to do up his bow-tie, at which point Alice managed a feeble laugh and wished him well.

Then, because Suzy was out, she went to the kitchen, took a large bag of biscuits from the larder and sat down in front of the TV where *MASH* was beginning. Watching the credits roll, she reminded herself, 'I don't mind spending an evening alone, I like my own company for a change.'

Ten minutes into the programme, she looked around the living-room and suddenly realized she was alone, that Eric had betrayed her and that she wanted to scream.

'Bloody bastard,' she muttered instead, 'fucking bloody bastard with his fucking bloody bow-tie.'

But because she wasn't one to believe her fury should be anyone else's problem for long, the accusations were at once turned in on herself: 'You self-pitying, narcissistic baby, maybe he's got better things to do than take a boring old fart like you along.'

For a few moments, she pulled herself together, sat up in the chair, ate a few more biscuits and stared at the screen with grim determination. Then, because this was simply untenable, she switched off the set, threw the biscuits into the bin in disgust and ran to her bedroom where she collapsed on to a heap of cushions and fell asleep sobbing her eyes out like a five-year-old.

The trajectory of paranoia had been a pathetic, tragi-comic drama in five acts:

1) Alice loved Eric.
2) He gave her cause to doubt he loved her by not inviting her.
3) Yet there was simply insufficient evidence in the real

world to mount a sane-sounding complaint. Unable to express her hatred and disappointment . . .

4) She began silently hating Eric.

5) Unable to tolerate her own aggression against him, she began to hate herself and took to bed.

The magic ingredients for lover's paranoia had been an interaction between the muffled fear that *You don't love me enough* explosively mixed together with the inherited psychological imperative that *I can't possibly bother you with my ridiculous worries*

—which are nevertheless, despite my best efforts to remain rational and mature, driving me silently mad . . .

POWER AND 007

Surprisingly perhaps, Alice had always said she wished for a relationship in which power would be evenly distributed. While all around her were couples in which one partner was manipulating or dominating another, she intended to assure a situation in which the scales would be balanced.

Her relationship with the bearded biologist had been markedly unequal. Older and supposedly wiser than she, he had acted as a surrogate father, alternately chiding and encouraging, but always from a position of significant superiority. When she met Eric, Alice was therefore determined that the work would be shared between them. No longer would she be abused and her needs left uncatered for in the name of pleasing a selfish partner. When Eric left a shirt at her house and joked she might iron it and bring it to his house when they next saw each other, the suggestion led Alice to spend a heated five minutes accusing him of a catalogue of Neanderthalian prejudices. A humbled Eric tried to make amends and invited her for dinner, which he cooked himself, wearing a bright apron with sunflowers to protect his shirt from the vegetable oil in which a couple of succulent trout fillets were frying.

Yet however good a trout might be, power in a relationship was a far more complex issue than who wore the apron or ironed the shirts. These were the obvious but now dated symbols of power imbalance. Everyone agreed that domestic work should be more evenly distributed, or that one partner beating up another was really not quite acceptable. But to focus only on spectacular cases of power abuse was like reducing the scope of medicine to gruesome first-aid casualties, rather than studying more pervasive but less dramatic varieties of illness.

The word power typically signifies a capacity for action. The *Oxford English Dictionary* tells us power lies in an 'ability to do or effect something or anything, or to act upon a person or thing'. The person who has power may influence the material or social environment, generally on the basis of possessing high-tech weapons, money, oil, superior intelligence or large muscles. In war, I am powerful because I can blow up your city walls or drop bombs on your airfields. In the financial world, I am powerful because I can buy up your shares and invade your markets. In boxing, I am more powerful because my punches outwit and exhaust yours. But in love, the issue appears to depend on a far more passive, negative definition; instead of looking at power as a capacity to do something, one may come to think of it as the capacity to do nothing.

The weekend after Eric's conference, Alice came to lie alongside him on the sofa and, while playing with his hand, said to him, 'I feel so comfortable being here with you.'

One might have expected him to answer likewise, but far from returning the thought, he asked her, 'What time is the Bond film on this evening?'

No one had been beaten up, there were no bruises or screams, and yet the balance of power had at once decisively shifted in Eric's favour. Measured on a scale, there was Alice's lighter, less powerful message on one end, and Eric's heavier, more powerful question on the other.

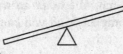

*I feel so comfortable being
here with you*

*What time is the Bond
film on this evenimg?*

To have equalized the imbalance, Eric might have said, 'And I'm comfortable with you too,' but, for whatever reason [and perhaps the timing of the Bond film really was a pressing concern], Alice was left holding none of the cards.

Power in love arises from the ability not to give a damn. I am powerful in love when you mention how comfortable you are with me, and I can afford not to notice I'm changing the subject to the evening's television. Unlike other spheres, the stronger in love is the one who has no designs upon the other, wants or needs nothing. Because love aims at communication and understanding, the one who blocks the process by changing the subject or answering a phone call two hours late at once effortlessly exercises a daunting power over the weaker, more reliable, more needy one.

Stendhal pessimistically suggested that there would always be one person who loved more the other and hence, by implication, that there would always be an awareness of power in a relationship. Only when both parties were placing equal stakes on the end of the scales, only when one partner said, 'I love you,' and the other answered quite naturally, 'I love you too,' could its existence be forgotten. It would otherwise take only the slightest divergence to signal its reappearance. Who could ignore the monstrous imbalance implied in the apparently inoffensive situation of one person whispering sweetly, 'Juliet, you know how much I love you,' and the other answering, 'Of course I do, Romeo my pumpkin. And you know how much I like you too . . .'?

When Alice was six years old, she lived next door to a very bright and very mischievous girl her own age. Out of a logic one forgets as adults, both girls had worked out a thrilling project with which to fill a Saturday afternoon, namely that they would run into the garden of a very bourgeois couple across the road and pull down their trousers, poke out their tongues and run away again. Much thought and preparation went into the plan, and when the appointed hour came, the two girls jumped over the low wooden fence and ran out on to the carefully manicured lawn.

Alice had already pulled down her trousers when she realized that her friend was no longer beside her and had fled the game to run over to the other side of the garden, where, with her trousers still firmly on, she had broken into a fit of giggles at the sight of poor Alice, standing alone with her trousers down in the middle of a stranger's garden, to the complete bewilderment of the bourgeois couple enjoying their martinis on the porch.

What is the relevance of this story? Only that Alice, left on the sofa next to Eric [now watching the famous spy in another of his adventures], felt a little like the girl she had once been. She had run out on to an exposed area, the neighbour's garden/the vulnerable earth of desire, and pulled down her trousers/declared she felt comfortable with her boyfriend, only to see her six-year-old friend/lover not involved in a similar risk or investment.

For a relationship to develop beyond the politeness of

strangers requires someone to make the move into the neighbour's garden and accept the danger therein. Someone has to summon the courage to ask, 'Would you like to come up for coffee?' or 'Have you seen that film yet?', someone has to clear their throat and say, 'I love being with you,' or 'Why don't we get married?' Someone needs to place their statement on the power scale and, terrified, hope the other comes up with material as heavy as their own load.

Yet responsibility is hard to ascribe. If a man breaks the law by stealing cars or distributing drugs, then his guilt is clear. But if he politely answers, 'No thanks, I've no time for coffee,' or, 'It's sweet of you to ask, but I'm just not the marrying type,' he cannot be accused of anything beyond a very excusable lack of interest.

Eric was not a criminal because he hadn't reached over to kiss Alice and told her that of course he too felt comfortable. He was simply betraying a very average, very understandable and very forgivable superior concern with the movements of 007 across the TV screen – a spy whose power he had thereby rivalled without the need for laser-guided projectiles or jet-propelled space modules.

RELIGIOUS
RELATIONSHIPS

However perverse the suggestion, Eric's reluctance to respond to his girlfriend's remark that she was comfortable with him might ultimately have served a certain [admittedly rather unhealthy] purpose. Though Alice argued she hated the experience of power, she nevertheless wanted a man she could respect, and though it ran counter to her every professed belief, the man she found herself most able to admire was one betraying no excessive admiration for her.

The couple were breakfasting together the Saturday after Eric's conference when the conversation led Eric to ask Alice what had been the most traumatic event of her childhood. Before she could swallow her mouthful of toast and reply, he happened to look across to his suit lying crumpled in a heap by the door, and exclaimed in shock, 'Christ, I've got to get this to the dry cleaner's before twelve o'clock. If I don't, I won't have it in time for the meeting on Monday.'

Some might have grown incensed by the disregard attending a possible answer to such a difficult question, but Alice lacked the conviction that her most traumatic childhood event should necessarily be of interest to another [even if this was her lover], and therefore replied, 'No, don't worry, there's another dry cleaner's on the Old Brompton Road and it's open until five this afternoon.'

When Eric's eyes drifted, Alice was rarely one to indignantly question why he had ceased to listen, accepting in all good faith that something more interesting had crossed his mind. Moreover, this apparent rudeness [it isn't nice to have someone ask a personal question, then find a pile of soiled laundry more interesting than the answer] did surprisingly little to tarnish Eric in her eyes. After all, he had tried to take an interest, he had asked some of the right questions, but could she really expect him to stay around and listen to her muddled reply when there was an urgent need to clean a suit for a Monday meeting?

Eric's distracted gaze reminded her of the privilege of being with someone who had higher things on his mind. He was distracted, distracted by other things, by bigger things, by better things than her. And if this man was in touch with bigger, better things, then surely he was worth loving [even if it meant leaving her story unheard]. It was a classic case of the love right angle:

$$A$$
$$\downarrow$$
$$B \longrightarrow C$$

The love right angle explains a devotion to someone focused on something or someone else. A loves B but B is more concerned with C. The interest lies in the way that far from working against B, B's attraction to C enhances B's desirability; to an extent, A loves B *because* of B's distraction with this object C, because B has the good taste to think A not worth listening to, because C is thought endowed with qualities that A, rarely a self-admiring person, is unsure they possess – but might feel connected to through the mediation of B.

Who or what was this C which superseded Alice? Was Eric involved in a project overwhelmingly more important than his girlfriend? There was no specific adultery to report, he had a rotating medley of concerns which lent him an air of distraction – at a dinner party it might be the red-head in the corner, in a restaurant it might be his food, during love making an incoming fax.

The distinctive feature was the way that this psychological absenteeism worked in Eric's favour. It seemed to suggest he had access to things which Alice, who was ready to listen, who was far more receptive than him, simply did not.

It was a bad case of a love right angle, it had all the signs of a Religious Relationship.

✝ ✡ ☪

In most languages and religions, the same word is used to denote both the act of worshipping God and attachment to a human being. Of course the nature of this love is far from equivalent, well-documented differences existing between religious and romantic brands. There are nevertheless certain stories which bear such resemblance to the variety of love typically seen in the course of holy worship that one may be forgiven if, rather than using the label of romantic, we choose to refer to the union as a Religious Relationship.

When devotion to God began to wane with the close of the Middle Ages, historians tell us that the love of one person for another took over as a dominant theme of art and literature. The Renaissance humanism which swept Europe in the fourteenth and fifteenth centuries emphasized the inner life of the individual, reorienting values in a way which indirectly but logically concluded in the Romanticism of the nineteenth century. God was replaced in the affections of humans by an earthly ideal, and the concept of sexual love grew tainted with some of the exalted and self-transcendent expectations previously attached to the love of God. In the course of the eighteenth and nineteenth centuries, finding the right partner ceased to be [for an educated and cultured minority at least] a matter of pedestrian consideration, simply a case of locating someone who could cook an acceptable fish pie, lay a table, farm a field or earn a decent living. It now had to do with the thought of loving a perfect being on earth, someone with whom one could engage in long silent prayer, take on lyrical country walks and love like an angel.

It is significant that the greatest yearning heroine in the history of the novel should have had [at different stages] three central longings: for God, for shopping, and for love. In her concerns, Madame Bovary was an archetypal modern, seeking a form of self-transcendence through all three. At an early stage in the book, Flaubert takes care to tell us that Emma spent her school years in a nunnery, and that her devotion to God was so passionate it contained [it is artfully suggested] elements of the erotic. Though many young women of the time were educated by nuns, Flaubert's detailing of this point is not coincidental. It illustrates something vital in Madame Bovary's attitude to love, for someone whose experience had descended indirectly from the worship of God would hold very different conceptions of kissing and the conjugal life to someone with access to a more earthly source. [It is worth noting that Emma's mother died in childbirth, tilting the balance of the daughter's affections towards the male parent, a well-documented connection existing between father and Father.]

The love Emma derived from religion bred a predictable intolerance of the earthly [as distinct from heavenly] male. Her husband Charles was unashamedly of this world rather than the next, not only in earning his living as a coarse country doctor used to sawing limbs off local peasants, but also in showing up on time, looking Emma in the eyes and avoiding the mystification of a religious partner, one who could provoke an array of agonizing questions ranging from 'Did he get my letter?' to 'Does he even know I exist?' One would always know where one stood with a man like Charles.

How wonderful. Or perhaps – how banal, how boring.

Charles had wished to make Emma happy by providing her with everything she needed, by listening to her stories and wiping her brow, but if her happiness was his goal, then he couldn't have chosen a more foolish route, for what she required in order to love was not his presence but his absence. Her religious love fed off the bitter-sweet pleasure arising from the distance between lover and beloved. She had a husband who loved her calmly and steadily, but he could generate none of the thrilling tension of her adulterous and unreliable companions, her religious love a reversal of Lysander's maxim in *A Midsummer Night's Dream* that 'the course of true love never did run smooth': in Emma's case, what nourished love [and it was Charles's downfall that he repeatedly missed the point] was precisely this unsmooth course.

What is peculiar to religious love is its emphasis on worship. But how may mere mortals come to be worshipped? By beginning to behave like gods. And how do gods behave? With notorious petulance and unreliability. Though not a god himself, we may look at Jesus's behaviour as an example. After he had been overdue for many hundreds of years, he eventually arrived in the Promised Land, but quite confounded his hosts' expectations by being dressed rather humbly, bringing few gifts beside a gamut of magic tricks and staging a series of melodramatic showdowns with the authorities. Then, after the briefest of stays, he vanished once more, promising to call back soon and leaving behind him many millions of followers waiting in vain for signs of return.

Nothing could have exceeded Jesus's *See you once every couple of thousand years* approach, but nor was Eric particularly noted for punctuality as regards Alice.

'Listen, I'll call you when I get out of my meeting, and we'll go and get some supper,' he told her when she rang him at five thirty on a Thursday afternoon. 'Did you have a good day?'

'Yeah, it was all right, and you?' asked Alice.

'Pretty busy, very hectic activity on the Deutschmark, but I think I came through it OK. Anyway listen, I've got to go, but I'll catch you later, at around seven or seven fifteen. I'll come by and pick you up and we'll go out somewhere, maybe drive into Soho or something.'

Why in that case was Alice still waiting by the telephone at nine o'clock? The delay started up theologically different groups within herself, each propounding rapidly alternating and conflicting beliefs—

✝ Main-line Christianity: 'He will call, but it will take a long time.'

✝ Agnosticism: 'I'll believe him when I see him.'

✝ Born-again Christianity: 'He tried to get through earlier, then decided to come straight here, but was held up in traffic. If I keep staring at the fading paintwork above the peep-hole, he's going to come through the door any minute. Perhaps he'll even have stopped off to buy a bunch of flowers to make up for the delay.'

✝ Atheism: 'Keep dreaming, honey.'

Because he still hadn't called by a quarter to ten, Alice phoned him. Expecting a certain complexity in the explanation, she was somewhat surprised by the response:

'Oh hi, it's you. Listen, can you hang on a second? The door bell's just rung, it's a pizza I ordered. [There was a pause, the sound of a motorcycle helmet being pulled off and an exchange of money.] Great, the ham looks wonderful . . .'

'What happened to you? I thought you were going to call and come round?'

'Listen, I'm sorry, I got caught up. Bill and Geoffrey wanted some help on a presentation they're giving to some Americans tomorrow, and then we ended up having a drink, and I've only just got back.'

'But I thought we were supposed to go out for dinner.'

'Yeah, we were, but you know how it is, I just had to help these people out. I mean, they'd do it for me . . . I'm sorry, OK. Do you forgive me?'

Faced with apparently irrational and hysterical devotions, po-faced rationalists have often tried to explain religion as a primitive way of accounting for evil in life, by fitting the evil into a wider theory of the good. The evil is simply a test, a hurdle to jump, like a child who must eat the ugly, rubbery broccoli so as to deserve the mouth-watering chocolate cake which awaits in the kitchen. It is a psychological structure built on the delay of gratification, on the belief that the good must always be earned, metaphoric chocolate cakes bearing a masochistically high price.

It had always been in Alice's disposition to sit and eat broccoli rather than complain dramatically if the promised chocolate cake was rather long in coming. She wasn't sure Jerusalem was owed to her right away, harbouring a sense of guilt which made her suspect she deserved some of the punishments life threw at her. If someone in a shop returned what she thought might be too little change, she rarely acted to correct the wrong. If she bought an appliance which broke down, she was not one to ring up the manufacturer enraged and demand her money back – she would think instead that perhaps she hadn't known how to use it.

'I have a problem getting angry,' Alice would recognize when unable to correct yet another infringement or wrongdoing of friends or colleagues. She frequently accepted unwished for offers, lent money because she was reluctant to say no, and was polite only because she hated to offend with her annoyance.

Alice's mother had no such problems. 'I'll give him one!' was her favourite rallying cry, swearing revenge on an unfortunate shopkeeper, husband or hairdresser. If, in a restaurant, the sauce was on the meat when she had asked for it on the side, she would call over the waiter and ask imperiously, 'Do you know what I am going to complain about?'

'Is everything all right, madam?'

'Is everything all right? My dear man, why would everything be all right when you've done the very opposite of what I told you to do but ten minutes ago?'

A huge fuss would follow, waiters would scurry, madam

would be appeased in every way possible – and Alice would blush and do her best to disappear behind a pot plant or Corinthian column.

The unfortunate Biblical anti-hero Job, who no doubt had a far sweeter nature than Alice, was sent the most unbelievable succession of troubles. The Bible tells us he was 'blameless and upright; he feared God and shunned evil'. And yet what torments descended on him! He lost his oxen, his sheep, his servants, his camels, his house, his sons and daughters, was covered in painful sores and suffered every imaginable pain – and yet the point of the story was that the man [albeit but for a few despairing moments] stayed faithful in his love of God. He didn't get angry, bang his fist and scowl, 'I asked for my escalope with the goddam sauce on the side,' or exclaim viciously, 'I didn't shell out for the synagogue extension to be paid back like this.'

What allowed Job to survive trouble without complaint was his undying faith that God was right, and he was wrong – or rather that whatever troubles God afflicted on him, He knew best, and there was therefore no excuse for a little old man like him to raise his hand and question Him [compare Job to his atheistic counterpart in modern literature, Joseph K, who experienced suffering as equally unquestionable, but simply absurd].

In daily life, we rarely have the patience of Job, because we lack his respect for those who do us wrong: the person who steals our parking space, or the colleague who gossips maliciously behind our back doesn't deserve to be forgiven, is worthy of the full force of our anger because they have no access to higher morality or wisdom.

But Alice didn't fight back because, like Job with God,

she typically respected and trusted the other more than herself. When Eric later told her, 'Listen, I don't want you to be upset that I didn't call you. I only said that we'd *maybe* go out for dinner if I had time, and well, in the end I didn't, so we didn't,' she herself forgot her complaint. She interpreted her suffering theologically, as a test of some obscure sort rather than as a miserable and highly contestable insult.

Though not religious herself, her behaviour revealed the bare structure of the religious impulse, shorn of holy books, organs and angels; namely, a predisposition to think that the Other [her lover, God] was running things in the sky, knew better than her what he/He was doing and therefore shouldn't suffer the indignity of her questions.

It is a feature of gods that they are often absent, or if not absent at least unattainable, people one communicates with via prayer or dream rather than a relaxed and honest chat in the kitchen over a mug of coffee.

Eric's religious distance was achieved by silence. He had never been a loquacious person, and would often keep his mouth shut during entire meetings or meals. His close friends would tease him about his pauses, would ask him if he'd exceeded his daily quota of words, but for those who didn't know him or were more impressionable, his behaviour could be intimidating. It led some to blame themselves for the lack of conversation, it was a conduit for the interlocutor's paranoias: 'Why am I so boring?' 'What is he thinking of me?' A silent person mirrors insecurities – faced with a silence, the guilty will take it to mean their crime is known, the stupid will suspect their idiocy has become obvious, the physically insecure will think their ugliness impossibly apparent.

Put a silent person in the middle of a dinner conversation, and slowly, imperceptibly, their silence [if skilfully and severely expressed] may unnerve everyone who is talking. The woman launching forth on a speech about American foreign policy, a topic she is cribbing from an editorial in the morning's paper, may suddenly catch the impassive eye of the silent person and feel ruthlessly judged and undressed. 'Does this silence mean he realizes I don't know the first thing I'm talking about?' And others looking on may think, Perhaps he is superior to us all because he talks so little, evidence for the unfortunate maxim that the best way to be thought intelligent may be to rarely open one's mouth.

Eric's silences provoked Alice into strenuous efforts to locate conversation topics, in the hope of landing on something to catch his attention.

If they went to the pub in the evening, she would typically be forced to scrape the barrel of her day's experiences.

'And then I called Suzy this afternoon.'

'Ehm.'

'You know, she might be going up to Nottingham with her friends for Christmas – that is, if she can get the time off.'

'Ehm.'

'I guess I should probably also ring John at some point, and see if he got that job in Brussels.'

'Yes.'

'I wonder if I'm ever going to hear back from the guy who gave an estimate for the TV. I told him I had to know by Tuesday, but he still hasn't gotten back to me. Do you think I should call him?'

'Maybe.'

'Are you tired?'

'A bit.'

The scenario could continue for a whole evening, but instead of throwing a glass of wine over this reluctant babbler, hitting him in the stomach and telling him to go find his tongue, Alice would walk home with the sense that rarely had she known anyone as dull as herself.

Though clarity and communication are commonly prized, one shouldn't forget a rather more puzzling attraction towards people or things that defy ease of understanding.

In certain academic spheres, there exists a long-standing prejudice against lucidity and a corresponding respect for difficult texts. The scholars poring over the dense prose of a Kant or Hegel, a Husserl or Heidegger are perhaps attracted not simply to the brilliant ideas they tell us lie therein, but also to the sheer difficulty of recovering these ideas from the contorted tangles of language impassable to the lay reader.

Hegel treats us to the following passage in his *Phenomenology of Spirit*:

The object is in part *immediate* being or, in general, a Thing – corresponding to immediate consciousness; in part, an othering of itself, its relationship or *being-for-an-other*, and being-for-itself, i.e. determinateness – corresponding to perception; and in part *essence*, or in the form of a universal – corresponding to the Understanding. It is, as a totality, a syllogism or the movement of the universal through determination to individuality, as also the reverse movement from individuality through superseded individuality, or through determination, to the universal.*

Picking a passage at random from a densely argued work of philosophy may be unjust, but there can be little doubt that with even the best will in the world and an eager and flexible intellect, Hegel's argumentation rarely rises above the enigmatic.

Yet a text which makes one suffer may be taken as somehow more valid, more profound and truer than one which reads with clarity and fluidity. The sensitive reader who dips into Heidegger or Husserl may think, How profound this text is; if I can't understand it, it is surely cleverer than me. If it's difficult to understand, it must no doubt be more worthy of understanding, – this rather than tossing the work to one side and declaring it a thing of intolerable nonsense.

Academic masochism reflects a metaphysical prejudice that the truth should be a hard-won treasure, that what is read or learnt easily must therefore be flighty and inconsequential. The truth should be like a mountain to be scaled, it is dangerous, obscure and demanding. Under the harsh light of the library reading room, the academics' motto reads: *the more a text makes me suffer, the truer it must be*.

The interpersonal corollary of this lies in the idea that the difficult lover may somehow be of more value than one who is open, clear, predictable and calls on time. To religious-romantic mentalities, such a type deserves only condemnation or avoidance, they behave like scholars who deride the ideas of a fine prose stylist simply because they could be understood by an enlightened twelve-year-old.

* G. W. F. Hegel, *Phenomenology of Spirit*, translated by A. V. Miller, OUP 1977

Similarly, far from understanding Eric's silences as a sign of how boring he was, Alice saw them as evidence of marked profundity and interest. She was like a scholar who devotes a lifetime to the works of Hegel, convinced of his genius – when an unkind critic might suggest the weighty German philosopher was ultimately only a most average thinker possessed of two or three good ideas and an atrocious inability to express himself.

ERIC'S BURDEN

Before condemning Eric [implicitly or otherwise] for his cruel silences and dinner arrangement betrayals, it is worth having a moment's sympathy for his position. He may have enjoyed the benefit of a woman who loved him dearly, but he had also been saddled with the burden of acting as the subject of another's zealous idealizations. He was being asked [sweetly and delicately, of course] to provide meaning for another's existence. No wonder he sometimes fluffed his lines.

'What did you think of me when you first saw me?' asked Alice when they lay in bed together late on a summer's night.

'I thought you were great, that's why I came to talk to you.'

Alice, like a stroked rabbit, gave off what might have been a purr.

'It's funny,' she continued, 'I liked you, but I didn't think you liked me. Remember the way you were talking to that other woman? I thought you'd have much preferred her to me.'

Alice alternated between moments of majestic reserve and the naïve honesty of a twelve-year-old. 'It was great when you did come over!' One needed a strong, unsentimental stomach to happily digest such sugary fare. One needed experience to deal with an alarmingly spontaneous compliment to the effect that 'I'm sure you've had lots of women running after you. Someone as handsome as you would.'

Eric was as vain as the next person; one might have expected that he too would begin purring like a rabbit on hearing such things, but flattery made him squirm uncomfortably. There was a certain paradox in a man who enjoyed the glances of women received in busy City streets, but was made uneasy by more forthright declarations made in his bed.

If he was often off-hand or distracted, if he sometimes failed to return Alice's calls, it was [beside sheer bad manners] because he felt in himself an insufficiency as an object of love, appalled by sentiments he was unable to respond to and which he therefore experienced as unacceptably [and accusingly] mawkish.

To return to the dry-cleaning of his suit, his reluctance to listen to Alice's answer reminds one of two forms of distraction:

—the distraction that arises when one is simply bored, when the topic fails to hold one's attention
—the distraction used in order not to dwell on what one has already noticed, a viable escape from the risk of an overwhelming situation, a socially acceptable reaction psychologically equivalent to running for the door.

When Alice threatened to start talking of her childhood, Eric looked away for the second rather than the first reason. Though he had asked it himself, the question of what had been her most painful childhood experience threatened to embroil him in unpleasantly sensitive material, which might have required a handkerchief or more to be contained.

Eric longed for Alice to be harsher with him, so he could

avoid the responsibilities created by her capacity for self-deprecation and denial. After he had been sulkily silent on a drive to Whitechapel on a weekend morning, she turned to him and asked, 'Sorry for bringing this up, but are you angry with me?'

There was no conceivable reason for him to be angry with her: they had only met at his apartment ten minutes earlier, and had not exchanged more than a few words while driving. In fact, his silence had at root a worrying article he had read in the newspaper at breakfast, suggesting a deal in which he had invested heavily the week before might turn sour.

'No, I'm not angry with you,' he replied gruffly.

'So is anything wrong?'

'I'm just tired.'

'That's fine, so long as it's not me.'

'No, of course it isn't, I'll get over it.'

Yet, in a sense, it was Alice's fault. Or rather, her behaviour helped to aggravate a grumpy predisposition. He was unused to the generosity [or, depending on one's point of view, the pliancy] implied in the question, 'Are you angry with me?' – this from a woman who had been blameless, good natured and sweet. He was being unfairly difficult, and though not mature enough to auto-inflict the message, recognized the need for another to chide him for it.

He was accustomed to women whose emotional generosity was more restrained than Alice's. He had had warm relationships, but always with an element of distance maintained; had he happened to be in a bad mood on a drive to Whitechapel on account of an article in a newspaper, he would either have had to explain his temper away or acted cheerfully enough to avoid a sharp exchange. He had always sought out sceptical lovers, those reluctant to take the blame instead of actively seeking it out – whereas Alice suffered from a self-defeating readiness to indulge him in his capriciousness.

He feared the defenceless way in which she loved him. Coy in his reception of affection, he would wait until he was at work to think of how much he felt for her, something that in her presence he had been unable to understand, let alone express. He needed time to answer her tenderness, like someone who grows tongue-tied on the telephone and requires the privacy of a sheet of paper to set down a response.

When they had first met, Alice complained that she wished to be more creative and would like to take up drawing again, something she had done successfully at school but had not continued thereafter. In an enthusiastic and flattering mood, Eric had patiently glanced through some of her charcoal drawings kept in a box in her room and watched her trace a bowl of dried flowers on the window ledge, after which he had declared her a natural talent whose skills reminded him a little of certain Degas sketches seen in a show in Paris the year before.

'No, you're kidding me. Tell me what you really think?' asked Alice.

'I'm telling you, I think they're really good. You've got a serious talent, and I wouldn't say so if I didn't believe it.'

'Really?' she asked, biting her lower lip.

'Of course. If you set your mind to it, you could make fantastic progress. You've got a natural gift for it.'

Eric's confusion between a set of muddy uninspired sketches and the charm of watching her delicately articulate a pencil across a sheet of paper cost him dear – for he became in her eyes something of an art critic. She showed him drawings she had done, and asked whether he detected improvements or could suggest possible directions. It gave Eric the feeling he was being asked to fill a role traditionally occupied by a father, someone whose authority he neither wanted nor trusted he had.

After she had spent a weekend painting a mural in a friend's bathroom, Alice brought him in to see it, and standing by the door in a pair of paint-splattered dungarees, asked him with an expectant grin, 'So? What do you think? Do you approve of me?'

The choice of words felt significant; not 'Do you like it?' or even 'Do you approve of it?' but 'Do you approve of *me*?', a personal note which hinted of a search for legitimacy, a childish cry, 'Am I OK?'

The need placed Eric in a position of strenuous responsibility: her sensitivity made him want to hurt her, tell her he didn't give a damn about a ridiculous mural in the hope she might cease to ascribe such respect to everything he said or did.

During lunch breaks, he and colleagues ate in a delicatessen near the bank, where conversation frequently focused on the opposite sex. On a particular Monday, over plates of pastrami sandwiches, the topic turned to female mammary glands.

'Big ones are nice, but you know, they're less sensitive than small ones,' observed Roger thoughtfully.

'Bullshit, you can get some massive tits that are seriously sensitive. You remember Carmen, the Spanish woman I was with? Well, I mean, she proved your theory completely wrong,' replied Bill.

'I don't know, Jodie's tits are big but you don't get any reaction from them. What do you think, Eric?' asked Roger.

'Well, it's obvious what I think, Alice has got quite small tits, I'm with Alice, so I must think they're OK. I mean, what's the point of being with a woman if you don't like her tits?'

Infantile and archaic beneath City suits, Eric and colleagues performed the age-old ritual of passing off emotional needs as sexual ones so as to lessen the weight of mutual dependence.

WHAT TO BE LOVED FOR?

Eric frequently referred to the physical aspect of women; this woman had a beautiful nose, that woman had great legs, the next delicate ankles. He also noted what he found ugly: this woman had sagging breasts, this one had thighs like tree trunks, the third had a crooked walk.

He and Alice were coming out of a supermarket when they passed a woman of whom he commented:

'God, isn't it amazing? All those women with really nice faces, then you look down and they have disgusting bodies. I mean, did you see how fat she was? It was incredible. And she didn't look like a fat person around her face, it was just the rest of her.'

Though always flattering towards her, such remarks made Alice feel awkward.

'Why do you have to talk like that all the time?' she asked.

'Like what?'

'I don't know – about everyone being fat or thin, this or that.'

'I'm just stating facts. I mean, did you see the way that woman's . . .'

'Yeah, well, I wish you wouldn't. It's awful that you're always thinking that way about people's bodies.'

'Don't you like it when I'm thinking of your body?' asked Eric in an exaggerated Californian accent. 'Come on, don't get heavy on me,' he said and placed an arm around her.

'I don't want to get heavy. It's just that . . . I don't know, let's forget it. Should we go and pick up some wine in the off-licence?' she asked, and coughed to clear her throat.

But Alice kept mulling over the issue on the way home. Eric had always been most generous towards her body. When they were naked in the bedroom, he would sometimes playfully ask her to pose like a sculpture or painting, and declare her to be his Venus or Aphrodite, Eve or Helen of Troy. After a few glasses of wine, he would take on a mock theatrical voice and call her bosom the fairest in the land, her eyes like jewels of the East, her triangle an inspiration to mankind.

'Stop exaggerating, you half-baked poet,' she would say and pull back the sheets to cover herself.

'Ah, Venus is clearly shy tonight, she isn't in the mood for coitus with Cupid.'

'If the fair Cupid wasn't such a dud shot with his arrows, maybe she would be . . .'

Alice's uneasiness emerged from the question of how much of a role her body was playing in Eric's feelings. She wished him to find her attractive, but paradoxically, didn't wish a bodily attraction to be what ultimately accounted for his presence.

She felt an implicit hierarchy of better and worse things to be loved for: though in every case she might be loved, according only to certain criteria could she accept that someone who claimed to love actually loved *her*.

[i] To be loved for one's body

The body is the locus of a stunning loss of control over the other's perception of oneself. It is the thing others most naturally and immediately identify as part of the 'I' without there being any chance of it reflecting an inner sense of self. Though only a collection of cells arranged according to the vagaries of our DNA structure, those who meet us cannot help but read meaning and personality within it. Prey to the pathetic fallacy, they call our features beautiful, cynical, honest or charming, much in the way that poets label the inanimate aspects of landscape according to emotional criteria, calling this mountain 'bold' or that stream 'merry'.

But though inwardly aware that our body may not represent us, we find it hard to apply such a lesson to our reading of others, whom we inevitably bond more tightly to their physical form. We lack empathy for their identity crises, because their identity is somehow much more obvious to us on the outside than to them within, based as it is on a materialistic, hence visually self-evident, footing.

Only on an introspective basis may we feel we have no more claim over our physical form than over the shape of a planet in a distant galaxy. No wonder Descartes should have surveyed the mind/body issue and in *The Discourse on the Method* declared in disgust, 'This *I*, that is to say the mind . . . is entirely distinct from the body' [though his biographers report a fondness for silk handkerchiefs and Flemish breeches which perhaps runs counter to an ortho-dox reading of his work].

There are of course those who accept without question

that their body reflects them, that there is a happy congruence between self-conception and the passport photo. They may pass a mirror, give a little wink and think cheerfully, Good old me. Eric's physical ease perhaps emerged from this fortunate sense of congruence rather than any particular vanity. He felt his face to be an accurate image of who he was, he was happy if people linked him to and loved him for his alert eyes, his short cropped hair, his strongly formed chin and boyish grin.

Then there are those strung along a spectrum of dissatisfaction ranging from 'I don't like my eyes,' to 'What the hell am I doing in here?' But no. Perhaps 'I don't like my eyes' isn't a good example, because the incongruity of body and self-concept goes beyond simply not *liking* one's eyes. It is more a question of a psychological, existential sense that 'These eyes are *not me*'. Alice didn't like her thumb for instance, but she accepted that it reflected who she was quite well. It had a character in line with her self-perception, a mixture of idealism around the nail, awkwardness around the joint, irony at the side, kept very often folded and somewhat nervously bitten. However, she couldn't have assumed the same fortuitous congruence in relation to her face. It was always going off on its own tangents, looking cheerful when it should have looked sad, flighty when it should have been thoughtful, vulnerable when toughness was required. She would catch sight of her face in a train and be appalled at a twelve-year-old's expression, only to then see her reflection in an office window and be surprised at a face that should have belonged to someone of sixty.

At adolescence, the age-old philosophical issue between the inside and outside had painfully opened up in front of the analytical truth of the mirror. Fleeing from it, she had run into books and into a period of her life she could now jokingly refer to with Eric as 'unbelievably repressed':

'I was just so screwed up about sex and everything. I hated myself and hated boys even more. I was so scared of them, if one came to talk to me, I'd blush from top to toe and break out in all sorts of nervous tics, I just sat in my room all day with the curtains drawn, mirrors covered, reading trash novels on my bed and screaming if anyone asked to come in.'

Alice's mother suffered from the ancient prejudice that girls of a certain age should devote their energies to impressing boys with an eventual view to marriage. Appalled by Alice's insistence on a pair of old jeans and a sweater, with her characteristic energy she would lead her daughter to a succession of clothes shops, storming into the boutique and asking the sales ladies with a melodramatic, despairing air, 'Is there *any*thing you think you can do for this young lady?'

And because these shops tended to be a half-century behind social taste, Alice would emerge something short of a wedding cake, full of bows, ribbon and frills, things more likely to repel a foaming male than induce him to relieve the mother of her awkward Lolita.

What Alice most resented in her incongruous body was that others would naturally assume congruence where none was felt. Whereas Alice read her physical form as a random phenomenon, men couldn't help but take it to be an extension of herself. When Eric jokingly sang the praises of her bosom, she couldn't identify with the praise, accepting it like an award for someone unable to attend a prize-giving ceremony.

'Your nose is so *you*,' Eric told Alice, tracing its outline in the bedroom.

'How do you mean?'

'The way it's small, and goes up ever so slightly, and the way it tapers off . . .'

'Did you take a course in nasal phrenology?'

'Of course. What the hell's that?'

However hard they tried, it would be hard for others to understand Alice if she told them, 'I am not really the way I look.' Forgivably puzzled, they might make all the right noises about of course not looking at her superficially and what did looks matter anyway, yet how could they do anything other than link her and her complaints to the physical form in which they were manifested?

Alice had recently read a magazine interview with a model whose face some would have auctioned their grandmother for, but who claimed her body was only a nuisance as far as relationships were concerned. She had married an unambiguously ugly man whom she could only have loved for something other than his body, thereby projecting in her choice of male the mentality she might have wished males to employ towards her.

Alice concluded that it might not matter whether one was ugly or beautiful – the body was still a curse because it opened up a gulf between the way one felt and the way one was seen. The Elephant Man and the top model, though at different ends of the fashion spectrum, shared a structurally identical psychological fate.

There was however a certain coyness in Alice's approach, particularly if one considered the extent of her annual investments in sets of lingerie or face soap.

Coyness could be here defined as a form of ambivalence whereby one both condemns something out of fear, because it is powerful, desired and one doesn't fully control it, and remains happy to derive the benefits from it. The successful artist is being coy when he or she stands up to condemn the capitalist system, yet cheerfully cashes the cheques from the sale of his or her work. 'You don't need to be pretty to be happy,' the multi-million-dollar model had said coyly, shortly after relating all the things that were currently making her happy [a shoot in Kenya, her own range of perfume] which had everything to do with looking the way she did. And Alice was being coy when she invested in seductive underwear but said, 'I would never judge anyone on their looks and I hope everyone around me would do the same.'

She knew the unfortunate rules of the game – a knowledge guiding her in clothes shops and hairdressers – yet when a man did notice her, she somehow wished to remove the knowledge from the equation of his desire. If her body attracted looks, she didn't wish a lover's glance to stop there. In her fantasy, and it had nothing to do with prudishness, the body would have been beside the point in a Cartesian sense – not ignored, for sex was wonderful, but beside the point. She would be loved for the mysterious rest one was left with after it was discounted, the confused welter of history, impressions, habits and temperament she called her self.

[ii] To be loved for one's money

Before he had lost all his in a bad investment, Alice's father had often warned his daughter about men who would be drawn to her on the basis of money. 'You're going to get all sorts of types trying to use you for it, and believe me, it's worse than being used for sex,' he had said, enriched with the experience of a wife whose love had proved as fickle as his income.

An awareness of the link between love and money had at origin given her father an incentive to grow rich, but the paradox, as in the case of a beautiful body, was that he could no longer trust the women he had attracted through such an external asset. Projecting his cynical view of human relations on to his daughter, the father had gone so far as to accuse her boyfriend at the age of seventeen of being a gold-digger because she would occasionally be the one to pay for a film or concert. The problem was now no longer so acute, a financial crash having lost her father his money and his wife, and made Alice reliant on an unenviable but less problematically lovable monthly salary.

Eric enjoyed a more affluent life-style, which had led Alice to remark on several occasions: 'What I enjoy about going out with you is that I get to see sides of London I never knew before – restaurants and theatres and stuff.'

Eric would smile benignly at such comments, though had he been of a different disposition he might well have questioned how long Alice would enjoy life with him if the sides of London it took an upper tax bracket to experience were thrown out of reach by unexpected insolvency.

Instead, lacking squeamish qualms as to the origins of love, he argued sportingly: 'As long as someone loves me, why should I start asking why?'

[iii] To be loved for one's achievements

In the period in which she met and began seeing Eric, Alice was promoted to a range of more important contracts, and was now overseeing clients' business worth in the region of half a million pounds. She was sent on trips to Dublin and Paris, talked to clients in Boston and Madrid and was given her own office and secretary.

Aware of the envy of others, she had a tendency to deprecate her achievements. If a friend said, 'I'd love to have a job like yours,' she would answer, 'No, you really wouldn't. You're much better off where you are.'

Eric was proud rather than envious of Alice [if in a rather paternalistic sense: the subtext was, 'Welcome to the real world of business of which I have always been a part']. The day she won the agency a new contract, he invited her out for dinner and showered her with praise and later with kisses. He was keen to boast to friends that he was going out with someone destined to become one of Britain's leading businesswomen, and news reached her through intermediaries of how flattering he had been behind her back.

However pleasant this attention, Alice felt a tinge of regret that Eric was always much sweeter with her when she was feeling strong and doing well than when she was weak and drained of self-confidence. She didn't need to be taken out for dinner when she could afford it, or told she looked beautiful when she could almost believe it.

Her parents had had a similar attitude towards achievement as Eric, namely that it produced from them a marked increase in affection. Till the age of thirteen, she had been slow at school and seemingly destined for academic oblivion. Her performance entailed unpopularity at home, where she was cast as the black sheep next to her scholastically superior younger sister. But at adolescence, she decided to confound expectations and began to produce excellent work, passing all her exams with top grades. Overnight, she became the family's new heroine and presents and attentions were showered upon her. 'Are you sure you don't want another holiday, another dress, a yet fancier bicycle?' the parents would ask. But the sullen adolescent would refuse everything, would dress in the shabbiest clothes and would treat parental offers like insults. Indeed, they were insults because they were the flip-side [the good side, but nevertheless only the flip-side] of the same approach which had condemned her to the role of black sheep simply on the basis of a school report card.

Her parents had sometimes explained the poverty of their parenting by saying, 'We were not good with children, we wanted someone we could talk to intelligently, like we can with you now. In one sense, we couldn't wait till you were grown up.'

Now that she could talk eloquently on any number of topics, they were keen to parade their beautiful, articulate daughter in front of friends, and were somewhat surprised by her marked reluctance to agree to such invitations. Toward her own achievements, she had the attitude of certain Hollywood stars who socialize exclusively with friends from before the time they were famous – 'If you loved me when I was down, you will love me always,' is their implicit attitude: 'If you begin to love me only now I'm respectable, how do I know that it's indeed *me* rather than the respectability you love?'

[iv] To be loved for one's weakness

Give someone enough success, offices, houses and yachts, sufficient eloquence, beauty or intelligence, someone will sooner or later fall in love with them. But love has as its idealized prototype what should be the unconditional love of a parent for their baby. Our earliest memory of love is of being cared for in a helpless and weak condition. Some babies are notably cute and cuddly, but they are by definition unable to bargain with the world on account of extrinsic characteristics. In so far as they are loved and looked after, they are therefore loved simply for who they are – which tends to be rather a messy business. They are loved for [or in spite of] their dribbling, shitting, peeing, vomiting, howling and selfish characters.

Only as the baby grows up does affection become conditional on a number of labours – saying thank you at table, fetching Mummy her glasses, scrubbing dishes and later, acquiring television stations, houses in Mustique and chalets in St Moritz. But though these things guarantee the interest of others, the true desire is not so much to gain the flatteries of starlets and chat-show hosts as to recreate the contract made by the parent with the child at infancy: a contract binding the parent to loyalty and fidelity, come what may.

Alice recognized the tension in her relationship with Eric, namely that one side of her wished to be the dribbling baby, complex, irrational, demanding – and another knew that in order to sustain his affections she would have to play the responsible, mature woman, attractive, witty and without need.

She sometimes had discussions with Eric on politics, in

which she would end up more to the left, he to the right. After the collapse of a giant and once proud car-making firm, the couple found themselves in a heated argument.

'Listen, the only justification for a business is if it's doing well,' declared Eric. 'When they could make the cars that people wanted, then it was a business worth keeping. But the fact is, they no longer can. They're without justification. Their models are outdated, they're overstaffed, inefficient, wasteful, badly managed, and they haven't invested enough in engineering and new equipment – so naturally, they're going to go the wall, and well they should.'

'How can you say that? Twenty thousand people are going to lose their jobs, a whole town is going to be decimated – and you think that's right?'

'It makes perfect economic sense: if Asian countries can make better and cheaper cars, there's no reason why they shouldn't be appropriately rewarded for doing so. A whole town in Korea or Malaysia is going to prosper at the expense of one here – but that's the way the game works. Korean companies spend huge amounts on machine tools which are much more advanced than anything you'd find in this country. Governments simply can't spend taxpayers' money propping up collapsing companies – it's survival of the fittest out there. You've got to keep an economy running on true demand, you're stimulating things artificially when you support businesses that the market deems should die.'

'But that's ridiculous, inhuman, cruel. It wouldn't hurt the taxpayer if the government could just give the company a loan to tide them over for a few years, till they get it together, then they'll be profitable again.'

Beneath an argument over the fate of an ailing car maker, one could detect a conflict that had nothing to do with bridging loans or Korean investment in machine tools. Alice's defence of the car maker was a defence of the right to be loved for weakness: Eric's attack was a form of capitalist Darwinianism she feared he implicitly supported as much in love as in business.

She feared the cruelty she detected in his economic logic, feared that one day, on account of collapsing thighs or droopy breasts, she too would be declared 'inefficient', 'wasteful' and 'without justification'. Whatever the true merits of the car maker, her defence of it was a trace of the childhood urge to be loved unconditionally [even if she was bankrupt], the state here in the role of a longed-for all-forgiving parent. Perhaps there had been sloppy management in the car factory, but didn't the firm belong to the nation, were its workers not citizens, and did the government not hence have a duty to nurse it back to economic health?

When a colleague at work had recently tried to pin the blame for a lost contract on Alice, Eric had been helpful in suggesting ways to report the incident to a superior without at the same time alienating those around her. When he decided she had a grievance, he took on his protective voice and rose to the challenge: but he was less ready to understand feelings of confusion unconnected to feuding at work, to sickness of friends or family. He couldn't accept free-floating sadness, sadness without any overarching explanation other than that she felt melancholy and wished for reassurance at a most primitive, most unreasonable level. Nor did she really want to burden him with this form of weakness, he knew how proud he could be when she was strong – though her real wish was to find room to express what she still could not, namely: *love me for my fears, my hangups, my neuroses, love me for who I am when I simply can't cope . . .'*

[v] To be loved for the details

On a holiday in Florence a few years before, Alice had been accosted by a man in the Palazzo Medici, who whispered to her while she contemplated a painting by Gozzoli that she had skin like an angel. Because his skin was not unangelic itself, and a pair of horn-rimmed spectacles made it seem seduction was not the only reason he toured galleries, she accepted his ensuing offer of a coffee, which developed into lunch, a stroll through the Uffizi and ended with a night in common.

In the morning, Giovanni fetched her coffee and a linen bath robe, and they sat on his veranda in a suburb of Florence. Then, in flavoured broken English, he embarked on an ambitious declaration of love. Following a North American custom of repeating the interlocutor's name at the end of each sentence, Giovanni peppered his apparently heartfelt declaration with this touch, except that the night with the English lady [or perhaps it was simply the coffee] had muddled his literary memory, so that he ended up referring to her not as Lewis Caroll's Alice but rather as Dante's Beatrice.

Because the declaration was in any case uncalled for and the unwritten convention of the one-night encounter clear, Alice didn't rush to offer a correction, nor was she unduly hurt by the implications of the impersonal nature of what they had shared. Yet on the train back to England, she chuckled at the contrast between the intensity of a very earnest-sounding declaration of love and the casual substitution of her name by that of the great Florentine heroine.

To Alice, a love became ever more genuine the more one person seemed to have learnt about another, the more evidence there was that love was something tethered to a knowledge of specifics. These were not necessarily the major elements of another's existence [age, job, nationality, etc.], but the little things that separated one person from another – an awareness of their taste in jam, the memory of their childhood anecdotes, their favourite flowers or brand of toothpaste.

She trusted those who had made an effort to learn about her and hence by extension, lent her a sense of identity. Their conversations would be filled with remarks like, 'Remember when I was telling you last week about . . .' rather than a hesitant, 'Was it you I was telling this story to or my flatmate?' They would remember the details of her life ['You said you went to Strasbourg with your mother as a child . . .' or even a trivial, 'You take two sugars with your tea, don't you?'] and hence hint at the dimensions she had assumed in their consciousness.

If a man remembered her way of pronouncing a certain word or a peculiarity in the way she used a fork, her tastes in books or choice of restaurants, it seemed to indicate better than expensive roses or extensive declarations that this was someone she could trust to care for her. It was out of more than modesty that she preferred a man to say, 'Those earrings really suit you. You were wearing them last Tuesday, weren't you?' than for him to say, 'You know, you're the most beautiful woman I've ever known.'

It was why when Eric happened to tell her, 'It's sweet watching the way you peel an orange,' she smiled and felt strangely warmed by the remark. In the hierarchy of 'I' related things, noticing her way of peeling an orange felt far more intimate, far more in touch with who she was than a possibly spectacular but less detailed compliment.

[vi] To be loved for anxieties

If two strangers meet at a party and confess how awkward they find it to talk to strangers at a party, the confession of a common problem of social difficulty may mysteriously remove any impediments to the flow of the conversation – the revelation of a risk of stilted dialogue avoiding it becoming a reality.

Anxieties reflect individual fears in the face of social pressures and expectations. Will I be as interesting as my companion expects? Will I say what he wants to hear? Will I fulfil the expectations of those I love?

Because these anxieties gather on the sensitive membrane between the individual and society, one imagines the loneliness when they cannot be confessed, when there is no one in the group able to understand fears engendered by others. There is the loneliness of saying to someone, 'I'm having an anxiety attack,' and them replying with a puzzled, hearty expression, 'What do you mean? What ever can there be to be anxious about?' And because we laugh at what makes us anxious, a failure to emphathize with anxieties robs us of a shared sense of humour, with the mind-set and anthropology this entails.

Alice recalled her attraction to Eric solidifying over a conversation about adolescence, night-clubs and football teams.

'God, I remember, I was one of those people who hated to dance,' said Alice. 'I loved the idea, but I used to get so self-conscious, the thought of actually going out on the dance floor would terrify me. I remember there was this boy at a summer camp I once went to, and he asked me to dance – but I was so nervous, I said no. I don't know what I missed: he could have been the man of my life . . .'

'I'm glad you did miss him,' answered Eric. 'I know what you mean about dancing though, you feel like such an idiot if you don't know how to do it properly. There are all these things that you have to do at that age, and feel like an alien if you don't want to. I was the same with football clubs. At my school, everyone had a football club they supported, and I couldn't give a damn about football and so didn't – but for a while I was considered something of a freak. I even remember asking my mother if it was all right not to have any club you wanted to support, if there wasn't anything wrong with me.'

Their discussion on night-clubs and football teams assumed a significance because around both of these activities centred a clannish, group pressure. To be able to confess uninterest or anxiety was to break away from convention, to admit discomfort with things society deemed one should be comfortable with, and thereby cement an alliance founded on common identity.

[vii] To be loved for one's mind

The modern chivalric code suggests the noblest form of love to be the love of the mind. The woman who introduces her girl friends to an aesthetically damaged suitor may later draw a hushed and admiring reaction by saying, 'You know, Maximilian is a *brilliant* man. It's his intelligence I find so dazzling.' Those more used to salivating over a well-toned body, an expensively furnished house or simply a helpful and good-natured partner will feel their insufficiency next to this paragon of virtuous love – the love of the mind.

If Alice didn't wish to be loved for her body, one might have expected that she wished to be loved for her mind. In a sense she did, but the issue was not so clear cut. Many people told her she was clever, because she had done well at school, had been to university and now held a responsible job. She herself recognized that her mind had its qualities: she was good at maths, able to draw up tables and charts for the weekly sales meetings and calculate projected yields and ratios. She also had a good memory, and an adequate command of language. But it was not this she wished to be loved for either: she knew that a headache or bad mood could quickly destroy her mental capacities, and that what others considered her mind was really just a form of mental acrobatics scarcely connected to her true self.

So perhaps the mind should have been divided further: into the intellect and then the other, more elusive, spongy substance one was left with afterwards.

[viii] To be loved for being

In essence, Alice only wanted to be loved for things which she was not logically able to lose without at the same time ceasing to be herself. She wanted to be loved for the irreducible elements about her.

Given sufficient time and bad luck, she would lose:

a) her looks
b) her job
c) her money
d) her reasoning abilities,

and yet still she would remain herself.

She therefore wished to exclude such criteria from the motives of love because they were extrinsic to her existence. They were dangerously beyond her control, charming for now perhaps, but likely one day to vanish – and along with them, the lover who sustained her.

One could force an analogy between this anxious search for the things to be loved for and Descartes' arduous journey to find truth. His legendary answer of the *cogito* was a tool located to transcend the scepticism introduced into philosophy by Montaigne, Galileo and Gassendi, and which teasingly asked the question, 'How do we know that anything really exists, that anything is really the way it seems to us through our senses?' [the corollary of the depressing 3 a.m. question, 'How do I know this love is genuine? That it really has anything to do with *me*?'].

Descartes pushed scepticism as far as it went and concluded that though he could doubt many things around him, the one thing he really couldn't doubt was that he was in fact currently in the process of thinking. Thinking beings could doubt everything from the colour of the trees to the shape of the earth, but they could nevertheless be certain of their existence by perceiving their own ideas. As Descartes expressed it in his *Discourse on the Method*, 'Even if I were to suppose that I was dreaming and that whatever I saw or imagined was false, yet I could not deny that the ideas were truly in my mind.'

'I think, therefore I am' should not be confused with its

later interpretation denoting rationality [the so-called 'Cartesian' spirit]. Descartes was far from suggesting that people could claim they existed only if they thought rigorously and preferably enrolled in advanced philosophy courses. The *cogito* was no value judgement, as implied when used to refer to different activities: i.e., 'I feel, therefore I am', 'I play squash, therefore I am', etc. It merely captured the minimum one could be absolutely certain was true when everything else was in doubt. It was a way of stripping away uncertainties until one was left with a single unassailable truth, from which premiss other truths might be resurrected.

The search to find the true criteria of love followed a somewhat similar trajectory. To be sceptical would have meant calling superficial and false the commonly accepted motives of love, that someone was beautiful and rich, intelligent or strong. These didn't provide the irreducible element one might look for in the other's desire, referring as they did to things which could be washed away by time or misfortune.

The problem, and it was one Descartes also ran into but didn't fret over, was that once one embarks on a stripping operation, be it to find the one certainty or the one true criterion of love, the surviving answer turns out to be so specific as to be very vague once more. Descartes doubted everything but realized he couldn't doubt the fact that he was himself thinking – this one certainty was wonderful indeed, but what did it really tell him about the nature of truth? What could he do with it? How could he apply it? It was undoubtedly correct, but at the same time somewhat irrelevant to the pursuit of knowledge.

And what was Alice left with when she excluded all the ephemeral criteria of love? What was there left to be loved for when she'd removed the body, the intelligence and the assets?

Like Descartes, not very much.

She was left with pure consciousness, a pure kernel of being, a desire to be loved for the simple fact she existed.

No wonder she kept buying makeup.

TRAVEL

Towards the end of October, Alice and Eric decided they would take a few weeks off work around Christmas. The relentless autumn rain, shortening days and bitter winds naturally suggested a trip to balmier climates, so they looked at brochures on the Far East, the coast of Thailand and India, the Polynesian islands, Mauritius and the Seychelles, but eventually settled on the Caribbean sea and a hotel on the island of Barbados whose style was described as 'relaxed', but with 'every modern amenity' and a price tag to prove it.

The prospect of the holiday took on mythic dimensions: it was a moment in the future which they could anticipate whenever the present looked problematic – if there was boredom, irritation or anxiety but no time to address the real issues, then the holiday would be invoked as a cure. Whenever Alice thought of how little she had managed to read recently, she would buy a book and add it to her 'holiday pile' which quickly grew so high it would have needed a year of holiday to consume. When Eric thought of how little exercise he had managed to take, the thought of diving into what the brochure described as 'idyllic turquoise waters' abated his fitness guilt. And because their respective work patterns prevented them spending much time together, they looked forward to the trip as a chance for them to do what the brochure eloquently described as 'rediscover one another' [adding a picture of an ageing couple raising their champagne glasses on a hotel veranda to confirm the point].

They planned for the journey meticulously: they bought tanning lotions and T-shirts, sun glasses and sandals, beach bags and novels. They behaved as if they would be going away for months, the size of their luggage symbolic of a wish for eternal reprieve.

Time – whose passage was measured in relation to enjoyment – passed painfully slowly, though eventually surrendered its long-awaited December departure date. They woke up in a holiday mood, sharing jokes and finding them funny without reason other than that they needed to laugh, and at the airport, buying yet more superfluities before boarding the flight. They felt close, gone were the doubts and questionings of their relationship. They once more had a will to find one another pleasant, to make the effort to minimize friction. Eric offered to carry her bags, Alice asked if he wanted to read one of her books or magazines. When the plane rolled down the runway, they found their fingers enlaced, touching each other's skin with all the joy of Columbus stumbling on new land.

'Isn't it amazing to think that in a few hours we'll be on the other side of the Earth?' said Eric.

'I almost can't imagine it, it seems so unreal.'

'Aren't aeroplanes fantastic?'

'Ehm.'

'Just think, this plane is as big as about ten houses, and yet is going to hurtle through the sky at five hundred miles an hour . . .'

The captain's voice came on over the loudspeakers, and pointed out their route. They would be flying down the M4 corridor towards Bristol, then heading out across the Atlantic, reaching Barbados nine hours and thousands of miles later. Alice was seated next to the window and looked out over the dull suburbs of London below them.

'God, I'm so happy to be leaving all this behind – those horrible streets and the clouds and rain.'

'You're so beautiful, I want to eat you,' said Eric.

'Can't you wait for lunch?'

'No. You're wonderful, you really are. I don't tell you this enough, I know, but you are. You are a scrumptious, delicious, delicate, wondrous water melon.'

'You've lost it – you're crazy . . .' laughed Alice as he drew her to him into a kiss whose intensity was enough to awaken the interest of even a blasé cabin attendant.

They slept for most of the flight, and awoke to find the plane banking low over the island, giving them a view of its deep greenness against light blue waters. The jet age made arrival abrupt and overwhelming. When the airlock of the aircraft opened, they felt a dramatic increase in temperature, the air humid and smelling of the sea. They had been transported as though by magic to a different land, their space module, the giant 747 dwarfing the airport buildings, its slowly rotating turbine blades giving no indication of the massive journey just undergone. A breeze was blowing the palm trees gently to one side, a few clouds floated across the azure blue sky.

'It's incredible, it's so hot,' exclaimed Alice in disbelief as they walked across the tarmac, quickly discarding as many of her layers of clothing as possible.

The airport was a dramatic rub of two cultures; on the one hand, the anxious Westerners whose race was insane enough to think of building giant tubes to hurl themselves through the sky, and on the other, the less chronologically driven West Indians, their limbs moving with languor and ease. After travelling at five hundred miles an hour, the passengers were in a hurry to pick up their suitcases and enjoy the holiday they had paid so much and waited so long for – the airport attendants had a different conception of time altogether, a view that if it didn't happen that day, it could always happen the next.

'When the hell are they going to get this conveyor belt working?' sighed Eric.

'Relax,' answered Alice, imitating the local accent and fanning herself with a copy of the airline magazine.

They were met at the airport by a minibus, whose driver introduced himself as David and drove them to the hotel on the north-west side of the island. On the radio, a DJ was introducing rap versions of Christmas carols and wishing his listeners greetings for the holiday season. They drove through the capital, Bridgetown, whose architecture bore traces of the colonial British influence.

'Isn't it amazing to think that just nine hours ago we were in London?' reflected Alice, looking out at the streets and squares and marvelling at the dislocation she had undergone. All the familiar guide-posts were absent: the billboards advertised unfamiliar goods, the vegetation was lush and deep green, old cars rattled down pot-holed streets. There was a riot of bright colours: gardens were filled with bushes of orange, pink and purple bougainvillaea, hibiscus and poinsettia.

They pulled up at the hotel and walked into the lobby area.

'Welcome to Crusoe's Hotel,' greeted the receptionist, and after the usual formalities, took them to their bungalow positioned just behind the main house, overlooking the sea and within earshot of the surf gently rolling on to the wide sandy beach.

The climate had inscribed itself on the architecture, for

the perennial mildness of the weather meant the bungalow had no windows: there were simply two large panels missing in the wall through which fresh air could blow. There was no rigid, northern division between what was inner and outer, no need for shutters, bolts and double-glazed panes. It was a trusting, unsuspicious architecture – and it instinctively appealed to Alice's hatred of the tomb-like qualities of northern houses.

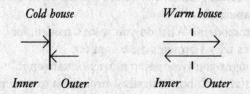

Eric, more attached to solid boundaries, started looking for an airconditioning unit, then called the reception desk only to learn that such appliances had been banned on the premises.

Alice undressed, wrapped herself in a dressing-gown she found hanging in the bathroom and went out on to the veranda. She felt the air against her skin, growing once more aware of a body so long wrapped up in layers to protect it from the fierce English winter.

'Do you want to go for a swim?' she asked.

'No, look, I've got a few things to sort out,' replied Eric inside the bedroom.

'All right, well I'll go, I'll be back in a little while.'

Without unpacking properly, she tore out a bathing costume and a towel, and headed for the beach a few yards down a sandy path. She ran into the water, splashing her feet against the sand and diving underwater when it was deep enough to do so. She articulated her limbs and moved powerfully through the water. After swimming from one end of the bay to the other, she returned to her towel and stretched it out on to the sand to catch the last rays of the day. Tired now [it was way past normal bedtime in London], she dozed for a few moments before heading back to the bungalow.

She returned to find Eric in something of a state.

'What's up?' she asked in response to his visible distress.

'This fucking hotel, they can't get the right modem for my computer.'

'What modem? What do you want a modem for?'

'That's why I brought the computer.'

'I thought you were going to write letters on it.'

'That as well, but basically I brought it to plug into the socket and get prices down the telephone – and now they tell me it won't work.'

'Oh well, don't worry. It can't be that much of a problem, surely something can be sorted out.'

'I doubt it. It's a disaster. And the shower doesn't work properly either.'

Alice sighed and sat down on the edge of the bed. Travel and the disruption of habit it entailed wasn't something Eric had been built for. If the tour operator who sold them the holiday in London had promised the phone socket would be compatible with the computer modem, then it was essential this turn out to be the case, and worthy of a large sulk if it didn't.

Eric was used to business hotels where he could count on finding a room with a large television in one corner, a couple of push-button telephones, an efficient laundry system, a helpful reception desk and a bathroom without stray hairs or rusty water. The chain he preferred was the Transcontinental group, which had branches in every large city. There was a Transcontinental in New York and one in Hong Kong, a branch in Bombay and one in Cape Town – and deposited in the lobby of these establishments, a guest could probably never know [apart from the language being spoken] which country they were in. Everything about them was designed to minimize difference and reassure guests that despite the rickshaws and temples outside, one could still dial nine and have a Danish and espresso sent up for breakfast. It was a philosophy reflected in the advertising slogan: *Transcontinental, Designed to make you feel at home everywhere*.

Those who go abroad might be divided into two groups.

→ *Tourists* have a cast of mind that hates surprise – they may like novelty, a handsome pyramid or a refreshing beach, but only if it conforms to expectation. They hate doubt, uncertainty, equivocation, they want the menu of the day to be clear and understandable, they can't stomach the uncertainties evoked by an exotic curry, emotion or fruit, clinging instead to preconceptions of place formed in an armchair before reaching the airport. Proust's narrator is perhaps the most famous tourist in modern literature: he spends pages of *A la Recherche* dreaming of going to Venice, a city which he has entirely constructed in his head from art and literature. He has a familiarity with this dream city which again and again delays him from actually going there for fear of testing the dream against reality, like a tourist who visits a country never straying from the pages of *Fodor* and *Michelin*.

→ *Travellers* on the other hand journey with fewer preconceptions, and are less upset if their ideas are contradicted by conditions on the ground. The difference is in the attitude towards the unknown. Whereas Eric hated the element of surprise represented by the difficult fit of a telephone socket, Alice didn't mind if the hotel in the brochure turned out to be quite different from the one she in fact stayed in – she was happier to abandon her routines, she could give up eating cornflakes and eat dried fish for breakfast if local custom required it.

And yet, if we are to draw an analogy with love, then Alice that day experienced a tinge of the same disgruntlement with Eric as he felt with the hotel – she recognized that in the territory of love she was perhaps herself a tourist. She too suffered from a lack of curiosity to test the dream, to venture outside the compound and explore what might be going on in her lover-country, daring not to think that the man she believed had everything was perhaps lacking in such basic amenities as a modem through which to communicate.

READING MATTER

Alice sat on the edge of the beach wondering, 'Did I put the six on my shoulders or the four?' It was the first day of sunbathing in paradise [though Eden had been lost], and she greeted it with a jet-lagged, slightly melancholic sigh. It was not an easy life; the perpetual balancing of different Protection Factor sun creams, the rotation of the deck-chairs in line with the drifting path of the sun, the need to alternate stomach and back, the tension that accompanied the inevitable hopes – 'Is my hair really going blond?' – and the compulsive need to check one's curls whenever a cloud crossed the sun. A light breeze was blowing in from the sea, and at the gate to the hotel a tall Negro was trimming a hedge. But there was work to be done. Alice reached for her Walkman and inserted a tape between the metal clips. A voice sang:

> Loving you ain't always right
> But baby, lovin' is the only light.

She and Eric had awoken early according to the time rhythm of another continent, unused to sleeping in a room where the birds could be heard rustling so distinctly outside and where nightly tropical showers beat down noisily on the palm-covered roof.

Eric's mood had recovered, and they spent a pleasant breakfast on the hotel's main terrace. By the time the sun was high in the sky, they had already swum a few laps of the bay, and returned to their chairs to dry.

'Will you pass me my book?' asked Eric, applying tanning lotion to his legs.

'Yeah, where is it?'

'It's in my bag. The Denis O'Donoghue. Under the towel.'

Eric read many books by authors with names like Denis O'Donoghue, large tomes hundreds of pages long filled with heroes who fought in mercenary wars, operated nuclear submarines, made love in foreign hotels and helicoptered down granite canyons.

Alice often teased him about his reading matter. 'Why do you spend your time reading books that make *Superman* look intellectual?'

Eric wasn't known for humorous responses, tending to give an answer along the lines that 'I read them because they're fun, light and why should everyone spend their time reading self-indulgent introspective bullshit?'

The bullshit referred to the literary genre Alice had lately started reading and which had brought her luggage to within grams of overweight on the flight to Barbados. They were brightly coloured books bearing such titles as *Learning Intimacy*, *I'm happy when you're happy*, and *Better Loving, Better Living*. To the reader who recalls Alice's objection to language within love, these books might appear somewhat incongruous, but her faith in intuitive understanding had recently waned enough to account for their presence – like an intuitive cook who nevertheless decides to glance in a recipe book to check the necessary measurements of flour and sugar.

Watching them side by side on their deck chairs, she reading *Understand Yourself and Your Partner*, he absorbed in

Operation Commando, a distinction came naturally to mind between two literary approaches.

📖 Reading to escape yourself

Unless they happened to have spent several decades in the Balkan division of the Secret Service, had travelled to Moscow as a spy during the Kruschev years, had a detailed knowledge of the inside of a nuclear processing plant, knew how to defuse a plastic explosive and were fascinated by the workings of the African arms trade, there was little in *Operation Commando* in danger of reminding readers of the texture or meaning of their own life. Despite well-researched accounts of such activities, the book lapsed into the most cursory descriptions of the sort of human affairs readers might conceivably have lived through. The reader was told how to work an Uzi sub-machine-gun and lower the undercarriage of an F-16 jet, but when it came to descriptions of the lowering of that other undercarriage, the writer brushed off possible emotional and physical complexities by informing us brusquely that the hero [complete with 'stubble showing he hadn't shaved since the debriefing with Mac aboard the destroyer . . .'] 'pressed himself against Bernice's quivering lips and squeezed her silken buttocks briskly'.

In the world of *Operation Commando*, no one was ever worried about dying, bored or vaguely and inconsequentially depressed. There was not time for biting nails and wondering if the phone would ring when there was forever a mission to undertake against Colombian drugs dealers, when there was yet another hijack to foil and only twenty minutes remained on the detonator beneath the Houses of

Parliament. Curiously, no one ever seemed overcome by the feelings of vague dissatisfaction revealed by a glance around a commuter carriage [T. S. Eliot's 'lives of quiet desperation'], no one ever wondered, 'Why doesn't something interesting ever happen to me?' or 'Will it go on like this till the day I die?' or quite simply, 'What the hell is this all about?'

And therefore readers potentially troubled by these concerns, as human beings perhaps must be [everyone must die, and as Montaigne pointed out, death forces everyone to become something of a philosopher], these readers were spared as much the joys as the travails of introspection.

Though Eric read many books, it wasn't unfair to say that this activity was free of all curiosity, for he read not in order to discover things, but primarily so as to avoid stumbling upon them. He wasn't looking for congruence; if he was fearful, the last thing he wished to read about was his own fear. He might have gained some relief from the fear of an African arms dealer pursued by a crack Marine unit – a fear perhaps, but not *his* fear.

There was tension in books like *Operation Commando*, but it was safe tension because it lacked all psychological, and hence personal, import. Eric could release his anxiety following a story of guerrilla warfare in South-East Asia while spared the need to untangle equally intricate but less distant conflicts. He had long held that the self-questioning, self-monitoring process served no purpose and had survived in the genetic make up of the species only by a freak of evolution comparable in redundancy to the spleen or appendix.

One might have expected Alice to follow him in his reading. Yet, however much she day-dreamed, she was searching. Her problems hadn't killed her curiosity.

She was messed up enough to have had problems to think about, but was not so messed up as not to have been able to think of them at all.

📖 *Reading to find yourself*

Books rarely address readers with the forthrightness a flesh and blood interlocutor may, but we are nevertheless familiar with works that seem to 'speak' to us. Rather than include us on rocket trips through black holes, they forgo the pleasures of intergalactic travel in order to sketch states of mind and situations of more human, more personal dimensions. A first kiss, hunger, the light on a cold autumn day, social isolation, jealousy, the sensation of boredom – these may provide us, in the hands of a skilled and honest author, with a feeling akin to a shock of self-recognition. The author has located words to depict a situation we thought ourselves alone in feeling and, like two lovers who are thrilled to discover congruencies, the reader may find themselves turning to the spine and exclaiming, 'My God, someone else feels this too! To have thought I was the only one to have the sense that . . .'

And for a brief moment, seated in a train carriage rattling through the darkened countryside or in a plane on an overnight flight, the reader may feel their loneliness alleviated, realizing their connection to a wider body than themselves, to humanity, feeling a sudden rush of sympathy and understanding for their fellow passengers and all those they had previously warded off as strangers – for a moment elated at the thought of the similarities between themselves and others outweighing the differences.

Alice was not in the process of consuming great literature

on her Caribbean deck-chair. *Understand Yourself and Your Partner* had none of the criteria we are taught to associate with the classics. Its sentences were blunt, direct and clumsily constructed. It abandoned claims to authorial objectivity and aimed for a niggling familiarity with the reader, chummily asking him or her, '*Do you remember sitting on your mother's lap and thinking that . . .?*' and, '*Have you ever thought that all the people you're interested in aren't interested in you?*' But far more offensively, *Understand Yourself and Your Partner* had a moral mission in hand, to tell the reader something that would change his or her life and to do it without the respectable incomprehensibility of the great moral works of classical philosophy. At the pinnacle of vulgarity, with all the forthrightness of a car-maintenance manual, the author advised the reader, '*Try and remember to ask your partner what is on their mind the next time that . . .*'

A very forgivable prejudice attends the sort of literature which 'tells' us something too directly. Stendhal once compared introducing ideas into a novel to letting a gun go off in a concert hall, and even outside the genteel world of the concert hall-novel, it is still thought best to cloak advice as other things – to render it abstract enough for it to become Sartrean philosophy, Symbolist poetry or a Scandinavian motion picture.

In Stendhal's language, the author of Alice's book was firing a sub-machine-gun in a concert hall [though it was not a novel], for she was currently working her way through a chapter entitled 'Realizing your Potential'. '*Most of us lead lives which don't allow us to fully express ourselves. We are filled with things we would like to say and do, but somehow never get around to them . . .*'

Alice only thought a book worth reading if it could in

some way help her live. She was thereby implicated in possibly the greatest sin a reader could commit with a book in the eyes of the educated literary critic – she wanted to get something out of it. After all, a reader shouldn't want anything, books had no *purpose* – vacuum cleaners and oil pumps had purposes, but surely there was agreement that art was for art's sake? One recalls Nabokov ridiculing those who read novels hoping to learn anything from them – learn from them! Was that not as ridiculous as trying to quench one's appetite on caviare?

Yet Alice could only spare a few hours to read each week, and wanted books to be relevant to her concerns, ones whose situations and descriptions she could apply without undue effort to her material and social settings. She looked for those that would 'hit the button', the button triggered by another's lines which matched what she had till then felt but had been unable to formulate herself. She searched for a more skilled articulation of her own experiences in the experiences of another. It was not necessarily physical congruence she sought [she was not going to put down a book simply because it was set in Barcelona and she lived in London, or it was about a man and she was a woman], but rather psychological congruence. It could have been someone else's story that gripped her, but it was her own story which [however obliquely] would be illuminated in the telling.

She was in this sense far more self-centred than Eric. Precisely because his self [of the 'Know thyself' injunction] was of no sustaining interest, he felt no loss or dispersal indulging in rugged safaris through the Kenyan bush, boat trips down the Amazon and balloon flights across Polar ice caps. But Alice couldn't project herself into situations so far removed from what she knew. She had no interest in reading yet another 'bold' and 'powerful' account of some-one's childhood and coming of age in Sunderland, she had no interest in another 'stunning' and 'elegant' portrait of ten generations of a wealthy Southern family or a 'stark' account of a repressed young man discovering his homosexuality in a New York bar.

She wanted to 'find herself'. The phrase was hers, and despite its confused and perhaps illiterate syntax, it captured something of the ambitions in her reading. She wanted to understand better why she felt certain things, why she loved and why she hated, why she was depressed and why she was happy, what it meant to be a woman and what it was to be a man, how two people could communicate and why they so often did not. She wanted stories whose characters would shed light on her experiences, who searched for love and meaning amidst the everyday clutter, and whose fates might, if at all possible, turn out to be moderately happy ones.

'Before you come fully to find yourself and perhaps even me, how would you feel about a piña colada?' asked Eric leaning over his chair and raising his sunglasses and eyebrows.

'Oh, that's very sweet, I'd feel very good about that,' answered Alice, putting down her copy of *Understand Yourself and Your Partner*.

'Great, well, I'll go and get some from the bar at the main house. I'll be back in a minute.'

She watched Eric walk across the beach and down

towards the hotel, his muscular frame showing the first signs of a tan.

He's really adorable, she thought to herself, ironic when only a minute before she had been thinking how unlike the ideal relationship described in her self-help book hers and Eric's appeared to be.

JOLLYISM

Eric returned carrying two pear-shaped glasses filled with a creamy white liquid topped with bright orange parasols.

'The barman was so friendly, he's a great guy, he's called RJ. He does a lot of fishing apparently, he was telling me about a barracuda he caught yesterday.'

'Really.'

'And then apparently they're organizing a huge Christmas party on the beach, with dancing and people are going to dress up and stuff.'

'Oh.'

'Isn't that great?'

'Yeah, sure.'

'Mmmm, this drink is fantastic, this has got to be the best piña colada I've ever had. Do you like yours?'

'Yeah, it's good. Bit sweet though.'

'Is it? Really? No, it isn't.'

'It is a bit for me.'

'I don't think it's sweet at all, it's just right.'

'Whatever . . .'

Alice's forehead acquired traces of thoughtful lines which attracted Eric's attention.

'What's up?'

'Nothing. Just thinking.'

'Isn't it all just brilliant. The beach and everything.'

'Yes.'

'Anyone who couldn't be happy here would have to be crazy, don't you think?'

'Depending on . . .'

'I think this holiday is going to be bliss from beginning to end.'

'It hasn't ended yet.'

'I know, but I can tell it will be.'

Ever since his modem crisis on the first evening, Eric had been full of manic gusto. Everything was 'wonderful' and 'terrific', 'fantastic' and 'great'. Alice was beautiful, the weather couldn't have been better, the food was delicious, the hotel was top class, this was paradise.

Alice was always apprehensive of occasions when happiness was a prerequisite, birthdays, feast days, reunions or weddings. She had difficulty enjoying things when under pressure to do so, there had to be a chance to declare something awful before she could begin to think it marvellous. Nothing made her sadder than someone who kept reminding her how happy she had to be.

However, Eric's view was that he was a happy man on a happy holiday and that there were therefore no grounds for him to feel anything but permanently contented. Despite earlier dissatisfactions, he was not going to dwell on such details if they failed to fit in with his contented self-image.

Alice's problem was very unfocused, for it centred precisely on her inability to tell Eric that however well disposed she was towards him, she at least had to be allowed to entertain the possibility of things not being fine. The potential to experience the island as paradise depended on her first having the opportunity to find it otherwise.

But there was little choice in the matter.

'What's wrong?' asked Eric, detecting a certain failure of enthusiasm before a tank full of eels on a trip to an aquarium that afternoon.

'Nothing, I'm just a little tired.'

'But we slept twelve hours.'

'You're right, I'll be fine in a second.'

Alice had often admired the way her friend Suzy and her boyfriend Matt dealt with difficulties between them. Their relationship was stormy, full of violent break-ups and passionate reconciliations. At the slightest provocation, they would accuse one another of violent crimes: 'You bastard,' she would say, 'I saw you flirting with her the whole evening.' 'You were flirting with him more like, you double-dealing, two-faced bitch,' he would answer, and walk out slamming the door.

When she had first witnessed these scenes, Alice was understandably worried, thinking that two people who screamed at one another in this way were destined for a bad end. Yet only moments later, the row would be made up and Suzy would tell her, 'You know, he's the sweetest little angel in the world' – this from a woman who had ten minutes before been accusing him of the most unforgivable offences. The couple had no trouble getting angry only to love one another an instant later, but accepting without problem that both things had happened.

'We make Romeo and Juliet look chilled out,' remarked Suzy, 'always screaming at one another, then doing the cuddling bit again. But we're a team, we really are.'

This scenario of passionate break-up and reconciliation was perhaps a way of dealing with an underlying fear of losing love, enacting theatrics in order to contain the danger of genuine drama. It was like mentioning a taboo word, and thereby alleviating its spell. By breaking up so many times, Suzy could make the experience familiar and hence less threatening: it integrated the end of love into the relationship – like shrugging off the fear of death by miming and laughing at the contortions of heart-attack victims.

Alice missed a similar acknowledgement with Eric. They had argued on the first night in the hotel, but it was hard for this event to find comfortable expression within a context of more cheerful times and simply delicious piña coladas. Eric had a nostalgic view of himself and his relationship which prevented the inevitable difficulties finding honest recollection.

He thereby evoked a certain psychological phenomenon one could term *jollyism*, of which he was by no means the only victim in the holiday resort.

The North American catering staff who managed the hotel dining-room were other notable examples.

'Hi, how are you folks doin' today?' the waitress asked Alice and Eric when they sat down for dinner on the hotel veranda that night. 'I'm Jackie, and I'll be bringing you everything you need this evening.'

'Thank you,' replied Alice, unsure whether or not this was a signal for her to introduce herself in turn.

'You bet,' answered the waitress. 'Now specials for today include calamari, sea bass and some great lobster.'

Jackie's face was frozen into a smile which made it seem vital to declare each dish a culinary triumph, so as not to let this miracle of facial muscle power collapse and reveal what might have been a ghastly pain.

Though happy sentiments are of course always desirable, jollyism could not comfortably have been equated with happiness. Whereas the happy soul would smile because he or she had a *choice* in the matter, because the sunset was nice or their lover had just called them, jollyists would be happy only *because they simply could not be unhappy*, because they suffered from a rigid inability to integrate the good and the bad.

There was something of this in the grim determination with which Jackie maintained the aerobic energy of her smile, and in Eric's repeated declarations over dinner – 'This is just fantastic lobster!' 'Isn't this the best holiday ever?' – though his girlfriend's expression might have suggested otherwise had he been tempted to study it.

In the course of their stay, Alice and Eric were befriended by a couple from Miami. Eric had met husband Bob in the fax room, where they had both been collecting material sent by their offices, and he had become friends with him and his wife Daisy. Daisy and Bob were lawyers celebrating their third wedding anniversary on the island [an achievement worthy of celebration in certain circles]. They had visited England the year before, and declared themselves committed Anglophiles, charmed by everything Alice and Eric chose to utter.

Bob had an irrepressible energy: he organized basketball games on the beach, table-tennis matches and chess tournaments for the evenings, trips to neighbouring islands and scuba-diving expeditions to outlying reefs. Neither he nor his wife ever had an off day, and Eric declared them the most entertaining guests in the hotel, people whom he would make an effort to stay in touch with on future visits to the States.

When Alice tried to make a joke about Bob's smile being almost as permanent as that of the waitress Jackie, Eric flared up.

'Why do you always have to be so cynical about people?

Why can't you just like them and treat them the way they treat you?'

'I haven't done anything nasty to them, I'm just remarking that, you know, well, they just seem so cheerful all the time. I asked Daisy how she was today and she said, "Actually, I am *so* well you know . . ."'

'I can't understand you, I don't know what's made you so bitter.'

Gossip is an exercise in trust: a person feels free to gossip when they feel they have someone to understand their objections. It is a colluding activity; two people leave the main group and open up their parcel of gossip material: 'Isn't she weird?' 'Don't you find him really cold?' 'Did you see her false eyelashes?' 'Is that a toupee?' 'Did she inherit that money?' Eric's refusal to collude in Alice's remarks therefore represented a symbolic shift of loyalty; it implied, 'I trust my new friends Daisy and Bob more than I do you. I won't join you in your gossip game for my loyalties are now elsewhere.'

On Christmas Eve, a giant barbecue was set up on the beach and a reggae band brought in to entertain the hotel guests. The management had decided to make the evening fancy dress, and guests now circulated around a bonfire in a variety of colourful costumes. Bob and Daisy had dressed up in a religion- and gender-confused vision of Indian attire, both wearing Sikh turbans, tikkis and saris, while Eric had put on a grass skirt and Hawaiian shirt. Alice watched them dancing around the fire, their arms interlaced, swinging their legs back and forth in the style of the French can-can.

If Alice didn't join the other guests singing around the beach bonfire, it was because she often fell prey to a version of the Nuremberg complex at such occasions. Looking at everyone chanting merrily, she would feel how easily groups that chant go on to chant not just 'Jingle Bells', but also 'Deutschland über alles'.

Bob motioned over to Alice.

'Come on, sweetheart, let's dance,' he said in a rum-punch drunken state.

'That's kind of you, Bob, but not just yet.'

'Come on, honey, why not?'

'Well, it would be a breach of my contract with the London Ballet. I'm not allowed to dance in public without their permission.'

'You dance for the London Ballet?'

'Yeah, sure, didn't you know?'

'No way.'

'Of course.'

'Ah! I think you're kidding me.'

'I think you may be right, Bob.'

'Hah, you English! You're so funny.'

Jollyists should not be thought a dull group of people: on the back of their enthusiasm and energy, countless Christmas and other parties have been set up and the social life of the community enriched. Yet there is a peculiarity to jollyist humour, a certain earnestness wedded to the mentality of the group, one which hints of the clean fun of the Scout movement or school hockey team.

However feeble Alice's joke about the London ballet, it was significant if Bob took longer than he might to realize her irony. Though jollyists find many things funny, the one thing they tend not to find funny is themselves. Attached to success and seriousness of activities on which they are engaged, their scope for ironic acknowledgement is necessarily curtailed. They can laugh at people slipping on banana skins, but grow more reluctant to self-deprecate, to declare themselves or the human project in which they are involved a deeply flawed and at times absurd exercise.

The thought that Eric and Bob, though jollyists, might be deeply humourless had struck Alice unexpectedly that afternoon in the course of a discussion on computers. After lunch, Eric had mentioned to Bob that he had brought over his laptop machine, and Bob had said he too had travelled with one. Both men had then returned to their bungalows to show off their respective equipment. Bob's machine turned out to be smaller, but Eric's had the thinnest colour screen yet made and an alarm to protect it from theft.

'This has revolutionized my life,' remarked Bob of his small grey box. 'You know, when I first got into computers ten years ago, you would have needed a huge desktop to do what this little thing can do. It's incredible the power they can fit into these chips now. And soon, these machines will seem like dinosaurs. We're on the edge of a complete computer revolution.'

'I think you're right,' replied Eric, 'this is only the beginning. Every sphere of life is going to be changed by technology. In a few years, everyone will be able to talk via computers sending information down fibre-optic cables. Everything will be electronic, there won't be any paper or ink left, and the productivity gains will be enormous.'

A hushed, earnest silence was to be expected in the wake of such predictions for the future of technology. The current flawed patterns of life would disappear under the influence of lasers, chips and fibre-optic cables. The world would enter a phase rendering everything before it a pale imitation of human possibility. Those prone to thinking that their life would not alter even if they had a computer the size of a bread crumb could be expected to lapse into silence at the prospect of this beatific, technological Jerusalem.

But Alice's scepticism was more enduring, which was perhaps why she asked Bob and Eric whether people would still be writing love letters to one another after this great computer revolution.

'Don't be silly,' answered Eric, picking up on, though not accepting her [admittedly uninspired] irony.

'Sure they will, Alice,' replied Bob missing the point completely, 'they'll be doing it through computers. If you wanted to write to Eric, you'd simply punch in his number, and perhaps even without writing, simply by thinking a love letter, a message could be sent to him – that's when they manage to hook up neurones to external data processors.'

On the way to Barbados, Eric had been greatly impressed by the technology of the Boeing 747 in which they had flown. He had talked about cruising speed and drag, ailerons and radars, Rolls-Royce engines and reverse thrust, and had then pointed out the wing of the aircraft and remarked: 'This is a feat of precision engineering.' Alice had to admit that it was remarkable to be able to fly from London to Barbados in a giant machine in half a day, but her enthusiasm knew bounds. Precision engineering was not about to change the fundamentals. She couldn't forget that this Boeing wing had been put together in Seattle, Washington, by a group of people who were at heart only a species of highly evolved apes, who cheated on their wives and husbands, had temper tantrums, jealousies, rivalries and insecurities, shitted daily and would later die.

Irony was her instinctive reaction to counteract the dangers of technological and other brands of humourless [and hence in some way cruel] self-importance. It was the pin brought in to pop the ever-present tendency towards balloons of seriousness.

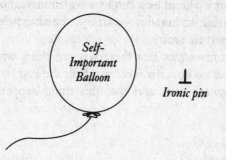

There had the previous day been a doubles table-tennis tournament in the hotel, in which Eric and Alice had entered themselves as a team. Her occasional skilled shot failed to disguise her weakness at the game, and after a good start, it became obvious that they wouldn't be proceeding too far in the tournament. Because he had counted on making an impression and perhaps reaching the quarter-finals [whose participants were to be rewarded with a free drink at the bar], Eric grew increasingly irritated by Alice's dud shots – so that at one point, she had to remind him, 'Don't worry, most people who went on to win Wimbledon came unstuck here, so I don't think your career is finished yet.'

'Concentrate, you're missing all the spinners.'

'It's just a game.'

'Only losers talk like that,' replied Eric abruptly, earnestly unwilling to pop the balloon.

Looking at Bob, Eric, Daisy and other guests dancing around the bonfire on Christmas Eve, Alice was reminded that simply because they lacked a sense of humour, people who took themselves too seriously still laughed. In fact, they might laugh all the more loudly and violently than others, but it would be a laughter which missed out on the richest source of humour – namely, the acknowledgement of their own absurdity.

It was only a pity that there was one thing which Alice could spare no humour for, for which she had no room for self-referential irony and that this thing happened to be love.

DIVING, ROUSSEAU AND
THINKING TOO MUCH

Back in the bungalow later that night, after they had made love, Alice leant her head softly against Eric's shoulder and asked, 'What are you thinking?'

'Ehm?'

'What are you thinking?'

'Nothing.'

'Nothing at all?'

'No, not really.'

The wind could be heard rustling through the foliage, the air humid before the nightly rainstorm. Alice's eyes drifted out of the veranda at the moon casting its light across the bay.

'Where do you think this relationship is going?'

'Alice, it's one thirty in the morning.'

'So?'

'So we're not going to start on this kind of discussion now. Why do you always have to make things so complicated? What do you want to know? Why I haven't asked you to marry me?'

Eric turned to the other side of the bed and readjusted his head on the pillow.

'You never look at me when we're making love.'

'Alice, please, can we leave this till tomorrow? I'm exhausted.'

*

The next morning, Alice told Eric she wasn't in the mood for breakfast and he should go on without her. When he returned from the hotel dining-room, he found her still in bed, absorbed in the final pages of *Understand Yourself and Your Partner*.

'Alice, you've got to get ready or else we're going to be late. Bob and Daisy will be waiting for us at the pier in ten minutes.'

'I don't know if I feel like scuba diving today.'

'You said yesterday you wanted to go.'

'That's a lie: you just assumed I wanted to go because you didn't hear otherwise.'

'What am I supposed to do? Read your thoughts?'

'No, but how about asking for them?'

'Why are you so aggressive this morning? Will you just relax.'

[Eric frequently told Alice she should relax, particularly when he was the cause of what was preventing her from doing so. The word was not coincidentally placed. Eric might have said, 'Will you just calm down . . .' but calming entailed an element of responsibility bypassed by a suggestion of relaxation. The person who *calms down* has something legitimate to be excited about, the person told to *relax* is cast as over-reacting to an objectively harmless situation – particularly when the command was given with the emphasis falling on the second syllable and a patronizingly elongated *a*.

A line might be traced from the Ancient Greek injunction to 'know thyself' through to the command to 'relax'. Much as the rational, self-conscious person was the envy and model of the ancient Greeks, so relaxation was the new Western psychological ideal. The difference was that Greek mastery of reason implied an effort, an overcoming of something [the passions] in the name of a rational life, whereas the command to relax simply implied the need to loosen one's muscles for the sake of a more comfortable evening in front of the television. One could relax in the way one slept, it was a passive state, not so much an interval as a pause.]

'No, I won't fucking relax.'

'Well, why not? What the hell do you want, Alice?'

'To know why I have to create a crisis before you'll ever ask that kind of question.'

'What kind of question?'

'What I might want. What this is all about. Where we're going.'

Eric looked out of the window at the surf. It was a brilliant blue day, almost windless but still cool enough to be pleasant. The vegetation glistened after the previous night's rain, and birds with highly pointed beaks dipped into long-stemmed flowers whose names he didn't know.

He felt a burst of resentment at Alice's psychological thrust. He disliked questions and felt burdened by her insistence on them. He longed to go swimming.

'Why do you never want to talk?' asked Alice.

'Because it's not good to talk about things too much.'

'Why?'

'Because it's not. Anyway, we're going to be seriously late if you don't start getting ready right now.'

'No, go on, tell me why?'

'Do you want to go on this scuba diving trip or not?'

'I don't know.'

'You've got to decide this minute.'

'In that case, I won't come. Just go alone.'

'God, you can be a drag,' snapped Eric and crossed into the bathroom to pick up a towel and a tube of sun cream.

'You know what your problem is, Alice? You complicate everything. You think too much. That's right, go on, stay home all day, I'm sure you're going to have a great time. It's not my problem if you miss out on seeing some of the greatest waters in the whole of the bloody Caribbean.'

And with this final attempt at inducing aquatic envy, Eric stormed out of the bungalow. He flip-flopped across the wooden veranda, down the sandy path leading through the trees to the pier at the water's edge, waving to the gardener on his way.

'How you doin', man?' answered the latter. 'You gotta lovely day for de beach.'

'Sure have,' mid-Atlanticked Eric, with a tone of almost aggressive bonhomie.

Eric's annoyance at Alice was perhaps understandable. He wanted to go scuba diving and swimming, he wanted a carefree holiday, he insisted on a carefree holiday, and yet [like poor old Charles Bovary] all he had was a sulky woman on his hands. No wonder he told her she thought too much.

It has often been said that pains and problems provoke thought. For instance, I don't feel my little toe until I stub it against a table, and then become acutely aware of it. I think of my toe and greater things besides only when they appear in some way problematic or painful. The psychological argument follows the model:

$$Problem/Pain \xrightarrow{\text{leads to}} Thought$$

However uncontentious this may seem, there exists a pervasive counter-argument that sees thought not as the *reaction* to a pain or problem, but instead as its *cause* and origin. According to this model, we find the equation reversed:

$$\text{Thought} \xrightarrow{\text{leads to}} \text{Problem/Pain}$$

For ease of use, one may call the first argument the *intellectual* one, the second the *naturalist*.

Did Hamlet think so much because he had problems, or did he have problems because he thought so much?

The intellectual would answer that Hamlet's thinking was problem-induced rather than problem-inducing, an argument betraying an implicit faith that thinking through a problem was the best chance a human had of solving it – the faith of Chamfort's formulation that '*La pensée console de tout.*'

The naturalist would on the other hand see thinking as a disease which predated and precisely initiated the problem it pretended to have been called in to solve. Thinking was a form of psychological hypochondria – only when Hamlet thought he might have a pain was a pain actually felt. The naturalist would hence advise the prince to indulge in minimal mental exercise so that things could return to the spontaneous simplicity and ease which reason had destroyed.

Naturalism has spent its long and glorious history arguing that things which happen without human, rational intervention are far superior to those polluted with the meddlesome touch of civilization. A wild waterfall in the Swiss Alps is superior to the rigid classicism of the Jardin du Luxembourg, the common sense of a ruddy farmer has more to teach us than the great books of philosophy, a carrot grown without fertilizer in the wild is better tasting than its commercial counterpart, an emotion left to flow unfettered by thought is richer and deeper than its analysed cousin.

Rousseau was perhaps the earliest and most revered spokesman for this naturalist position, attacking such products of civilization as luxury, art, science, modern government and thought. Paradoxically for someone whose collected works ran to over a dozen volumes, he was of the view that books gave people pains they didn't know they had: 'In instinct alone, man had all he required for living in the state of nature; and with a developed understanding, he has only just enough to support life in society.' 'Our first impulses are always good,' he declared, only social life and the intellect had robbed us of our spontaneous virtues. He pointed to the example of a murder committed at the window of a philosopher who had only to 'argue with himself a little to prevent nature identifying with the unfortunate sufferer'. By contrast with this unwholesome academic, Rousseau argued sportingly that 'The honest man is an athlete, who loves to wrestle stark naked.'

Though he didn't wrestle stark naked [and only occasionally indulged in games of table-tennis], in the choice between the two models, Eric was by temperament strongly inclined towards naturalism. This didn't mean he loved nature – he rarely went into the countryside, and when he did, what he saw didn't touch him deeply. Far from worshipping the simple life, he wanted advanced telecommunications and state of the art plumbing, nor was he someone to go soft at the thought of fertilizer-free vegetables or gardens left to the ways of nature. Rather, his attachment centred around emotional naturalism, the idea that feelings were better if left to flow unfettered. But again, we shouldn't paint him as a mystic indulging in spiritual communion in contrast to Alice's somewhat crude concern with self-help philosophy. He didn't lie back and listen to his inner pulses with the silent and reverent countenance of certain audiences at performances of Chopin or Schubert. His attachment to emotional naturalism was limited to his manner of accounting for [rather than dealing with] the sort of unpleasant emotions that sounded like nails being scratched across a blackboard.

When he guessed that Alice was experiencing emotional nails across a blackboard [as she had that scuba diving morning], his reaction inclined towards diagnosis not aid, and his diagnosis towards a naturalist accusation of excessive cerebral activity. He suggested that Alice's afflictions were not part of her lot *per se*, but merely the temporary and extrinsic result of too much cogitation. They could no more be considered her problem [and hence his] than the erratic behaviour of a person acting under the influence of drugs – an explicatory manoeuvre akin to Rousseau's helpful suggestion that the evils of mankind were unnatural, merely the product of civilization and money, commerce and history.

Eric's emotional naturalism could less generously have been explained as a brand of *common-sensism*, the attachment to a cluster of reductive ideas suggesting simplicity to be the essence of wisdom, the truth 'obvious' and hence beyond analysis. Under the guise of calling a spade a spade, commonsensists would declare all garden implements spades because differentiation entailed too great an effort – reductionism passed off as clarification.

To ask a commonsensist why wars occurred or people fell in or out of love, or did a host of everyday but immensely complex things, one would learn that it was simply quite natural to do so. Common-sensism would mark off areas as 'beyond thought' on the grounds not of their *complexity*, but of their excessive *simplicity*, their sheer *obviousness*. If Eric didn't wish to talk to Alice, he told himself that it was not because things between them were too complicated, but rather because they were too basic to waste breath on.

His view of human psychology implied that unless people were openly starving, homeless or had had a leg amputated, their problems had a fictitious and hence analytically unworthy quality. It helped explain why on the first day in Barbados, he had called Alice's reading matter 'self-indulgent introspective bullshit'. Using a somewhat curious argument given that they were on holiday, Eric condemned her reading matter not because it was patronizingly written and simplistic but on account of it leading to excessive pleasure, an unforgivable brand of pleasure, the self-indulgent variety.

But why was introspection self-indulgent in the way that scuba diving or piña colada drinking was not? Because it suggested a narcissistic enjoyment with oneself, a form of masturbation [always the shady cousin of intercourse], carrying with it ancient connotations of the religious condemnation of the self [when Augustine divided the world, he declared that two loves had created two cities, 'Love of self, to the contempt of God, the earthly city, love of God, to the contempt of self, the heavenly' – a theme taken up by Pascal in his narcissistically deprived '*le moi est haïssable*'].

To think of oneself was taken by Eric to be far worse than eating an ice-cream, because it involved a vanity-filled session in front of the mirror. The condemnation was of course premissed on a crucial assumption – that one would necessarily admire the image one saw in the mirror. Only if one thought oneself wonderful would introspection become an ecstatic affair, truly a self-indulgent activity, a pastime where one would sigh and say, 'Look how intelligent I am! Am I not kind and gentle too? And what of my wit? Goodness, I am brilliant!' Eric hadn't stopped to consider that for Alice, introspection might be a wholly different and far less pleasurable game.

Alice too had her own enthusiasms for the naturalist project. She was a great lover of the countryside, she liked to go diving, always took care to buy ingredients without additives, gave money to anti-whaling charities and grew enraged if she read about developments to pour concrete on another stretch of landscape. We may also recall her attachment to intuitive understanding, and her annoyance with the poverty of language ['It's so nice being here with you . . .']. Nor was she someone who liked to complicate things unduly – but simplification could as much imply reduction as clarification.

She and Eric had been talking at lunch the previous day about his friend Josh with whom he had recently argued. Eric had explained, 'It's not that I'm not annoyed with him. I wouldn't be annoyed with him because he hasn't consciously done anything to annoy me. However, his behaviour has contributed to my annoyance, though it's not clear whether I can hold him responsible for what I'm feeling, though what I'm feeling isn't necessarily what he meant me to feel, because he doesn't know I'm annoyed.'

'You mean you're pissed off,' said Alice.

'Right,' replied Eric, surprised to find another knowing better than him what he happened to be feeling.

Then there was another kind of simplification, the reduction Eric performed when Alice asked him why it was good not to think too much and he answered quite simply, 'Because.'

Had her union with Eric been problem-free, she would have been the last to ask where they were going or criticized him for not wishing to talk about things or indeed missed out on the rare chance of a scuba diving trip. But given that these questions had arisen, her only recourse had been to annoy Eric and cancel the morning's diving, so as to be able to follow instead some of the multicoloured and strangely threatening fish she felt paddling through her consciousness.

ADOLESCENCE

Daisy and Bob were waiting for Eric by the pier, to which was tethered a small rubber boat owned by the barman RJ. He was to take them to a neighbouring reef, where they would dive and admire coral and fish. They had with them towels, cameras, a picnic and a crate of beer and soft drinks.

'Hi, Eric. Alice not coming?' greeted Bob cheerfully.

'Er, no, you know how they can be . . .' answered Eric.

'I sure do,' winked Bob, an appeal to the age-old myth of women's inherent natural difficulty, a myth that comfortably absolved men from any causal role therein.

While the boat picked up speed and headed west, the three passengers sat on a small wooden bench at the back, watching the engine carve its wake through the water.

'She's a nice girl,' remarked Daisy, holding down her large straw hat from a jealous wind.

'Yeah, really terrific,' echoed Bob.

There was a silence, hesitation before gossip they were waiting to initiate. By staying on shore, Alice had delivered a rejection for which she could expect to be punished in some way.

'How long did you say you folks had known one another?' asked Daisy.

'Oh, I'd say almost a year now.'

'That's great,' reflected Bob for no obvious reason.

'I guess all relationships can be difficult,' philosophized Daisy with pointed abstraction. 'It takes time and effort.'

'And you've got to be so mature.'

'How old did you say Alice was?'

'She's twenty-four.'

'And how old are you?'

'I'm thirty-one. Well, almost thirty-two actually, in February I'll turn thirty-two.'

'Yep, well, Bob and I aren't getting any younger either,' said Daisy, 'add our two ages together and you get a little over seventy, isn't that right, Bob?'

'You bet.'

'Well, she's a sweet girl, anyway,' concluded Daisy, unconsciously signalling with her 'anyway' a prior desire to add something less than polite.

The fact that Alice was some eight years younger than him had never bothered Eric before; in fact, he had always liked the idea of younger women, something which had led to a reputation of cradle snatching amongst his male friends. Apart from what he called their 'lithe bodies', he was perhaps attracted to younger women because they enabled him to pass over certain assets as achievements rather than things which time would naturally bring. The maturity a thirty-one-year-old would develop by simple fact of having been on earth for a decent stretch of time could appear impressive to a twenty-four-year-old used to the greater awkwardness of the younger man.

Eric had an admirable command of those around him. Extended travel and constant contact with others had led to an ease and authority in boardrooms and dining-rooms, hotels and offices. It gave him an impression of maturity which was simply the result of chronological accident.

Differences of age or of race may set up positions of manufactured superiority: the manual worker from Germany flies to Thailand and because of the historical advantage of his economy and exchange rate, feels and behaves like a millionaire. The plodding Englishman arrives in a small North American town and, simply on account of his exotic accent, may be welcomed as charmingly original and sophisticated.

'There's a certain side of her that can be very adolescent,' resumed Eric after the conversation had lapsed. 'You know, she gets into moods, gets very introspective, and there's nothing I can do really.'

'It's absolutely an age thing,' confirmed Daisy. 'She's at a difficult time of her life: just starting out in her career, making choices, trying to look at all the options, and that can be hard for anyone. I can remember myself at her age, boy was I a nightmare! Always changing my mind on things, not knowing what I wanted, putting my boyfriends through hell. Gee, Bob, it was lucky you didn't know me then, otherwise you'd have been going through the same as poor Eric here.'

Eric didn't protest when Alice's problems were parcelled off as the result of a particular chronological stage. He was happy to see the emphasis placed on the stage rather than the problem, it made arguments and sulks seem in the course of things rather than directed at an offence he had committed. He couldn't have done anything wrong, because whatever his behaviour, her stage of life meant she would in any case be difficult. Her complaints were merely the by-products of development. 'We're not understanding one another properly,' Alice might say: but this surface message was irrelevant, what she really wanted to say was,

'I'm at that stage of life when I will naturally be inclined to ask a lover whether or not we understand one another properly . . .'

Whatever the merits of the adolescent accusation, it at once flattened the complexity of human agonies. Had it been extended to the great works of literature, it would have thrown every literary critic in the world out of a job. What made Hamlet, Raskolnikov or Young Werther tick? Adolescent angst, of course. And what of Don Quixote or Humbert Humbert? Mid-life crises, naturally. So how could one explain dear old Anna Karenina? Quite simple, really, PMT and tricky hormones.

MISOGYNY

If anyone had accused Eric of misogyny, he would have considered the charge shockingly inappropriate. Besides recognizing the social unacceptability of such a position, he took positive action to affirm the abilities of women. In his office, he had argued vigorously for equal rights and had ensured that several women were now on the board of directors. He was full of praise for their greater efficiency, and liked to joke with his secretary that she could do the work of five men put together. He had many women friends, with whom he played the role of mascot and confidant. Yet whatever his admiration, it was essential for Eric to know that this could be delivered from a position of superiority. He could afford to be generous to women against a more fundamental and reassuring belief in their inferiority [ironically, nothing could have better proved his basic belief that men and women were not equal than his zeal to promote them at work].

This attachment to male superiority may appear contradictory when we recall that Eric preferred Alice when she was strong than when she was weak. Why did he need to be superior when he was happiest with Alice in her independent and successful phases? A closer definition of strength and weakness may be required, for there were perhaps two ways in which Alice could be strong, and only one of these left Eric comfortable.

The first we may call *autonomous strength*, the confident

and undemanding demeanour Alice would assume when in a good mood and in control of the leading aspects of her life. Instead of sulkily staying home to read, she would take part in scuba diving expeditions [both metaphoric and real], charming all those who came into contact with her. This was the Alice Eric liked to boast was destined to become one of Britain's leading businesswomen. This was the woman who reminded him of his deep love for her when she gave him an affectionate wink in the midst of a party or, in the course of a stiff dinner, cheekily pulled out her tongue at him.

Then there was another form of strength one may call *Olympian strength*, so labelled after Edouard Manet's legendary portrait first exhibited in Paris at the Salon of 1865. When it was shown, the *Olympia* caused a furore in the art world and was at once condemned as obscene and immoral by critics. Manet was accused of parodying and caricaturing the traditional painterly genres with the vulgar incongruity of the model's pose. But what really worried critics was not so much the formal transgressions as the more unmentionable issue of the expression on the face of the model, Victorine Meurent. The [male] art history of the female nude had until then almost always placed the model in the seductive, docile position. In a boudoir or classical garden, the woman was shown naked, waiting for a male to initiate sex and wearing an expression akin to an undemanding yet alluringly coy fifteen-year-old's. The viewer could salivate over the beautiful nymph while apparently only engaged in the contemplation of Great Art, with all the pure intentions the pre-Freudian age attached to such an activity. This was the painterly tradition of Titian's *Venus of Urbino*, which Manet had made a sketch of in his youth, and which showed a woman both soft and innocent yet clearly ready for coitus when the viewer felt like it. He could undress her with his gaze, corrupt her at his leisure and have no worries concerning her appetites.

Olympia was a different case altogether: this was clearly no shrinking violet, but a woman confident and knowledgeable of her desires. If anyone was going to initiate anything, it was likely to be her rather than a male viewer, the expression painted into her eyes and mouth suggesting she might even add a little joke or two [funny for her, devastating for him] about size or performance.

The strength that Alice sometimes assumed in Eric's eyes was akin to the threat contained in Victorine Meurent's expression – but in his case, it was not so much a sexual as an emotional threat. The side of Alice he feared was her desire to strip him of his subterfuges, her asking him such questions as, 'What do you want out of this relationship?' or, 'Why do you never look at me when we make love?'

He felt threatened by an aspect of women that might be termed [in respect to his experience rather than male–female relationships generally] a superior emotional maturity. He resented the thrust of Alice's questions, her desire to 'talk things through', her asking him how he felt or why he acted in certain ways. She wanted something of him which he would have preferred to surrender in his own time, she was like the Olympia who initiated sex with male viewers used to controlling seduction themselves. He then experienced her as probing, demanding and [though it was impossible for him to admit it] a little frightening. He would withdraw into his shell, wished to answer nothing and would have fled the room were it possible. Instead he normally changed the subject, turned up the music or feigned a need to make a phone call. Somewhere at the back of his mind lay the thought that Alice was dangerously more mature and wise than him, that she could in her more lucid moments see him for what he feared he might be; a naked emperor.

Every man has a mother before he has a female lover – in that sense, every man experiences the omnipotence of the mother *vis-à-vis* the helpless child before a more equal [or indeed abusive] relationship is established. Eric's mother had been a powerful woman, whom he had been slightly afraid of as a child. She reared four sons with immense energy, was eminently practical, used to turning up trousers, curing minor ailments and cooking jams and cakes. She had also been somewhat suffocating, a worrier, forever fretting if her sons had enough scarves or pullovers, whether they had taken their medicine or done their homework.

It had given Eric a fierce desire for independence, and though he now wore suits and cuff-links, tipped taxi-drivers and carried business cards, his attitude to women still had about it something of the little boy who in front of the school gate pushes away the mother who is trying to give him a kiss and close his coat.

When Eric was seven, he had wanted one February to go and play in the snow by a tributary of the Thames with his older brothers. His mother, fearing for his health, told 'Little Man' [as he was known in the family] that as he had only just recovered from the flu, he would have to stay home. But because his mother was away from the house all day, Eric went with his brothers anyway. The game went well. He could keep up with them, he threw snowballs like the best of them, he felt like a man, not the little man of his mother's nickname, but a champion like his brothers. They had been playing on the river – throwing snowballs from one bank to the other – when the ice beneath Eric cracked. He had fallen into the freezing water, only down to his waist, but it was painful and he had cried all the way home. His brothers had put him to bed and he had awoken to meet the gaze of his mother, with her broad shoulders and large moon face. She wore her usual severe smile, wiping his brow and asking in a plaintive monotone: 'Why didn't you listen to Mummy, Little Man?'

It was such images that lay at the root of Eric's misogyny: the fear of the nurse, the fear of the all-powerful mother. But as if to release him from this image, he had another image to identify with, that of his father who would shout his mother into submission, and with whom she grew strangely docile. It had always surprised him how easily she bowed to his father, how he could be rude about the evening shepherd's pie, could tell her the house was looking dirty or accuse her of plain untruths, and this powerful woman would accept the charges without complaint.

Eric knew how simple it could sometimes be to reduce otherwise independent and strong women to docility and fragility by an appeal to these archaic patriarchal models. Whatever his intentions, however many women friends he may have had, Eric was strung by his history between two poles which defined his approach to the opposite sex: on the one hand, the mother with her large moon face, and on the other, this same woman turned to jelly at the hands of a bullying father.

When Eric returned from scuba diving, he sensed that the moral initiative had passed to Alice, and that instead of her fitting the role of the sulky adolescent, it was he who now appeared defensive, an immature male who had fled the situation to indulge in childish scuba affairs.

'You missed some great fish,' remarked Eric in a conciliatory tone as he wrung sea water out of his bathing suit in the bathroom sink.

'I'm sure I did,' replied Alice, regretting nothing.

'What did you do with your day?'

'I was taken out water-skiing by a couple of Canadian guys at the hotel.'

'Was it nice?'

'Yeah, fantastic.'

'You didn't catch too much sun? It was really hot out there today.'

'No, I was fine. And Brad lent me his T-shirt.'

'Oh, I'm glad. It's good you got to water-ski, you said how much you wanted to do that, didn't you?'

'I'm going out with Brad and Danny again tomorrow, they want to go down the coast towards Bridgetown.'

'That sounds like a great idea.'

'Yeah, I think I'm going to have an excellent time.'

A HOLIDAY FROM ONESELF

'Alice! Jesus! Hi! Come in, how are you?'

'I'm fine, it's so good to see you.'

'God, look what a great tan you've got – bitch.'

'I know, I've been getting such dirty looks from people all day.'

Alice had dropped in to see Suzy [who was house-sitting for her boyfriend] on the way back from her first day at work, and they stood in the hallway and embraced one another like long lost companions, though it was scarcely ten days since Alice's flight had taken off from Heathrow.

'God, I'm jealous, you're looking so well.'

'You are too, Suzy.'

'No, I'm not: I'm so white I glow in the dark, actually I'm more green than white, and I haven't done any exercise in ages. But tell me all about it. How was the island, the hotel, everything?'

'Oh, it was nice, Barbados was lovely, we had this bungalow with no windows, just kind of open to the elements, with a view on the sea, and the hotel had tons of things you could do like water-skiing and stuff.'

'It makes my skin tingle just to hear it – it all sounds so sexy.'

'Yeah, I guess it was.'

'And did you eat lots of tropical fruit and stay up and dance reggae?'

'Yeah, that kind of thing.'

'And was Romeo behaving himself?'

'More or less.'

'And how about the weather?'

'Oh, it was really hot all the time, it sometimes rained at night and in the morning it could be a bit overcast, but basically it was perfect.'

'I bet it was. Oh, Alice, I'm so happy for you! Give me another hug.'

The visit was Alice's first chance to narrate in detail the story of her holiday. She had provided a few potted accounts of it at work, but planned that with Suzy she would explore the diversity of her feelings and the extent of her ambivalence.

She had often observed how important the first narration of an event could be, as though what mattered was not so much the moment itself as the way it was narratively arranged. She had until then simply lived the story, and the memories of it hovered without order.

'Look, I've pinned your postcard to Matt's holder,' said Suzy, pointing to the card she had slipped into the hotel mail box a week earlier. It showed the main beach, an expanse of yellow sand ringed by lush vegetation and tall palm trees. The sea was a turquoise green, the sky a perfect blue.

'I'd love to go away somewhere like that with Matt: it's just so hard to get the money together at the moment. But look at the colour of that sea, and the sky – it's impossible not to be happy when you think about a place like that.'

By a form of identification with her friend's perceptions, Alice was reminded of her anticipation of the holiday, which made her current ambivalence all the more inexplicable. Overwhelmed by Suzy's desire to read the trip as everyone's dream experience, the plan for a complex narrative therefore gave way [under the weight of the listener's anticipation] to a simplified account of a Utopic Caribbean sojourn.

Travel may more interestingly be read as a psychological rather than a geographic effort – the outer journey a metaphor for the desired inner one. Trekking in Nepal, scuba diving in the Caribbean, skiing in the Rockies, surfing in Australia – these may be exotic and enlightening but may only be paltry excuses for far deeper motivations, namely the wish that the person enjoying these activities could be someone other than the one booking the holiday.

Though travel agents pretend to deal in such material trivia as flight times, hotel rooms and insurance, their underlying trade is founded on the more subtle illusion that buying a holiday will somehow miraculously allow one to leave oneself behind. The idea is not for 'I' to have a holiday, but for the holiday to change the 'I'.

The holidaying self that Alice had pictured from London had been without all the things that made living with herself difficult – she imagined someone free of self-doubt, tiredness, anxiety, boredom and longing. Because the temperature would rise to twenty-five degrees, because nothing of the vegetation or routines of her holiday existence would bear any resemblance to London life, she had dreamt of slipping effortlessly into the role demanded of such scenery, the role of Rousseau's Noble Savage, untroubled by the problems of Western civilization, unburdened by her psychological history, the overweight of her neuroses. But instead, though the bungalow was idyllic, the fruit succulent and the sand warm and soft, nothing of significance was shirked. However wonderful, these were but details next to her interior decoration, the clutter of her inner geography.

If Alice wondered why her experience of the holiday had been so different from its anticipation, why, despite all the qualities of the island and the hotel, she had found herself as confused as ever, it was perhaps because she had forgotten to leave one vital thing behind when packing her suntan lotions, self-help books, bikinis and sunglasses – namely, her own self.

In her state of anticipation, she had sat in London and looked forward to the island without thinking that she would be included in the equation of the future, focusing simply on the beach, the palm trees, the breeze . . .

And then had come the realization that she had cleared Barbadian customs without shedding the one thing she had come to avoid, a realization that she had arrived on a perfect clear day in the West Indies carrying with her the only thing she had really wanted to leave behind [who in the end cares about a grey sky anyway?] – that is, *herself*.

In his essay *Of Solitude*, Montaigne recounted that 'someone said to Socrates that a certain man had grown no better by his travels. 'I should think not,' he said; 'he took himself along with him.' Or, as Horace asked in the same essay,

> Why should we move to find
> Countries and climates of another kind?
> What exile leaves himself behind?

The fact that people talk of 'escaping themselves' has a significance missed by simply talking of escaping this or that problem. The self is here understood as the locus of a host of inherent, intractable difficulties. These cannot be focused on any specific thing – otherwise one would talk of escaping 'the job', 'the weather' or 'my husband'. The use of 'oneself' captures a vague existential weariness, a frustration at the heaviness of always inhabiting the same body and encountering a familiar cage of thoughts when the mind is activated.

Alice had forgotten that the eye watching a scene wouldn't alter though the scene itself might. She had surveyed the future impersonally, as though benefiting from it without the agony of actually partaking. In retrospect, she was shocked at how poor her imagination had been – she would only have had to subtract from her current anxieties those problems directly linked to being in London and at work to realize that even on a paradise island she would have had plenty of material to cause her sleepless nights. Instead, she had pinned her hopes on the weather and the scenery's transforming effects, like a bad actor who imagines his soliloquies would improve if only the costumes and stage sets were richer.

She might have recognized the process of disillusion. Just before leaving London, she had been flicking through a copy of a magazine and had seen a section entitled 'Beach Beauties'. Five glossy full-page spreads showed a tall blonde model walking along a beach in a long white linen dress worn over a yellow bathing suit. Not prone to wearing either white dresses or yellow bathing suits and feeling too poor to allow herself much indulgence, something about the pictures had nevertheless captivated her, and she had noted down the shop and designer on the back of an envelope.

However, when she reached Barbados and a beach which looked roughly like the one the photographer had shot, she realized the shocking redundancy of the outfit. She was simply not tall enough for it, the material dirtied itself in the sand, it seemed the most inappropriate of garments, too dressed up for the day, too beach-like for the evening. 'Why the hell did I buy this crap?' she wondered, and mentally consigned it to the [tragically large] section of her wardrobe devoted to unwearable clothes, garments she had bought on rejection or self-hate rebounds and that had revealed themselves as wholly unsuitable when looked at in a more lucid, practical light [when the imperative to expend money on something, *anything*, had abated somewhat].

In buying a linen dress or Caribbean holiday, Alice had fallen into the classic trap of consumption. When things are bought out of more than sheer necessity, the unconscious goal may not simply be to acquire a product, but to be transformed by the acquisition. What she had wanted from a dress and bathing suit on which she had lavished eighty hard-earned pounds were not the miserable overpriced garments cut by a cynical, untalented designer and hyped by a fashion magazine, but rather the more elusive *being* of the person who she had seen wearing them – it sounded ridiculous, but what she had wanted was not the model's clothes, but the model's *self*.

And what had happened instead? She had unpacked the dress, and realized that what would be slipping into it was not the wonderfully toned and tanned moving sculpture of the photographs, but her own familiar blobby shape, with its imperfect, too short legs, its unglamorous hips, its unaerobic stomach and stunted breasts. What a deception! She could spend all the money she had, but the only thing she wanted was the thing no one could sell her, *someone who was not her*. It was a cruel dilemma, for how could one admit to such an intention in a clothes shop, asking not for this or that size but for a different self – or for that matter maintain a straight face while asking a travel agent for a holiday destination 'anywhere so long as it's away from myself'?

The Greek meaning of the word Utopia was 'no such place exists'. But the reasons for this non existence were quite specific in Alice's case. She believed Utopias could exist *per se* [the Robinson Crusoe hotel *had* been idyllic], she simply concluded that she herself would never fully partake in them. There was no social or financial reason, simply the paradox that in order for her to enjoy something, she would have to include herself in the equation and thereby spoil the thing to be enjoyed.

'The only possible paradises are those we have lost,' said the nostalgic Proust: less morose writers have preferred anticipated ones, but the point about the past or future [about yearning over a brochure of a holiday to come or a postcard of a holiday just past] was that they were scenarios one could envisage without being actively present to soil them.

While she watched her holiday tan fade over the coming

weeks, Alice recognized the old truth that the man who gives up a wife to marry his mistress nevertheless has to find a new mistress – and that the person who flies off to a Caribbean island still needs a paradise of the mind to appease the inevitable, sun-and-sea-withstanding disappointments.

PROVINCIALISM

Alice's background wasn't tethered to a particular patch of the Earth. Though she had lived in London for many years, her mother had been born in England of French and Italian parents, and her father was an American from Chicago whose grandparents had originally come from Russia. There was no ancestral home to return to, no graveyard where five generations of relatives were buried and which might provide a central focus of genealogy.

Because her father had worked in a multinational company, Alice had spent her childhood shuttling across the globe, attending different schools every few years, learning to speak English, French and Spanish, and living in a home visited by a variety of guests: diplomats and academics, businessmen and painters, architects and accountants. She had grown up unattached to any one location, her memories were scattered over a confused geographic chronology. She had witnessed spring in a house in Barcelona, she remembered the smell of autumn in a garden in Neuilly, she knew the sandy dunes of Long Island beaches and the icy stillness of Norwegian fjords. She had read the fairy tales, monsters and wicked witches from children's books of many languages, Babar and Grimm, Potter and Zipe y Zape.

Her allegiances were confused: she was often asked, 'What do you feel?', as though nationality was something one felt in one's bones. But she couldn't limit her feelings to one passport: she had known too many homes, too many schools, too many sweets in different countries to feel any one nationality. Her friendships had been brutally dislocated: she had had to leave her best friend Sophie behind at the age of five, her friend Maria at the age of seven, her first love Thomas at the age of eight.

'What are your roots?' others would ask. What is it to have roots? To feel one has come from a specific soil, to have an identification with a particular climate, with particular cultural products, with the idealized mentality a race calls its 'national character'. Alice recognized only diversity: when she was in London, she understood the relativity of its buildings, its streets, its ways of life – she could fit them into an awareness of other cities and places. She could compare the experience of a bar mitzvah in San Francisco with communion in Seville, the taste of bread in Paris with that in Chicago, the colour of the sky in New York and in London; she had in mind the prejudices of bigots from many lands.

Eric had by contrast grown up in as settled a way as was still possible in the twentieth century. His family had lived in London for five generations, and before that had come from a village in Hampshire where his grandparents had still owned a farm. His parents had never moved from the house in which he had lived as a child, in an area between Notting Hill and Holland Park where shop keepers recognized him when he walked into their premises, where his mother knew the name of the milkman and the butcher, where there existed an almost feudal allegiance between server and served. Eric was surrounded by friends whom he had known since childhood: he worked in his office with someone he had been to nursery school with, he had been moving in essentially the same circle of friends since early adolescence, a continuity of surroundings negating certain questions of identity.

'I don't know what I feel,' answered Alice when Eric asked her about the issue of countries one evening, 'what do you feel?'

'I suppose I feel English. I mean, I could hardly feel anything else.'

'Yeah, but what does that signify for you, to be English?'

'God, I don't know, it's just normal. It's a set of impressions and feelings. For instance, last weekend, when we were coming back from Heathrow, I felt a kind of bond with the landscape, that this was my country. It has a lot to do with the countryside and with the buildings. Also, when you're abroad, you see British people or British things, and you feel a kind of bond. I got that sense in Barbados when I found a copy of the *Financial Times* or listened to the BBC World Service.'

A person cannot arrive singly in a relationship – with them comes the whole accumulated cultural baggage of infancy and youth, a network of relations and traditions, something one could perhaps call their particular *province*. A province is made up not only of national characteristics, but fragments further into a welter of class, regional and family traits. It is the set of largely unconscious elements a person will think of as normal: the normal appearance of a high street or post office counter, the normal evening news bulletin and manner of filling out a tax return, the normal way to greet a friend, make a bed, butter bread, keep a house clean, choose furniture, order a meal, arrange cassettes in a car, do the washing up, find a holiday destination, end a phone conversation, plan a Saturday.

'Why do you always want to see films in the afternoon?' Eric asked Alice on a January weekend when she wanted to go to the two o'clock show and he to the nine o'clock one.

'What's wrong with seeing films in the afternoon?' replied Alice, whose slender relationship with her father had been largely based on trips to the cinema on Saturday afternoons, a time which remained unconsciously linked to the memory of her father and his movies.

'I don't know, it's really weird to do that,' answered Eric, whose family had always harboured suspicions of what his mother called 'the moving pictures', and for whom weekend afternoons had traditionally been taken up with watching or playing rugby, football and cricket.

'Why weird? It's just more convenient because it's so much less crowded and also cheaper,' replied Alice, the inherited tastes of the father contradicting the inherited tastes of the boyfriend.

'But it's so strange to come out of a film and see it's still light,' said Eric. 'When you see a film, you want to come out in darkness, not bright sunshine, you want to be ready to go to sleep, not still have to have dinner and everything.'

A relationship necessarily involves the meeting of two provinces. Even Alice's confused background had given her a province, though it couldn't handily be identified with a single country: one couldn't say she was 'so English' or 'so American' or 'so middle class'.

What was distinctive in this relationship was Alice's gradual realization that Eric handled the differences as though the onus of otherness effectively lay with her. The implication was that the benchmark of normality was settled in his province, and that it was her taste in cinema-going or food or colours or etiquette which, if there was divergence, deserved to be called the strange one.

In short, in the inevitable case of two provinces colliding, she noticed Eric's tendency to become *provincial* – that is, to form an attachment to his own traditions which precluded the equal legitimacy of the other province. Unwilling to admit the relativity of his position, he identified his values as the centre of a monotheistic universe.

'There's an antiques fair at a convention centre in Islington this weekend,' Alice told Eric while she looked through the paper on a Tuesday morning. 'It sounds excellent. They're going to have antique dealers from all over the country, and apparently you can get a ten per cent reduction if you bring along this coupon. We could go on the way back from lunch with those friends of yours, couldn't we?'

'It doesn't sound much good.'

'I think it sounds excellent.'

'I'm going to have a lot of work to do this weekend.'

'I can go alone then.'

The issue seemed to be decided and silence fell upon the breakfast table.

'But why do you want to go to an antiques fair anyway?' asked Eric a moment later.

'What's wrong with going to an antiques fair?'

'I don't know, it's so . . . so . . .'

'So what?'

'So sort of old grannyish. Only old grannies are interested in antique furniture.'

'Maybe your granny was, my granny was into De Stijl.'

'Really? Mine couldn't spell Stijl if you paid her. But those antique fairs, they're full of musty dark brown furniture, it's all second-rate junk sold by provincial crooks who bang on about some table being done by an assistant of Chippendale. You're just going to get ripped off; if you need furniture, why don't you just go to some modern place, get a good contemporary designer, you might have to pay a bit more but it would be quality stuff.'

'That's not really my taste.'

'Well, why don't you get good taste?'

'Because I like my taste.'

'Even if it's crap?'

'For God's sake, why can't you just be happy that I'm going to be doing something I enjoy this weekend?'

The answer, though Eric wasn't about to admit it, was because Alice was going to be made happy by something unrelated to him, and which hence catalysed a tinge of jealousy at the independent source of her pleasure.

She had recently become aware of Eric's tendency towards provincial jealousy, his decrying aspects of her province out of a form of xenophobia. Her awareness was part of a broader sensitivity to the tastes and expectations of others – expectations to which she was highly prone to moulding herself.

'I change with whoever I'm with,' she admitted, and one could indeed register subtle differences in the way she acted in company, her response to what others wanted to hear rather than she to say. Her mother liked her to be sophisticated and socially adept, and Alice helped confirm this image by telling her of invitations she had received, she knew Eric favoured remarks on how she had filled up the tyres on her car or handled a presentation at work, she sensed that her friend Lucy didn't like hearing of her successes, and would hence try to appear always a little depressed so as not to offend. When she was talking to her wealthy friend Lavinia her accent shifted to west London, when she was with her artist friend Gordon it dropped to Lewisham.

Alice's speech bent itself around the particularities of

others: it registered their distastes and enthusiasms, and struggled to fill them. It was a nervous speech, it kept pace rather than followed its own course, it had to impress rather than stay constant.

She had in the past been hesitant in revealing those parts of her province which didn't match Eric's. She would down-play her objections to his minimalist taste in furniture and political allegiances, she was wary of telling him he should buy different ties or drive more slowly in urban areas. She was reluctant to assert her own enthusiasms; for walks in London parks or trips to the country to see historic houses, for baking bread or taking action to save threatened Amazonian tribes. She hesitated to cook Eric her vegetarian moussaka, to play him her James Taylor albums or tell him to handle foreplay differently.

On returning from holiday, this lack of province-assertion led Alice to question the extent to which she had ever really articulated a correct character within the relationship.

What does it mean to be a character? Go to a dinner party, and the person whom everyone calls a 'character' is the one who tells the dirty jokes, laughs uproariously, performs a magic trick with a napkin and ends up drunkenly seducing the hostess. No one will call a character the one who simply talked to the neighbour on the right, then the one on the left, then quietly made their excuses and left. Their status as a human being wouldn't be in question, simply their status as a character.

Character emerges on the basis of difference and divergence. With every difference from the next person, someone becomes more of a character: announce you like to eat raw worms or can sing out of your ears, and you will at once become remarkable, someone who is not *every person*.

Literature is full of men and women, but there are far fewer 'characters'. Don Quixote is a 'character', Joseph K is not: the former could be instantly spotted at a cocktail party, the latter would simply be nibbling peanuts unobtrusively at the door, his palm a little sweaty, his expression a little anxious, desperate to seem just another clerk.

Alice's mother was a 'real character', described as such by friends who appreciated her tendency to gossip relentlessly, tell schoolgirl jokes which seemed shocking in elegant surroundings and snort amusingly when she laughed. She could be recognized anywhere on account of the long pink outfits and strong perfume she wore – all these were signals of just how much of a character she was.

Her daughter was less spectacular with the elements defining her character. Because they were not founded on a blind desire for difference, she had no obvious markers; her quirks took time to get to know.

One such unspectacular marker was that she happened to have a taste for antique furniture – a taste which was apparently a cause of deep offence to her lover. Though objectively concerned for her welfare, Eric would have preferred to consign this particular enthusiasm to character*istic* oblivion, so little did it match his idea of who she should be.

'Who gives a damn if he doesn't want to go with you?' asked Suzy when Alice told her she would like to have gone to the antiques fair, but Eric objected to the plan. 'Just go yourself, you'll have a great time.'

'I don't know if I want to go after all,' said Alice.

'Yes, you do. Of course you do, you said so yourself.'

'Did I?'

'Yes, otherwise why would you have complained about it?'

'I guess you're right.'

'Of course I'm right. And you know what? Matt's got this good friend of his, Philip. He works as a sound engineer on classical recordings. He's really nice and I remember he likes antiques, so maybe you should go along with him. That way you'd have someone to go with. I'll try and fix it up.'

WHO DO YOU ALLOW
ME TO BE?

Philip called Alice's house later that week and arranged to meet her outside Victoria Station on the Saturday.

'How are we going to recognize each other?' asked Alice. 'What do you look like?'

'Oh, when I'm in a good mood, I think I have a passing resemblance to Robert de Niro. I don't know. What a question! How am I going to recognize you?'

'I'll be in a plain brown envelope.'

'Sounds wonderful.'

On the appointed day, after more detailed descriptions, they found each other without problem, and made their way to north London in Philip's bright green Mini. The antiques fair was taking place in a large convention centre in Islington, and seemed filled with just the sort of musty furniture that Eric had predicted.

'What I'm really looking for is a kitchen table,' Philip told Alice as they surveyed the hall from one of the upper galleries.

'Do you think you're going to find one?'

'Doesn't look good, does it? But maybe. It's amazing what you find quite by chance sometimes. I once found a great four-poster bed in a fair like this, and got it ridiculously cheap.'

'You sleep in a four-poster bed?'

'I know, it's embarrassing, but I do.'

'I don't think it's embarrassing, that's really romantic.

Oh, look at this table, this would be great next to my bed,' remarked Alice, as they passed a stand displaying a small wooden table in the shape of a cello.

'Only twenty pounds,' announced the predatory salesman.

'That's pretty good.'

'So get it.'

'Should I?'

'Yeah, sure. If you like it, why not?'

An hour and a half later, a cello night-table under Philip's arm [but without a suitable kitchen table], they came out of the crowded convention centre into the sunny High Street. Because it was shortly after midday, Philip proposed they leave the cello in the Mini and go on to have lunch in a fish restaurant near by.

'Isn't the sea amazing, when you look at it, it's just this vast thing, and it puts everything into proportion,' said Alice, looking at a seascape that took up a whole wall adjacent to their table.

'Puts what into proportion?' asked Philip.

'I don't know, things, all our little problems and worries. What we lose sleep over and fret about during the day.'

'Do you lose a lot of sleep?'

'Well, not tons, but I do worry, don't you? Sometimes I feel I'm living with the handbrake on. You know how it is, when you're driving and you notice there's a kind of heaviness to the car, then you realize you'd forgotten to take the handbrake off, I'm always doing that. But anyway, I'm burbling on.'

'Not at all,' replied Philip, and Alice smiled weakly. She took up the salt cellar and poured a small amount into her hand, then let it run out into a little pile on her bread plate.

There was a silence and they both returned their gazes to the sea.

'You know, there's this fish I read about,' said Alice, 'which lives deep at the bottom of the ocean floor and hardly ever comes across another fish of the same species. But then when it does, the two fish immediately make love, after which the female fish devours the male one.'

'That's a brutal way to end an affair. No wonder they're such a rare species.'

'Isn't that weird?' asked Alice. 'I'm always thinking about that, two lonely fish in a huge ocean, then they meet and one eats the other.'

'The Dover sole?' asked the waitress.

'That's for me,' replied Alice.

Philip and Alice soon found themselves talking of things beyond their civil status, circumventing conventional layers typically endured before sincere bedrock is reached.

More remarkably, Alice realized it was she who was doing most of the talking, remarkable because she usually asked the questions without having any addressed back – something which had earned her the nickname of 'the interviewer' in certain circles. If weakness is linked to self-revelation and power to self-containment, then the interviewer is always in the powerful role. But power suggests Alice asked all the questions for Machiavellian reasons, though she ended up in this position only out of a certain fear of self disclosure. She needed to share her inner life, she was simply reluctant to press its details upon anyone. And because others sensed a willingness to listen, they tended to use her as an economical form of therapist rather than as a true companion.

But in Philip she detected a curiosity which made her

want to talk, and an honesty which made her feel free to do so. Over two courses, they covered large tracts of her childhood which she had rarely discussed so frankly [and certainly not so quickly] with anyone.

'He was this amazingly clever man,' recalled Alice of her father, 'everyone admired him as well as thinking he was crazy. He was always busy running round the world, he worked for a department store chain, then bought up a business building fixtures for shop windows. I very rarely saw him as a child, and when I did, I was always panicked by it, I was so desperate to make a good impression. I remember his birthday when I was about eight. Everyone always got him these sumptuous presents, and I too wanted to get him something special. Of course I had no money, so I remember just finding some enormous boxes and wrapping them up, completely empty boxes to give to him. I was so frantic, I ended up with about fifty boxes. But I never got to give them, he got held up on a trip to Canada and didn't make it back for his birthday. My mother said they were taking too much space, so she threw them all away.'

'Sounds as if she was jealous.'

'In a way probably, yes, she was always creating obstacles between my father and me. But she didn't use her jealousy productively. I mean, she would stop me from seeing him, but didn't put in the effort to know me better. She was destructive in that sense. She always wanted to break people apart, without being able to draw value from them when they were single.'

'Did she like children?'

'Well, originally my father hadn't liked the idea of children, and only had them because my mother tricked him into it. She was desperate to have kids, but also wanted his approval, which she slightly lost by having them, so I think she took out some of her aggression on us. She felt we had been her idea, and anything that was wrong with us, she took personally. I was a pretty slow child, I hardly spoke till I was twelve, I was very shy and my mother was annoyed at that because she thought my father was brilliant and if his kids weren't, then she had been the one to bring "bad genes" into the family.'

'Was she happy in her marriage?'

'To my father?'

'Why, were there others?'

'She's on her third.'

'Well, then to your father.'

'No, I don't think so. I wasn't sad when she went off with Avner, because I never laid much store on us being a family. We were never the type to sit around the kitchen table and play Happy Families. She's a very cold woman, almost macho in a way. You see, her own father died when she was quite young, and she was the oldest, and I think she had to sort of take over the running of the family. She was only twelve when it happened, and she had to grow up very fast. Which is why one side of her is this very tough and worldly one, and the other is just this frightened twelve-year-old who won't admit she's frightened.'

'So why did your father marry her?'

'I think she represented a certain security for him. They met when he was just starting up in business. They were both living in New York, and my mother was sort of glamorous, at the time she was working for a TV company and doing very well for herself, and they both wanted to get married. They met at a party, and within three weeks they were married, which is crazy really, but it shows how desperate they both were to find some kind of security.

And then it took them years to work out that perhaps it wasn't quite right.'

'Can I be rude? Are you as screwed up as you should be according to all this?'

'You're funny. Of course I am, yeah, but you know, I get suspicious of anyone who says their family was happy. It simply isn't possible, and at least our family was messed up in a very open way. No one could have spent five minutes in our house without realizing there was something seriously wrong. It wasn't like one of those very polite places where everyone is saying, "How lovely, dear," but grinding their teeth and entertaining murderous fantasies. Those kind of places remind me of that joke, you know the one where the man says to his analyst, "Dr Speigeleier, I committed an interesting slip the other day. I was having tea with my mother, and I wanted to say, 'Mother dear, could you please pass the sugar?' But to my complete surprise, what I in fact ended up saying was, 'Mother, you bloody fucking bitch, you ruined my life.'"'

After lunch, they took a walk along the High Street, and browsed through a succession of bookshops. Then, because it had begun raining lightly, they headed for the car and wound their way back into central London.

'Shall I give you a hand setting up your cello piece?' asked Philip when they arrived at her flat in Earl's Court.

'No, that's fine. I can do it on my own.'

'Whatever you like.'

'It's really sweet of you to give me a lift and everything – I'll have to pay you back some day.'

'Sure. You can help me find my kitchen table.'

'Great, so we'll be in touch.'

Alice stepped out of the car, took the cello out of the

back and gave a small wave before disappearing through the front door. She carried the night-table into her room, placed a small lamp and her alarm clock on it and smiled when she saw how well it fitted by the bedside – a smile wiped off by Eric's predictable remark [delivered over dinner that night] that the table sounded like the most kitschy thing anyone could find to waste twenty pounds on.

The incident served to remind Alice that she wasn't a single person. This wasn't to say there were hundreds of clones running round London, Paris or New York with more or less the same history and lifestyle, but rather that she contained more than one version of herself depending on the people she was with. And what was more, she recognized that some of these versions were better, *more her*, than others.

The pictures Eric and she had taken on holiday were finally back from the printers, and after dinner, they went into the living-room to look through them. Amongst the Barbados snaps was a shot of them on the veranda outside their bungalow, taken early on in their stay judging from the colour of their skin.

'Look at this. This is a great one of you,' remarked Eric. 'You look wonderful.'

'I look monstrous. It doesn't look like me at all. That's so weird.'

Eric hadn't misidentified her in the picture, the expression she wore certainly belonged to her [rather than being airbrushed in by a cruel photo-lab]. Nor was it a distinctly unflattering shot, it simply revealed sides to her face that Alice was unused to seeing, over which she hadn't extended ownership.

Her reaction revealed a certain propriety about a correct 'me'. Not just any old picture, and certainly not the particular shot of her by the Barbadian bungalow wall could be considered a true likeness. The self-timer had picked up on a side of her features [and by extension a side of her nature] she didn't identify with. She had never laid claim to this sort of smile, she hadn't made friends with her cheeks flushed in such a manner, her hair wasn't remembered in this wind-buffeted style – and she didn't wish to have these aspects arrogantly attributed to her by the sham literalness of the camera.

Yet such feelings weren't limited to photographs, for it wasn't simply her body, but also her character which could be read from different angles – in different lights, through different lenses, through different lovers. There were people around whom she felt more 'herself' than others. Around Suzy for instance, she had always felt particularly understood for who she wished to be. Suzy was full of psychological insight, would say, 'Alice, I know you, you only like him because he's unavailable,' or, 'You're just trying to get someone else to do what you want to do yourself . . .' Then there was her friend Gordon, sympathetic for the side of her which longed to shop and vanish into the pages of a magazine, a side which he treated with gentle irony, jokingly asking, 'How's life with you today, Emma B.?' When she sighed, he would sigh even louder in imitation.

'Stop making fun of me,' she would protest.

'I'm not, I'm heartbroken that M&S has run out of the tights you wanted,' he would answer.

'You're being sarcastic.'

'Is that so wrong, your honour?' Gordon would answer gravely, drawing a laugh from both of them.

Perhaps because her friends responded to Alice's foibles by making jokes of them, they turned her from an everyday neurotic into something of a comic. It was a point between them that Alice had difficulty being organized, but instead of getting cross with her, they would send her invitations to parties with the ordinary time substituted by 'Alice-time', an hour or so before so as to allow for her disorganization. They took on funny accents to exaggerate her desire to find herself, to become a Hollywood starlet or save the Brazilian rainforests. They made her feel understood, forgiven and liked for her foibles.

She wondered why a similar process was not at work in her relationship with Eric: there, the tensions appeared unmentionable or liable to spill over into humourless disagreement.

Because she had spent such a pleasant day with Philip, because she had felt so herself around him, she had tried that night to continue her mood in interaction with Eric. There had been a tender jokiness about Philip. He had quickly picked up on her characteristics and treated them with intelligent irony. Lightly teasing about her notorious indecision in restaurants, he had asked the waitress midway through the main course if they could start studying the dessert menu now so as to reach a decision in time.

She had left in buoyant spirits, and on entering Eric's apartment, had behaved with confidence and ease:

'What's up, swotty? Have you finished your work?' she asked Eric.

'Yeah. What's wrong with you?'

'Nothing. Why?' answered Alice.

'I don't know, you seem in a strange mood.'

'I'm not, I'm just in a good mood.'

'Oh.'

'Do you want to hear a joke this guy Philip told me?'

'Go on.'

'OK, so there are these two Jews standing outside a bath house, and one says to the other, "Did you take a bath?" and the other one answers nervously, "No, why? Is there one missing?"'

'Oh.'

'Do you get it, "Is there one missing?"'

'Yeah, yeah, thanks, I get it – there's some of that cake left in the fridge if you want some.'

'Great . . .'

To adapt Wittgenstein, the limits of others' understanding of ourselves marks the limits of our world. We cannot help but exist within the parameters of others' perceptions – they allow us to be funny by their understanding of our humour, they allow us to be intelligent by their own intelligence, their generosity allows us to be generous, their irony to be ironic. Character operates like a language which requires both reader and writer. Shakespeare is a jumble of nonsense to a class of seven-year-olds, and as long as he is read only by seven-year-olds, he cannot be appreciated for anything beyond that which a seven-year-old could under-stand – much as Alice's possibilities could stretch only as far as her lover's empathy.

There was a playful, clownish side to her which Philip had responded to and encouraged, but how could she continue in this mode if her jokes fell on flat ears? She couldn't help but return to the assigned mould Eric's perception entailed.

Relationships might be based not so much on the quali-ties of others as on the effect that these qualities have on our self-image – on their ability to return to us an adequate self-image. Who did Eric make Alice feel? How did he suggest this? She wasn't sure how the process operated, whether it was all in her head or had external validity, but she had long had an impression of unworthiness around him. The Alice she experienced was materially spoilt, of no great intelligence, fixated on emotional issues and suffering from an irritating dependence on others.

Eric never told her as much: these were simply things she felt about *herself* when with him. When scientists wish to know the cause behind an effect, they set up controlled experiments, where only one thing changes at a time and the contributing cause can be isolated. In a controlled experiment, Alice would very quickly have seen how Eric was affecting her self-concept – for how else could she have explained her marked sensations of inadequacy around him? But she didn't register the connection. Her feelings towards him could remain warm [or steaming with the heat of religious passion] even when feelings about herself had grown cold and damp. Eric affected her self-concept long before affecting her Eric-concept.

When A looks at B, B can't help but be affected by the assumptions carried by A's gaze. If A thinks B an adorable, soft-skinned little angel, B will probably begin to feel some of the effect of being thought an adorable, soft-skinned little angel. If A thinks B a blithering idiot who couldn't add two and two, B will in all likelihood find his or her capacities diminished in accordance with expectations, and may therefore conclude that two and two make roughly six.

What puzzled Alice was the subtlety with which this process operated. After all, A who thinks B a blithering idiot rarely has to say, 'You're a blithering idiot' for this assumption to be communicated – but in such an incorpo-

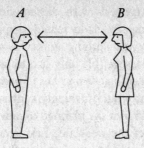

A   *B*

real way as to leave a self-questioning B wondering whether 'It's all just simply in my head or . . .?'

Communication is seldom made up of bold declarations – rarely does anyone have to linguistically explain their feelings to another. So how can a message be suggested without being stated?

When Alice speculated to Eric that their friends Claire and Miles behaved as though he was the child and she the mother, Eric [who had known Miles ever since school] rejected the idea out of hand and said, 'Oh, nonsense. You're reading too much into it as usual.'

'But you've got to admit, there *is* something odd going on between them. He seems to moan all the time, and then she'll come along and help him out – and it's as though they both like playing those roles.'

'Rubbish. They're really great people.'

'That's not my point.'

'Well, what is your point?'

'Just that their behaviour is balanced so that . . .'

'You love to make things complicated, don't you?'

'I don't, I just wanted to say. Oh, what's the use? Forget it.'

Repeated often enough, the lesson of Eric's reaction [though there was no statement to that effect] was to deem eccentric Alice's concern with the emotional lives of her friends, suggesting she hallucinated shapes and shadows where the healthy saw nothing amiss. He was never forced to spell out the message. He only had to brusquely dismiss her thoughts on a sufficient number of occasions for such a verdict to be silently but crushingly conveyed.

When Alice told him she planned to move a pile of books into her room over the weekend, Eric later referred to her intentions by asking, 'Are you going off to move all your first editions now?' There was no lumbering open declaration to the effect that she was over-educated or read too much. Nevertheless, to refer to her books as first editions when they were ordinary cheap paperbacks was to lightly accuse her of pretension, the pretension of those who buy old volumes to show off rather than imbibe their contents.

Of course, Alice had no time to decode this [and other] attacks. Her unwillingness to believe her lover could be attacking her prevented a measured enquiry: 'I don't own any first editions, you know that, so spare me the jealous sarcasm. I like books and if you have a problem with that, maybe we should talk about it.' Instead, she returned home saddened, without knowing for what or by whom.

Even without such catty remarks, the person Alice felt she could be around Eric was limited by his conversational inclinations. If he felt happy discussing the state of the yen and the performance of a new engine in the next generation of BMWs, then she soon grasped the message that things she would have preferred to talk about were out of bounds. He didn't forbid her to tell her stories, he simply indicated by the stories he himself told that to do so would mean falling on deaf ears.

She therefore forgot the extent to which she might have been more interesting in the presence of others, and concluded that she had grown most uninspiring. Instead of sitting at dinner with Eric confident there were things she wished to chat about if only a more appropriate companion could be found, *she simply forgot she had anything to say* – evidence that others shape not so much what we *can* say, but what we *feel* like saying, *what we are capable of wanting to say*.

The following week, Alice met Philip for lunch, and because her office colleague Xandra had just announced she would be marrying her boyfriend in June, the conversation turned to marriage.

'I think a lot of people just get married because they're afraid of being alone,' speculated Alice, and Philip carried the thought into his slice of dialogue, enriched it, then passed it back to her.

One could liken conversational potential to a tree-shaped structure where dialogue may run down any number of different branches according to whom one is with; the same night, Alice had dinner with Eric, and because her colleague had announced marriage only that morning, Alice for the second time that day initiated a conversation on the topic.

To compare the two conversational trees, one could align the paths taken by Alice and Philip on the left, and Alice and Eric on the right.

Though a trivial example, the conversational tree nevertheless produced two separate Alices. Philip's receptivity to the topic of marriage, company and loneliness allowed Alice to articulate certain thoughts that Eric's responses did not permit – and hence indirectly left her feeling a slightly different, and in this case slightly richer, person. Eric never forbade her to talk about what it felt like to be alone with

SHE: *I think a lot of people just get married because they're afraid of being alone.*

↓

HE: My friend Jill admitted as much to me the other day: she said she couldn't stand to be by herself, so she'd rather get married even if he wasn't necessarily perfect. How about you? Can you be alone without a problem?

↓

SHE: I don't mind at all. In fact, I find I can't really deal with people unless I've actually been alone for hours before. My most productive times are always when I'm alone.

↓

HE: I guess there's a difference between being alone and being lonely.

↓

SHE: That's right: I can be alone sometimes, and yet I feel I'm with lots of people, because they're in my head talking: I'm thinking about what people have said to me, things we've done together and stuff – so then I don't have any sense of being isolated.

↓

HE: I suppose that if you're happy alone, you've got a choice in the matter. You've got a sense that there would be lots of people you could call up if you needed a chat.

↓

SHE: It's funny you say that because at university, I was always manic about seeing people, I was really sociable, but deep down I was always a bit afraid that I didn't really belong. I had to rush to the college bar all the time, because I was afraid of being left out.

↓

HE: So what changed?

↓

SHE: Lots of things, really. I started working, for one. So the time I had to socialize shrank, and then I became very good friends with a few people, but stopped being part of a really big gang. I just stopped being so worried about what the clan thought. I realized the world was a big place, that it didn't really matter where you spent Saturday night.

13.31 p.m., Dean Street Restaurant, London W1

HE: People are marrying younger again. I read it in the paper today.

↓

SHE: Do you think people are getting more scared of being alone?

↓

HE: No, it's just economic. Whenever there's a downturn, people marry younger: to save money.

↓

SHE: It's really weird how economics can affect relationships.

↓

HE: In Asian countries, they're now marrying much later, because GDP is rising. Did I tell you? The garage called today. In the end, it was something in the transmission.

↓

SHE: Oh really, that's great.

20.07 p.m., Onslow Square, London SW7

lots of people in one's head, he simply closed the conversational gate that would have led down such a path, he failed to pick up on the latent potential of her original statement.

So which did she prefer, lunch or dinner?

SOUL

Philip, who hadn't been invited for dinner in Onslow Square [he had spent it in the tedious company of a group of German record executives in a restaurant off Baker Street], was certain which meal he preferred. He had kept returning to the thought of Alice throughout the day and much of the one following. It was a most innocent thought, a simple brush of consciousness against the mental image of her sitting opposite him in the restaurant, her frequent smiles alternating with an unusually serious, almost melancholic countenance.

Philip had a friend called Peter with whom he often spent evenings in the pub discussing the central constituents of happiness – work and love – and he found himself talking of Alice when they met the following week.

'I met her through Matt's flatmate Suzy. They've known one another for ages, she works in marketing or something. We went to see an antiques fair in Islington together the other day. She's really wonderful.'

'In what way?'

'It's hard to say, I don't really know.'

'Is she beautiful?'

'No, not especially. I mean, she's very attractive in her own way, but she's certainly not beautiful.'

'Does she make you laugh?'

'Yeah, sort of, but she's not about to make it as a stand-up comedian.'

'So is she really dynamic, sort of charming or something?'

'It's strange, I don't know what it is about her. When I think about it, there just seems to be a real depth to her, it's sort of undefinable. She sort of has *soul*, if you know what I mean?'

'Soul?' echoed Peter, who clearly didn't.

When the French Enlightenment philosopher La Mettrie [1709–1751] published his book *L'Homme Machine* in 1748, he outraged educated public opinion by asserting most brutally [for his was still a largely spiritual age] that human beings were at heart only complicated machinery, little other than an arrangement of gates, sluices, cogs, pipes and atoms – such as could be found in reptiles, amoebas or maritime chronometers.

'Man is a machine and in the whole universe there is but a single substance variously modified,' declared La Mettrie, this substance of course being humble *matter*. The claim challenged the dualism which had reigned more or less unquestioned since Plato and argued that all human beings were made up of both matter and soul. It was clear which part was more important; it was soul which gave humans life and dignity, without it they would be simple machines, doomed to eternal death if they suffered a fatal coronary at the shareholders' meeting.

But what then was this soul? It was like the spacecraft at the head of the rocket which carried out the first manned lunar landing, in 1969. The spacecraft was only one of three parts of the giant Apollo 11: with all its sections, the spaceship measured one hundred and eleven metres, but when the astronauts returned to earth after their eight-day mission, they took with them only the tip of the craft, a minuscule cone measuring a little over three metres in height. The rest of Apollo had served to fire the astronauts into orbit, but the animating and critical feature was the module containing the one-small-step-for-man astronauts.

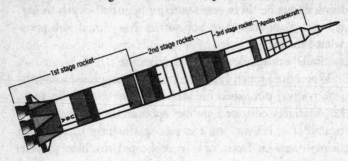

Theorists of the soul similarly saw human beings as divided into large but spiritually useless bodies, and smaller but infinitely precious souls. The body was the equivalent of a rocket, concerned with moving the soul around, fired by the consumption of coarse-grained bread and double cheeseburgers. Though the body was often impressive [though rarely standing one hundred and eleven metres tall], it was in the end superfluous to the human mission on Earth. After a decades-long life journey, the only thing to survive would be the tiny soul–spacecraft, invisible to even the most powerful microscope.

Most philosophers agreed that humans were divided into eternal souls and rocket–bodies, but they were not so unanimous about who or what sat in the valuable space-craft. The thing in the craft would naturally be the most important part of a human being, but what exactly consti-tuted this?

Plato came on to the philosophical scene arguing that reason was critically important, and therefore made a case for the soul being a *rational* spacecraft. Augustine, for whom God was far more vital, saw the soul–craft as belonging to God and aspiring to Heaven – a view which remained popular among astronomers and laymen for centuries hence. However, as the influence of God waned with the Enlightenment, so too the role of the soul in its theological sense began to change. If the most important part of a person was their soul, but God was no longer so important, then to what would the soul now be devoted?

Of course, not everyone was so convinced that the soul–craft should even continue to be of separate interest, and scientists and hard-nosed philosophers like La Mettrie curtly agreed to drop the subject in favour of materialistic allegiances. It was left to more mystical thinkers and dewy-eyed poets to continue with the idea of filling the soul–craft, something they quickly began to pack with *feeling*.

From being an item one automatically had as a human being, the soul became something one had to a greater or lesser extent – in relation to how much one *felt*. A crude person who picked their nose, burped during operas and had nothing but scorn for poetry would henceforth be known as someone with 'no soul', a fate that had been spared even the most base simpleton of old. 'To have no soul' came to mean one was lacking in sensibility to such things as art, literature and music. It explains why the dramatist John Dryden [1631–1700] could write of Shake-speare that 'he was the man who, of all moderns, and perhaps ancient poets, had the largest and most comprehen-sive soul.' According to Keats, the soul had its very own nourishment [no double cheeseburger here], and con-veniently for him and his publisher, it came in poetic stanzas: 'Poetry should be great and unobtrusive, a thing which enters into one's soul . . .'

Looked at sexually, loving someone for their soul came

to seem infinitely more worthy than loving them for their body–rocket – though the two might equally well end up with sighs in the bedroom. When Marilyn Monroe [1926–1962] wished to show up the moral bankruptcy of the film industry, she articulated a post-Enlightenment understanding of the soul by claiming that Hollywood was 'A place where they'll pay you a thousand dollars for a kiss, and fifty cents for your soul.'

Therefore, when Philip told Peter that Alice had much soul, he was pointing to an alluring sense that she felt much and deeply. But how could he claim such a thing after only a few meetings, none of which had included a performance of Ravel or readings of Wordsworth's *Prelude*?

Though feeling is a subjective experience, some have argued that the soul may be visible, inscribing itself on the physical features of a face, leaving a sediment on the material vessel. In Richardson's *Clarissa* [1747], we are told that Clarissa's eyes were full of soul, and poets down the ages have called these organs the soul's windows. But what in Richardson's name is a soulful *eye*?

The representation of soulful faces has more or less disappeared from Western art – faces are now typically presented as smiling, sultry or pouting – yet in certain portraits of the Virgin Mary painted in early modern Europe, we may find prime examples of soulful expressions. A walk around London's National Gallery reveals Van der Weyden's *Magdalen Reading* [painted in the 1430s], in which Mary Magdalen's eyes hint at an almost untouchable sorrow; she seems strangely removed from the book she is reading, lost in the netherworld of the soulful person. One thinks of Botticelli's *Virgin and Child* [painted 1475–1510], a picture where the Virgin is infused with the mood of a late Bach aria or the opening of Pergolesi's *Stabat Mater*.

'Listen, Philip, what's going on here? Are you trying to bed the bloody Virgin Mary?' interrupted Peter.

'Don't be silly,' replied Philip, 'I didn't say she *was* the Virgin Mary, I just said she's got this kind of expression that made me think of some of those Virgin Marys you sometimes see.'

'I just don't get it.'

'You don't get much?'

'Probably not. Ever since you renounced going out with the most beautiful woman in the Western world, I've got to admit, everything's been a bit of a mystery.'

Peter was alluding to Philip's ex-girlfriend Catherine, whom he had been seeing for some months before ending the liaison. Catherine was tall, blonde and gifted with a perfectly structured face and body. To earn money, she had in the past appeared as a model in several publications, and was generally agreed to be an almost ideal specimen of human beauty. Nor was she simply a pretty face. At twenty-seven, she was a fully-fledged doctor who had passed all her exams with top grades, and had begun delivering research papers to seminars of senior academics. Her character appeared equally flawless: she was never spiteful, kept up with old friends and wrote charming letters to thank those who invited her for dinner – so why in that case had she left Philip with the distinct feeling she had no soul?

It might have stemmed from her La Mettriean unsentimental *literalness*, an outgrowth of a medical training which left her unwilling to mince words or stray far from the essential components of life and death. Beside Catherine,

Alice's speech appeared *poetic* – not that she spoke in rhyming couplets but that it carried resonances in the way poetry may and prose usually does not.

Alice could relate a banal fishing holiday she had taken as a child, a prose event if ever there was one, and yet it would come across as somehow poetic – as though there was more to this fishing trip than sailing tackle and a beach hut in Norway. She didn't exhaust Philip's interest with her literalness, her privacy suggested a sorrow just out of reach, she maintained a degree of mystery essential to ignite desire.

At lunch a few days before, she and Philip had first had a drink with a prospective client of hers: the man was telling her about his business ['We import exhaust pipes from the Netherlands, fit the new converters, and then re-export them all over the European Union . . .'] and Alice had nodded and interspersed 'I sees' and 'How interest-ings', and yet had all the while seemed on another planet altogether – one to which Philip longed to propel himself, if only the correct Apollo could be found.

But though this might have sounded most innocent, there was potentially a darker side to Philip's enthusiasm for Alice's soul.

If the concept of soul came to be linked to *feeling* during the Romantic period, then it was significant that feeling was soon associated with feeling *pain* rather than pleasure. Experiencing things intensely rarely meant being happy, whistling in the shower or singing in the garden – to have soul was an indicator of a susceptibility to suffering.

It was no coincidence if the 'soul music' originating with Ray Charles and culminating in Aretha Franklin ['The First Lady of Soul'] should have been a predominantly black movement. Ever since the blues, black musicians were said to have had more soul than white ones: it was as if centuries of oppression, the slave ships and the cotton fields, had enabled them to understand and hence express suffering and emotion better than more pampered whites.

The link between black oppression and soul music was part of a wider Romantic assumption of the artist [the one who feels] as tortured creator, someone whose work could emerge only out of long trials and suffering. The American philosopher George Santayana [1863–1952] suggested the development of the soul could arise only through an initiation of pain: 'The soul, too, has her virginity and must bleed a little before bearing fruit.' Cyril Connolly remarked he would liked to have been Baudelaire or Rimbaud without undergoing the suffering he held had been a prerequisite [rather than an obstacle heroically conquered] of their artistic production. It was an assumption that artists did not create in spite of their sufferings, but precisely *because* of them.

Might Philip's love of soul not therefore have hidden a certain love of sadness, that most classical and lyrical aphrodisiac?

But how could sadness be attractive? Because while a woman seen laughing in the company of others clearly could not be in need of attention, the unhappy one staring at her coffee alone in a diner would allow a seducer to hope she might be acquainted with, and hence responsive to, his own sorrows. Her pain will lead her to understand my pain, he might imagine from the far side of the deserted diner.

Happiness is exclusive, unhappiness potentially inclusive. The lover who needs to be needed may therefore choose an unhappy expression over a happy one, hoping thereby to avoid the independence, the insensitivity to suffering, entailed by gaiety. To seek out unhappiness might be to seek to escape the competition suggested by self-sufficient expressions.

'I get it,' interrupted Peter, 'it's a complete rescue fantasy. Here's a woman who's getting a bad time at the hands of her boyfriend, and you want to ride in on your white horse and save her. You're one of those sick people who gets off on other people's unhappiness. I've seen couples like that, where the woman is unhappy and the man finds it charming. And you know what happens? It's terrible, the woman ends up even more unhappy because the man drives her into it – because he's so happy to see her unhappy.'

'Peter, I know the type, and believe me, it's not the case here. I don't want to rescue Alice, that's the last thing on my mind, I'm sure she'd be shocked by the idea she even needs rescuing. She's unbelievably independent, if anyone tried to rescue her, she'd probably bite their head off and say, "Look, I can do it on my own, thanks very much." I've got to tell you, it's bizarre, but the only excuse I have for liking her is the idea, and it's probably a ridiculous one, that because of the way she looks, because she looks soulful, she's somehow more profound and more interesting than a lot of other women I know.'

'I just think you'd better be careful trying to seduce someone who looks like something out of a Van der Weyden painting.'

'Hey, just a minute. I may have said she's wonderful, but the last thing I'm going to do is try to *seduce* her.' '

'How do you mean? You've just been banging on for half an hour about how great this girl is, and now you're saying your intentions are purely amicable? I can't believe it.'

'Look, she's got a boyfriend, and you know how I feel

about that kind of situation. I refuse to get involved with a woman who's already involved with someone else, it's too messy, life's too short for that kind of thing. She's more or less happy with this guy, and I'm happy to be her friend, to chat with her, that kind of thing. She's an intelligent, interesting soulful friend, and that's absolutely the way I intend to keep things.'

TRUTHFUL LEVELS

For much of life, one may muddle by without a coherent value-system, the absence of moral dilemmas absolving one from the responsibility of choice. What are one's true literary allegiances, free of the culture guilt induced by literary sections of quality papers? Until we have to pack our bags for a lifetime on a desert island, are we in any position to judge? Which does one prize more, power or honesty? Unless one has been forced to choose between the two, can one and does one really wish to know [no wonder Faust leaves us squirming in our seats]?

We shy away from stark choices, for they prevent us doing what comes most naturally, namely believing a dozen different completely incongruous and comfortably flattering things. What if one considered oneself a lover of intellectual literature, and realized at the desert island moment that one's favourite book was an airport novel? What if one thought oneself a person of integrity, then saw how easily ten million dollars could lead to frightening economies with the truth?

How did Alice feel about Philip? *Oh, he's really quite nice, thank you. Sort of friendly, he works as a sound engineer on classical recordings. He was recently with Midori in Berlin, Bach I think it was. Are you sure you won't have any tea? I went to an antiques fair with him the other day, we had a really nice chat. Is there a particular reason you're asking or are you just . . .?*

However, in the Freudian understanding, despite huge

areas of self-ignorance and unresolved conflicts, there exists a certain dynamic which aims at self-knowledge and resolution. Dreams and slips of the tongue are, in this framework, explained as confused but ultimately highly logical attempts on the part of wishful elements to find expression. The military general who thinks himself straight as a line-rule dreams at night of buggering the blue-eyed lieutenant he played pool with earlier that evening – and is thereby initiated into his own homosexuality. The man who cannot stop secretly thinking of his best friend's wife means to casually ask this friend how he is, but in the process recognizes his overwhelming concern with his spouse, 'How's your wife, Bill? I mean your *l*ife, Bill?'

Since she had met Philip, Alice's dream patterns showed no marked anomalies. She had had a dream about being in an aeroplane which crashed into a mountain. She had dreamt of being five and the excitement of going on holiday to the seaside near La Rochelle. She had dreamt of walking on stage in a school production of *Helen of Troy*, and nothing but soap bubbles coming out of her mouth when she tried to speak. It was the usual mixture of anxiety and fantasy, but nothing she would have withheld from Eric on waking up beside him. Nor had there been any marked forgettings or slips of the tongue; she had forgotten the name of an unpleasant accountant she had had to call at a rival firm, but then Shrivangajuri was an easy name to misplace. She had by error referred to her colleague *L*ucy as her flatmate *S*uzy, but then the linguistic equation was marked enough to supersede any psychological reading. And yet despite an absence of classical parapraxes, Alice's wish nevertheless revealed itself in the course of a phenomenon known as the *answerphone slip*.

When Freud died in London in 1939, the telephone was

still a primitive and exclusive instrument. Many calls were not directly dialled, but handled through an operator, lines had to be booked hours in advance and international services were prohibitively expensive. Moreover, if someone called when one was out of the house, there was no way of retrieving a message unless a butler was there to pick it up. Because the dominant method of recording sound was via the wax impression, it proved impossible to connect the telephone to a recording machine. Until the enclosed reel-to-reel cassette became widespread in the 1970s, there was hence no way for a caller to leave a message if the prospective interlocutor was out to lunch. However, the development of the cassette enabled a number of electronic firms to pioneer the manufacture of the *telephone answering machine*, a box which could be connected to the telephone and activated in response to an incoming call, standing in as a form of auditory mailbox. Before their integration with telephones themselves [a move dated to the mid-1980s], these machines tended to be small rectangular boxes containing two cassettes, one to record the outgoing message the other the incoming, a selection of controls [including play, review and record] and a small LED display showing the number of calls logged during one's absence.

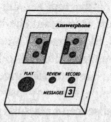

It was only a chronological accident which prevented Freud from investigating the enormous psychological significance of this appliance, for the telephone answering machine provided [in much the same way as dreams] a royal road into the subject's unconscious. Because of the construction of the machine, the order in which the owner confronted the news they had been called entailed first knowing they had been contacted [because the LED would display a certain number] and only then learning who was responsible. Inherent within the design was therefore a crucial delay between the excitement of knowing one had been called and the revelation of the identity of the caller – a delay which facilitated and encouraged the gestation of fantasy, revealing not who had called, but who one *wished* had called. The owner of a machine might frequently be unaware of the hopes they had pinned on a certain person, because of the danger of admitting a need only to see it unfulfilled. However, when they returned home after an evening with friends, and saw the LED light glowing with a bright and promising ④, the *answerphone slip* would inevitably reveal the identity of the wished-for-caller: the owner could not prevent the thought racing through their mind [while they fumbled for the replay button] that at last the desired he or she had called.

It was in this context that we approach the news of Alice's interpretation of the LED display on her answering machine as a sign she had received calls from Philip during her absence, an orthodox wish-fulfilment of the type defined by Laplanche and Pontalis as 'a psychological formulation in which the wish seems to the imagination to have been realized'.*

The wish was not based on untenable foundations: Philip

* J. Laplanche, J. Pontalis, *The Language of Psychoanalysis*, Karnac Books 1988

had after all taken her number and at the end of lunch in Dean Street promised to call her in the course of the following week to arrange to see a film or visit the new exhibition at the Royal Academy. No wonder then that when she returned home to find a ③ on the machine, she instinctively imagined one of them to be from Philip, even though they turned out to be from her mother, the plumber and her bank manager. And no wonder that when no less than ⑤ people rang the next day, the same thought occurred to her once more, though the callers proved equally disappointing [yet how actively disappointed could she be when she was in fact deeply in love with Eric, when she had more than enough friends, a hectic work schedule and had anyway seen Philip only a few days before?].

The following week, Eric planned a drinks party at his apartment, and asked Alice to add a few names to the invitation list. She bought an elegant black dress for the evening, and appeared unusually cheerful at the prospect, whistling the theme tune to a nature programme while applying make up in front of Eric's bathroom mirror.

Midway through the party, the phone rang in the kitchen and Alice went to pick it up. It was Philip apologizing for his delay, regretting that it would be impossible for him to make it. A recording he had been working on at King's College in Cambridge had massively overrun, and there was simply no way for him to return to London in time. Moreover, he was off for a three-week project in Cologne the next day, the cinema and Royal Academy would therefore have to wait, but he would call her when he got back.

When Alice rejoined the conversation she had left a few

minutes before, the topic had turned to UK working practices. A tall, bearded journalist was speaking:

'I think the idea that the British aren't reliable is as outdated as the idea they all go to Eton and have posh accents. Britain has one of the highest levels of productivity in Europe. It has a very low incidence of strikes when compared with other countries, and a highly developed and efficient communication system. British companies usually deliver on time, at the right price and in the right quantities.'

The other guests were too bored to agree or disagree and the conversation seemed ready to lapse.

'That's complete rubbish,' said Alice suddenly, 'there's inefficiency everywhere. Everywhere you go, you see contracts not being fulfilled, people reneging on promises. I was reading just yesterday of a company that was twenty-four hours late with a contract and they lost a deal worth three-quarters of a million pounds to an American firm.'

Alice's passionate attack on British inefficiency surprised her guests, who had thought the issue either uncontentious or dull beyond consideration. Several of them were astute enough to judge that perhaps their hostess was a little too excited on this matter to make it polite to pursue, and headed for more neutral topics, eventually alighting on sailing holidays in Cornwall.

Alice was furious with Philip – but no, how could she be furious with Philip when she didn't care for him? In fact, if she was annoyed, it was only because here was a journalist who believed in British efficiency, when daily she was made aware of stunning British inefficiency. And because the bespectacled guest was in a combative mood, what more natural reaction than to spend part of the evening passionately debating a cause she had never known she felt so strongly about?

It was as if a compromise had been reached amongst the various desires in Alice's mind. On the one hand, the anger accruing from Philip's rejection was fighting for expression, but on the other, the censor was deeming expression impossible on account of what it said of her feelings for him. A deal had therefore been struck, one side of the mind telling the other, 'I'll allow you to get angry, but only if you don't realize what you're getting angry about: only if you get angry while ignoring the true cause of your anger.' How much easier it was to say she was annoyed at British inefficiency than that she was annoyed at the particular inefficiency of a particular Briton she cared about though she was deeply in love with someone else.

Eric came up to her in the midst of her discussion, gently put his arm around her and asked if she was enjoying the party.

'Definitely, it's great, there are really interesting people here.'

'Who was that on the phone earlier?'

'On the phone earlier?'

'Yeah, who was it?'

'Oh, no one, I mean, it was Philip, it's nothing, he was just saying he wouldn't be able to make it.'

'That's a pity, I was looking forward to meeting him. You must be annoyed.'

'Annoyed, no why?'

'I don't know, because you invited him.'

'I don't care. That's completely his problem not mine. The only thing that gets me frustrated is when people agree to come to something and then don't.'

And the matter was dropped, the hurt passed off as a

respectably administrative, rather than shamefully emotional, gripe.

The distinct feature of self-deception is a failure within a single person to be coherent about two beliefs which together should have cancelled themselves out. Stated philosophically, it implies a situation where a person acts in a certain manner [manner x] only because of a prior but hidden belief in x's opposite [x is made possible by not-x]. The classic example is that of the fat man who likes to believe he is thin, who deceives himself he is thin, and in order to do so tucks in his stomach just before looking at himself in the mirror. The mirror doesn't show the extent of his beer belly, yet the disguise is premissed on a prior awareness of the belly's existence and dimensions. The man wouldn't have been able to consider himself thin without first knowing he was fat [and therefore drawing in his breath to hide the uncomfortable fact].

Though she had no beer belly, Alice was involved in a similar manoeuvre, for her unusual lack of surface annoyance with Philip's absence was premissed on the knowledge of a far deeper and unacceptable anger arising from it. She cared less than usual whether or not Philip came, precisely because at one level she knew she cared about it more than usual and far more than was advisable [a case where thought x was made possible only by the thought that not-x].

But how could the same person both produce and swallow an untruth? The answer in Alice's case could only lie with the feeble but legendary *at one level*. Did Alice love Eric? Or course she did – at one level. How did she feel about Philip? Pretty warmly perhaps – at one level. Was she aware of all this? Maybe – at one level.

Her mind could have been compared to a lift shaft connecting many floors, where the contents of one floor

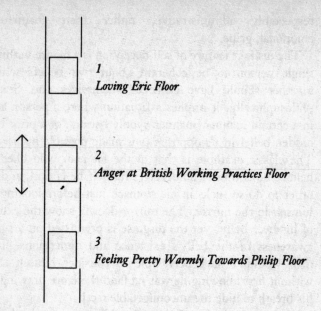

1
Loving Eric Floor

2
Anger at British Working Practices Floor

3
Feeling Pretty Warmly Towards Philip Floor

didn't necessarily negate those of another. Quite incompatible things might be happening at each layer, the lift simply shifted beneath floors without logical continuity.

The evening of the party was hence one of paradoxes: an evening when Alice hadn't, at one level, cared whether or not Philip had come because, at another level, she cared about it too much to admit, and an evening where she had loved Eric less than usual but made love to him more passionately than usual, so as to prevent the realization of a drop in her affections which she must, at one level, already have known of to make such passionate love making possible.

It was simply a pity there were other people involved at each floor . . .

QUESTIONS

Philip never denied he found Alice attractive; from the very outset, he simply asserted a quiet but firm refusal to become involved with a woman already involved with someone else.

When he returned from Germany a few weeks later, he and Alice began seeing one another regularly for lunch, the proximity of their two offices in Soho granting the meetings a certain geographical rationale.

'How was your weekend?' asked Philip one lunchtime.

'Oh, whatever. How was yours? Did you go down to Cornwall in the end or did you end up staying here?'

'I asked first.'

'Well, it was just another weekend, you know . . . Have we ordered? I really feel like an avocado today, I've had this real craving for avocados all day.'

'Are you doing this on purpose?'

'What?'

'Changing the subject.'

'No, not really. Look, I don't know what to say. The weekend wasn't so hot. Eric was in another of his "don't talk to me, I'm feeling uncommunicative" moods, which was a pity because he'd expressly asked me to stay in London and not spend the weekend with Suzy. He gets into these moods where he ignores me, as though I'd done something terrible, but if I ask him what the matter is, he just flies off the handle and tells me to stop bothering him.

I was at this cake shop yesterday, and because I know how much he likes cheesecake, I bought him a slice and took it back to his place. But when I put it down on his desk next to him, he didn't even look up, and when I came back later, he'd gone out and the cake was still there untouched. Anyway, I can't imagine any of this sordid, boring stuff is of any interest to you. I'm famished. Can we order now?'

However sordid and painful, our culture teaches us to look kindly upon unrequited love. Though largely intolerant of failure in professional spheres, society maintains a certain respect for grief in the emotional one. The great disappointed lovers of literature [Bovary, Young Werther] derive admiration from their audience for the generosity they display towards their unwilling, insufficient or cruel targets of affection. In feeling pity for Alice, Philip was therefore following an ancient and well-known societal path. Here was a sad case of a woman loving a man unable to respond to the affection bestowed on him. Eric was the evil monster, Alice the one bringing the cheesecake, and because she had undeniably beautiful eyes and an arguably soulful face, Philip had predictably little difficulty finding sympathy for the unfortunate maiden.

'Don't let him walk all over you: it's the worst thing you can possibly do. He won't respect you if you're a doormat.'

'What should I do then?'

'Just act a bit tougher with him. You know, if he's in a bad mood, just be in an even worse mood, rather than waiting on him and being passive. He's only acting like this because he knows he can get away with it.'

There were many such sessions of advice: Alice would sheepishly mention something Eric had done, and Philip would try to suggest remedies.

However innocent these sessions seemed, they nevertheless implied complicated questions. What was Alice doing spending her time complaining of her current lover? If she complained about him, then clearly things were not going too well, and if they were not going too well, then perhaps she was looking to find someone with whom they might go better. In that case, what was Philip's role in this? Why had he been chosen as the friend/therapist who would listen to the tales of woe? Was it because he was a good listener, or because the patient might have wished to drive things beyond the amicable? Was Alice complaining about Eric so as to suggest she wouldn't be averse to Philip's attentions, or were these lunchtime discussions simply innocent opportunities for Alice to vent frustrations in an essentially happy relationship?

Given the minefields, Philip had a careful line to tread.

'Eric's always so negative about my tastes, you know, I'll choose a movie and ask him if he wants to go, and it always feels like he's rejecting it because it's my movie.'

'Hhm.'

'What do you think?'

'Perhaps he just doesn't like Bergman films.'

'No no, I think it's more, it's like he's using Bergman to make a point about our relationship.'

'What point?'

'Like he doesn't respect me.'

'Could you never talk these kinds of things over?'

'How do you mean?'

'I mean, are all tensions just completely unmentionable?'

'No, why?'

'I don't know, you just made it sound that way.'

'Did I?'

'Yeah.'

There was a pause, the waiter arrived with a tomato and mozzarella salad.

'You know, things may not always be brilliant with Eric,' said Alice brushing back her hair, 'but basically, we both know we love one another, there's a real commitment between us. He's brought me things no man ever brought me before, I respect him for that.'

Why in that case did Alice spend much of her time hinting at the opposite, and defending the relationship only when Philip attacked it too directly? Why were catalogues of injuries followed by sudden assertions of love?

Whatever the answer to such tortuous questions, their presence at least had one notable side-effect: they made a mockery of Philip's claim never to be involved with a woman involved with another man. Though he had tried to resist the lure of Alice's attraction on the very rational basis that it would only lead to complications, a situation full of indecision and prohibition had unwittingly grown highly charged.

PASSING THE GUILT

Eric went away on business to Athens for a few days, so Alice rang up Philip and asked him if he wouldn't mind accompanying her to a film her other friends had already seen.

'I don't know why he keeps calling me,' she said to Suzy on her way out of the house.

'Why shouldn't he?'

'No reason. I just hope he's not getting the wrong idea.'

'What wrong idea?'

'That it's only, you know, friendly.'

'What's wrong with thinking it's only "you know, friendly"?'

'Oh, don't be silly.'

The cinema was only a few yards from Philip's house, so after the performance, Alice remarked that she should finally take the opportunity to have a look at his flat.

They sat side by side on a large green sofa in the living-room, their conversation assuming chronological dimensions unusual for a mid-week evening. They talked of politics, cooking, parents, illness, they even asked themselves the name of the world's longest river and diligently poured over a large atlas [their knees lightly touching] in order to check.

'My guess is it's the Mississippi,' said Alice.

'No way, it's the Amazon, everyone knows that.'

'The Amazon may be the windiest river, but it isn't the longest.'

'Look in the back, it's all written there.'

'OK, here's the page, populations, lake areas, mountain heights, oceans, seas and, there, rivers. How weird. Neither of us was right.'

'Was it the Yangtze?'

'No, it's the Nile.'

'Christ, the Nile, how could I forget? It's so obvious.'

'Almost too obvious.'

'So how long is it?'

'Six thousand six hundred and ninety kilometres, a hundred and twenty kilometres more than the Amazon.'

'Well, I was nearly right.'

'There's no nearly right in this game: you're a hundred and twenty kilometres out, my friend.'

Their fluvial researches over, Alice cleared an obstruction in her throat, threw a conspicuous glance at her watch, sighed and uttered a sentence made up of the following words:

'*I'm tired.*'

The semantic content of such a sentence typically causes its listeners few problems. In most languages, 'I'm tired' indicates a biological disposition to wrap oneself in a soft blanket and extinguish consciousness for several hours.

But given the setting and delivery, 'I'm tired' contained a denotational potential rich enough to rival the most expressive constructions in the language.

It might have been a way for Alice to suggest any one of the following:

1) It could have signalled an impatient, 'Listen Philip, don't you realize I realize what's going on? Do you really think it

amuses me to sit here all night and talk about the length of the world's rivers? Do something. Some of us have to be at our desks at nine o'clock tomorrow morning.'

2) Or, it could have been a way of reminding Philip that though she was sitting on a sofa beside him and had recently brushed her knee against his, she had no desire to see things proceed any way beyond that.

3) Or, it could have been a way for her to bring up the matter of departure, not out of any desire to leave, simply to prompt Philip into preventing her from doing so.

4) Or, lastly [and in such circumstances, most unbelievably], it might simply have meant that Alice was tired.

After sustained effort to unpack these complex words, Philip finally settled on an interpretation optimistically hovering around [1] and [3]. It explained the sudden pilgrimage of his right hand towards Alice's open palm, whose lines it caressed without protest. It explained the move of his upper body an instant later, a reorientation allowing his mouth to land softly against hers, grazing the outlines of her orifice with his lips, and eliciting an unmistakably sympathetic, even enthusiastic response.

'Listen Philip, this is impossible, it's crazy,' protested Alice a few moments later, though the moments had been long enough to suggest it wasn't.

As if it might be news to both of them, she added, 'You can't expect me to do this kind of thing, I'm involved with someone else.'

A classic parlour game exists called Passing the Guilt – a game requiring two partners, a taboo or risk and the possibility of guilt and recrimination. Its purpose is for one player to subtly construct a situation which will lead another to be liable for the blame stemming from the fulfilment of their own wishes.

Let's suppose a given action requires four steps, but cannot be identified as an action before the fourth move has been made. Though the other party may have made steps one to three, the person ultimately responsible for the action [i.e. the person to whom the blame can be wedded] is taken to be the author of the fourth step. A skilful player will therefore initiate the first three steps, then stand back and watch the other execute the final stage of the game, thereby avoiding liability for the resolution of their desires.

Imagine that Alice wasn't really so tired, but that kissing Philip carried an imposing burden of guilt given her involvement with Eric. What better idea than to be a party to a kiss, but then suggest the plan had originated elsewhere? After all, hers hadn't been the lips to cross the decisive threshold; what had she been doing but sitting on a sofa and sighing she was tired?

Philip was by nature averse to carrying sacks of guilt which weren't his own, and therefore said to Alice, 'Oh, please. Don't spoil things by playing the innocent. We've been wanting this to happen for weeks. I agree it's a big problem, but it belongs to both of us.'

And with this counsel, he gently drew Alice back to him.

'Philip, it simply isn't like that. I'm sorry. What happened tonight really shouldn't have happened, and I don't know how I let it. I've got responsibilities towards Eric, I can't forget that.'

'You're suddenly talking as if he never let you down.'

'I don't know whether he has.'

'Is that why you spend so much of your time complaining about him to me?'

'You're being unfair.'

'Have you thought what you're being?'

'You don't understand. I love Eric.'

'Well, excuse me for getting a slightly different impression, no fault of your own, of course. Let me tell you something Alice; in future, I'd be grateful if you saved your confusion and hypocrisy for someone else.'

'In that case, I'm sorry I ever bothered you.'

And with these words, the kissers parted frostily, Alice burying her ambivalence under the well-known narrative of a friendship spoiled by one party short-sightedly confusing the amicable for the romantic.

PRIVATE LANGUAGES

The fiasco with Philip encouraged Alice to recall her affections for the man who had made such a fiasco so necessary.

When Eric returned from Athens, she embraced him with a fervour whose intensity might have aroused his suspicion, had it not been for his charmingly naïve [if not slightly vain] predisposition to think himself an eminently suitable target for fervent embraces.

Her efforts manifested themselves in a number of speeches delivered [in the bath, on the way to work, before falling asleep] to an internal representation of Eric. These speeches concisely laid out everything amiss between them, amounting to a bold plan to turn their relationship into a paragon of modern openness and communication. They began with the declaration, 'I want to feel I can be honest with you . . .' Maturely she would outline the areas of tension between them, balancing criticisms with assertions of love, invoking the familiar, 'You know I'm saying this only because . . .'

She planned to deliver the speech one evening after work. Eric would return home, set down his briefcase and walk into the kitchen to get a glass of water. He would sit next to her on the sofa, and then quietly but confidently she would begin, 'Eric, there's things we should talk about . . .' She imagined his surprise at her eloquence, the way her bottled feelings would demand a response. She would set out her case like a trial lawyer, and when she had finished, the eyes of the entire courtroom would be with her.

Wittgenstein denied the possibility of a private language by arguing that language was by definition a shared system of communication, and was therefore unimaginable outside a society.

But whatever Wittgenstein thought, Alice was gradually forced to recognize that these speeches were being delivered in what could only have been described as a private language. What did this language consist of? It wasn't an incomprehensible system of grunts or clicks, but rather a tangle of words whose message proved incapable of expression let alone understanding.

In objective reality, Eric returned home as predicted, went into the kitchen to fetch a glass of water, then turned on the television, and while images of riots in South Africa and shootings in Northern Ireland rolled by, Alice told herself that perhaps the following night would after all be a more suitable moment to deliver such an important message.

And when she finally spoke, her voice refused to find the fluidity it had earlier assured the mind it could command. It sounded strangulated, intense, desperate, far from the aspired lawyerly tone. Nor was Eric the pliant interlocutor she had imagined. While she had counted on his listening patiently, understanding, then giving a considered response, she recognized how far her initial reluctance to speak had stemmed from an unconscious but painfully correct sense it would get her nowhere.

HE: I've got to do something about my car tyres.
SHE: Eric, I've got to talk to you.

HE: What's the problem?
SHE: I think you know.
HE: The car tyres?

Their dialogues had the absurd feel of exchanges by Harold Pinter or Tom Stoppard, in whose plays characters seem doomed to talk at cross-purposes – one character answers a different question to the one currently being asked, or unknowingly continues a conversation the other has abandoned ten minutes ago [a discrepancy shown not even to matter, so enclosed in a solipsistic world is each character, benignly assuming the other to be on their wavelength without bothering to enquire].

Behind every complaint expressed one might premiss an optimistic belief in the other's capacity to atone for wrong. Complaining implies a faith in dialogue, the idea that though one has been hurt, the other has a [retrospective] capacity to understand their offence.

Alice's allegiance to the art of complaining wavered between messianic and autistic phases.

[i] The messianic phase

In this phase, she held that conflicts, however grave, would invariably reach resolution through dialogue. Disagreements were simply failures of one party to see the other's point of view, but if both could be brought to the table and calmly given time to explain themselves, an understanding would naturally follow.

When Alice had first shared her apartment, Suzy had had the irritating habit of using the same knife to butter her toast and to scoop out the honey, leaving small white globules throughout the jar. The origin of Alice's irritation was no doubt complex, but the politics of expressing it were even more so. How could Suzy possibly understand the extent of her flatmate's frustration at the sight of these blobs, the silent anger they elicited each morning?

Yet when Alice finally confronted the issue, a hesitant, 'I know this will sound ridiculous . . .' successfully built up into, 'Perhaps we could designate one knife for the jam or honey, and then another knife we'd use just for buttering and spreading.'

'Sure. What a good idea,' replied Suzy, unaware of the extraordinary inner turmoils Alice had had to go through to deliver such a suggestion.

Her relationship with her mother had been one long round of metaphoric butter knives in the honey, but one which had rarely benefited from efforts at messianic conversion. But because Alice now saw her mother rarely enough for her image to blur nostalgically, she had recently greeted news that she was visiting London by deciding to break the customary polite hypocrisy of the adult relationship in order to speak honestly of what had gone on between them in childhood.

[ii] Autistic phases

Alice and her mother had had dinner in a restaurant in Wandsworth, and after a salad of small-talk, Alice had steered the conversation to the past.

'Your father and I were always very busy. It wasn't that we didn't care for you, just that we had no time to show how much we cared,' explained the mother.

'But was it really a question of time?'

'You're right. I can't defend how we behaved. Looking back on it, it was selfish. But we were young, we were in such a hurry to get everything out of life, to have children and build up careers and money. It all seems so worthless in retrospect. Now that I'm a shrivelled-up old prune.'

'Oh, Mum, you're not.'

'I am dear, nothing but a shrivelled-up old prune. No doctor or face cream can help me now.'

'But you're one of the most beautiful women I know.'

'Kind of you to say so, dear, but flattery can't help me at my age. I just look at the mirror and realize it's all over. But where were we? Oh yes, your childhood. What I meant to say is that I realize now that the most important thing in my life is my children, that nothing else really matters. Didn't we order water without gas?'

'No, gas is fine for me.'

'It affects my stomach terribly.'

'We'll get another then.'

'No, no, dear. I'll just take it in little sips.'

Alice returned home believing that in her own way her mother had begun to recognize the buried grievances between them. She had indicated a development in her sense of value; her children mattered more than she had realized – a departure from her attitude of old, where even a game of golf had seemed to hold greater priority.

Why in that case did a third party subsequently report that her mother had judged her to have had 'something of a nervous breakdown'? 'The poor girl is clearly still most disturbed, anyone who in their twenties bursts into tears at the mention of things that happened decades back should really be seeking qualified help. I did what I could to reassure her, but she's still so very vulnerable, so very over-sensitive.'

It was experiences such as these which flung Alice violently back into her autistic moods, where she was convinced people would never really understand each other, however eloquent the dialogue, however much reasoning, pleading and persuading was involved. She could have spoken to her mother for days, the woman would have given encouraging signs of life and empathy, but would in the end have remained as blind as she had ever been, as self-centred in her prune years as in her youth. There were simply things she could never grasp, and it was best to accept and mourn this rather than risk further disappointment.

So what was Alice's approach to Eric? She had from the start been more inclined towards messianism than autism, though this perhaps carried too strong an implication of conversion for someone who rarely broke forth into dialogue and was prey only to stifled [some might say almost mystical] hopes for Eric's understanding.

They had recently been to see a film together, a moralistic story in which a man neglected his partner and friends before realizing he had been escaping commitment and changed his ways. Though the message was crudely put, Alice watched Eric's face in the dark and hoped he had drawn the same parallels between art and life as her. But on emerging from the cinema, it was clear that the hoped-for identification had failed to materialize. Far from the film producing a shock of self-recognition, it merely gave Eric a comforting sense that it had shown up the faults of a man a million miles away from his own situation.

Alice might have been aware of Eric's faults, but if this understanding didn't tally with his self-perception, then it was cruelly ineffective. It was the old dilemma of being able to bring a horse to water [or cinema], but having no power to make it drink.

She had for instance noticed how often Eric blamed people's problems on their own incompetence rather than accepting the broader factors at play. She also had a dozen theories as to why this might be.

'It's because you're so harsh on yourself that you've got to be harsh on others,' she told him after he had fired another employee.

'It's got nothing to do with harshness, Alice. It's got to do with the fact that I can't keep working with staff who treat basics of administration as some kind of joke. I know you'd like to expand this into a large and worthy debate on my character, your character and probably the state of the nation too, but I'm afraid the issue is much simpler, and much less interesting, than that.'

Alice might have made an accurate appraisal of Eric's psychological make-up, but her epistemic advantage was useless if she expected him to act on its revelations. Her insights had all the pitiful capacity for provoking self-recognition as that of showing a person their DNA structure. Wise scientists might tell someone the genes were theirs, but because they couldn't *feel* the matter subjectively, they might understandably reply, 'This double-helix rubbish has nothing to do with me.'

With her analyses of Eric's character, Alice was akin to an observer looking down from a helicopter at a maze, therefore able to see the problematic heart of the tangled hedge hidden from someone on the ground.

But her solution to the maze [whatever its validity] was sadly ineffectual. Eric might decades later have realized while lying in the bath that a past girlfriend had had some remarkable insights into his character, but Alice couldn't

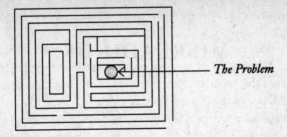

The Problem

simply helicopter him into the middle of his psychological
puzzle, point to the heart of the problem and expect him to
tell her how right she was. Having not made the journey
himself, unable to see the steps linking this information to
the rest of his make up, he might forgiveably declare, 'I'd
appreciate it if you kept your pop psychology to yourself.'

MISREADINGS

When one loves someone with a problem [they don't love back, they're jealous, insensitive, more interested in the other sex, married to someone else . . .], there is no more common reaction than to declare the problem doesn't really belong to them. They have it, of course, but it isn't a central feature of their character, it's there rather by chance, like an ingrown toenail that can be removed, a small impediment time will erode.

Suppose one is in love with an emotionally distant being who rarely answers phone calls, never reveals vulnerability nor shares anything of value. What matter. These are but small details next to what one takes to be the central constituents of their character – namely, the sensitivity in their eyes, the way they once took our hand in a busy shopping street, the time we saw them cry in a film, the traumas of a childhood for which we feel so much empathy . . .

Alice had always performed an original, perhaps oblique reading of Eric's character, whereby certain facets of his nature, though taking up proportionately less space than others, were judged to be the essence of who he was. Her iceberg approach meant that if he had been funny only once or twice, she nevertheless believed him to have had an impressive, though largely submerged, humorous core.

But a question now arose whether the so called obstacles to him being funny, sensitive or kind on more than rare occasions were really obstacles at all. Might they not have had as much claim to the title of Eric's true self as the delicious nuggets she had till then identified it with?

Looking is always supplemented, some would say even superseded, by knowing or wishing. We rarely rely on what is in front of our eyes, proceeding instead with quick glances overshadowed by images already imbibed. Take Alice's journey to work: she knew it so well, she rarely noticed it was happening, she sometimes arrived at the office without recollection of having crossed half of London to get to her desk. All she needed was a quick bleary-eyed gaze at the basic shapes of the station platforms, and the rest would follow: she knew how many Underground stops she had to pass, which direction the escalators operated, and which tunnels the crowds avoided. She had no will to register the colour of the carriages, the shape of the clouds as they floated above the London skyline or the texture of the clothes around her. Though charming and no doubt poetic, these were luxuries in the overall design of her journey to work.

If Alice was a lazy Underground traveller, the poverty of her perception stemmed from a reliance on habit. She saw what she had grown used to seeing rather than what might have unfolded to an innocent gaze.

Visual tricks reveal how when a word is missing or repeated in a familiar or authoritative sentence, the reader will often overlook it in expectation of a correct text. Take a sentence in a daily newspaper from a recent article on the Middle East:

> The foreign secretary declared that
> only when both sides were prepared

> to talk could a settlement be
> reached, adding that bloodshed
> in the province would never be
> be stopped by external pressure only.

A reader might be so accustomed to sentences with only one verb, particularly typed sentences in a daily newspaper, they would overlook the repetition. Knowing what they wanted to read [a correct English sentence], they would overrule the visual information which didn't fit their prejudice.

Observation is concluded on the basis of a clash or mixture of two inputs of information:

1) What something looks like.
2) What we know *or wish* of objects which tend to look like this.

Ideally of course we would judiciously balance the two, mixing precedent and perception. Delusion [the abandonment of outer reality in favour of inner wish] would start only when we focused exclusively on the second point. The reader who had missed the double 'be' might then [like Alice in another context] be accused of a small but distant fantasy.

In May, Alice and Eric were invited to a dinner at which they arrived separately, Eric from his office, Alice from home. They were seated at opposite ends of the table, she next to the host, he next to a frosty lawyer and a bubbly PR lady. During a lull in her conversation, she looked across the table and overheard Eric telling a story:

'We were coming into Hong Kong during one of those flashfloods they have in the rainy season, and the whole plane was juddering. They warned us it would be a bumpy landing, and when the wheels hit the ground there was spray everywhere. You couldn't see anything out of the windows. Then, just when the plane was losing speed and we thought everything would be all right, we noticed it wasn't really stopping enough. The plane overshot the runway and came to a stop just before the sea, the front wheel completely buried in mud.'

'You must have been scared.'

'It was a lucky escape.'

Though constantly looking at people, one rarely forms new impressions of them, impressions implying the registration of novelty rather than the confirmation of prejudice. At only a few stages do we actively sketch a picture of someone – on first meeting, after a long absence, in the course of a furious row, after an illness, something to break the laziness of photographic habit.

The result was bewildering, for in the space of a sentence or two Eric suddenly struck Alice as incredibly *ordinary*. His manners no longer seemed a symbol of greater magnificence, nor his conversation worthy of particular respect or attention. While the host poured more wine and Eric reached for another serving of peas, she found herself thinking [as though it was an extraordinary insight], *He's just another human being* – the curdled echo of George Bernard Shaw's famous maxim that love was only a curious process of exaggerating the difference between one person and another.

WHO MAKES THE EFFORT?

Eric couldn't have ignored the decline in Alice's affections. He had noted her many lunches with Philip, and even when these had abruptly ceased her behaviour retained a flirtatious edge. Having rarely shown interest in parties, she now attended them regularly, arriving without Eric in tow and later receiving calls from men not previously identified as friends.

He might well have felt and expressed jealousy at this departure from her once devoted state, asking sourly [as some men will], 'Why were you all over that bass guitarist tonight?' or, 'Who is this Luke character who calls here all the time?'

But Eric had always held jealousy to be a most vulgar emotion, the recourse of those without refinement or shame. Children and adolescents felt jealous, not grown men secure of their position in the world.

Such lack of jealousy might have been considered admirable, it at least saved Alice from the more grotesque scenes of certain paranoid liaisons. However, it could equally well have been read as a blatant insult, a refusal on Eric's part to assert and defend his love, for to experience jealousy required him to admit two things:

Firstly: that he cared desperately about another human being,
Secondly: [and this was where pride came in] that this person no longer cared too much about him.

If Alice wasn't delighted by the absence of jealousy, it was because she experienced it as a reflection of a stubborn inability to acknowledge the first point, something which ironically helped to pave the way for the scenario of the second.

Eric's behaviour nevertheless underwent certain changes. Alice had always spent nights in his apartment, very conveniently for him, less so for her. It had been her responsibility to pack a bag and leave Earl's Court as a result of the mysterious [and of course tacit] game of brinkmanship whereby both partners pushed to see how far they might go in getting the other to make an effort before reluctantly making the trip themselves. Their phone conversations on the issue ran something like this.

SHE: What are you doing tonight?
HE: Just hanging out at home. How about you?
SHE: I don't know. Do you want to do something?
HE: OK.
SHE: Do you want to come here or shall I come to you?
HE: I'm quite tired tonight.
SHE: Are you?
HE: Yeah. A heavy day at work.
SHE: Me too.
HE: Ehm.
SHE: So?
HE: What?
SHE: Ok, well should I come to you then?
HE: Yeah, that's a great idea.

Somewhere in the folds of the conversation, Alice would detect evidence that if she didn't push herself to leave her apartment, then Eric was unlikely to leave his. His desire to spend the evening together was fractionally, but decisively, weaker than hers. He would have tolerated an evening alone, she couldn't as easily – and hence the effort was hers to make. Perhaps if she hadn't backed down, if she had said, 'Why the hell don't you come to me for once?' then Eric would have driven to her door that instant. But she was in no position to try such brinkmanship: she cared too much to risk encountering a refusal.

But as her affections waned she was freer to gamble on Eric's reactions. When the issue came up she no longer rushed to offer a visit and Eric therefore learnt the logic of travelling himself. The conversation now ran more like this:

HE: What are you doing tonight?
SHE: I might be going out with Gordon, or Suzy. Why?
HE: Do you want to come over here?
SHE: Sorry, Eric, I'm really too knackered.
HE: But I haven't seen you since Thursday.
SHE: So.
HE: So that's a long time.
SHE: Is it?
HE: Sure it is.
Pause
HE: What about if I came over later?
SHE: What about it?
HE: Well, would that be OK?
SHE: Yeah, I suppose so, but then don't come before about eleven, I'll be out in the pub till then.

The brinkmanship could have been likened to the game seen in certain American films, where two cars head towards each other on a narrow road and compete to be the last to swerve on to the grassy bank. Each driver has to evaluate the likelihood of the other swerving before he or she does, but if neither car swerves, both drivers die.

Though no lives were at stake, Alice and Eric were involved in a game where the decision of who should cross

London depended on an evaluation of how tempted the other partner would be to prevent both of them spending a night alone. Shifting on to the grassy bank meant making an effort to avoid collision, leaving one's apartment or one's pride, in short, abandoning one's selfish desires for the sake of the couple. The person who most often shifted off the selfish road was of course Alice, for her fear was greater. Eric was invincible for he appeared not to mind slaughtering love.

But when it now came to getting off the phone, taking the worst seat at the cinema, doing the shopping or answering the door, Eric noticed Alice growing more reckless than him. It was logical to drive dangerously only so long as he was certain to be the only one ready for love's demise. If Alice was joining him at his game, then kamikaze techniques represented an unsustainable risk for someone who simply wished to rid himself of effort rather than of his girlfriend.

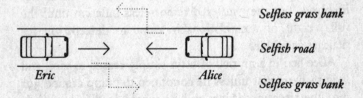

Selfless grass bank

Selfish road

Eric   Alice

Selfless grass bank

Relationships might be said to have an inherent and cruel desire for self-balance. Looked at in terms of an equation, to keep two people together might require 40 units of effort [here labelled x] from both partners.

Alice $20x$ + *Eric* $20x$ = *Relationship* of $40x$

$40x$ would imply the relationship was a going concern, the cruel point was that the sum would not have to be equally paid. In only the most sensible liaisons would both parties cough up 20 units of effort; typically one party would make more effort than another. But how or why? How was the person who paid less chosen? By a very cynical sense of how much the other person cared. Each partner would intuitively weigh up the other, asking, 'What is the minimum effort I can make? How far can I push the other to pay more than me before they refuse and love is lost?'

For most of their relationship, Eric avoided paying his due because he knew Alice would pay when he didn't. If he paid only 10 units, she would come up with the other 30. If he didn't feel like driving over to her house, then she would come to his. If he didn't wish to break a deadlock after an argument, he could count on her to play the mediator.

But he miscalculated just how far he could push Alice. Her share of the $40x$ began to slowly decline, leaving him to make up the shortfall. Only small amounts were at first involved, but they suffered remorseless inflation until the full weight of the relationship came to descend on his delicate shoulders.

Alice had in a myriad of ways simply ceased to care, and Eric realized that unless he continued to pump around $39x$ into the situation, Alice and he would inevitably collide and break up.

ROMANTIC PUZZLES

It was a strange and melancholy thought, the idea of 'outgrowing someone', like one would outgrow a pair of trousers or an overcoat. It was a reminder of emotional development which risked outpacing a partner of slower step. The answers love was asked to provide changed as Alice changed, time revealed possibilities which required the recasting of a relationship's initial contract. By simple virtue of her own altered capacities, a once adored figure could assume the role of romantic dinosaur.

Alice loved in order to make up for her own insufficiencies, she searched in others for qualities she aspired to, respected but lacked. Her emotional needs were like a puzzle incomplete without a segment brought by another, but the dimensions of the void altered in response to self-development, the piece which fitted at fifteen would no longer fit at thirty. The gap redrew its contours, and unless the puzzle-person kept up she would be left to divorce or awkwardly force the issue.

The myriad of differing solutions might have been tabled thus:

Age	Gap to be filled	Masculine solution
8	Desire to find someone with whom to climb trees, light matches and introduce her to the most fashionable gang in school.	A sophisticated nine-year-old called Thomas who sported a leather jacket and rally bicycle. They planned to marry and have twelve children. He once allowed her to watch him pee in the garden.

Age	Gap to be filled	Masculine solution
13–16	Desire to learn about sex and kissing: corresponding terror of actually kissing or having sex.	A succession of sebacious teenagers furtively groping on top of her, then writing love letters packed with intensity and spelling mistakes [the second of which she corrected].
16	The vagina.	The first man who looked capable of taking her virginity: the son of friends of her parents – a twenty-four-year-old Yale graduate who was none too delicate, finished in five minutes and refused to answer her letters after she fell hopelessly if predictably in love with him.
18	Desire to take mind-expanding drugs and listen to obscure music in dark basements.	A twenty-year-old Herman Hesse reading student, nicknamed 'the good doctor' by his friends for his cabinet of pills and grasses. Named Alice after a Hindu goddess of fertility, though was himself impotent.
19	Wish to improve her sex life, and in the process shock her parents [relics of Marx's historically doomed bourgeois class].	A Jamaican saxophonist called Trevor who claimed to have slept with two hundred women, was involved in 'business' in Notting Hill, took her to ecstasy and back – and so appalled the relics of Marx's historically doomed bourgeois class that they threatened to have him followed by the police.
20–23	Search for intellectually superior father figures.	A bearded biology professor at university: preached sermons on Darwinian evolution, and screamed names of fossils at orgasm.
24	Ill at ease in London, desire for a confident, prosperous and good-looking lover to counter her own insecurities.	Eric.

The Evolving Romantic Puzzle

What Alice loved in Eric represented a historically relative solution to the missing puzzle-piece within her. Their affair was doomed to resemble a meeting of two roads aiming in different directions, roads which had nevertheless briefly [and in many ways very pleasantly] joined up at a junction.

Alice's Path

Eric's Path

LOVE

The pain arose out of growth differentials, how two people meeting at a compatible *stage* might with time discover they were not in fact headed in the same *direction* – compatibility at one stage only a fortuitous congruence along a wider, divergent path.

What Eric could offer no longer appealed. A knowledge of London's restaurants, an elegant apartment, an established position on the social ladder, these had grown both more attainable and less necessary. Success at work meant her partner's career was a subsidiary consideration next to his ability to make her laugh or surprise her with his kindness. And though the bearded biologist had for a time alienated Alice from the cerebral mentality, Eric's psychological lightness had proved differently but as intensely wearing. She hoped for a companion for whom the mind would be neither a frightening irrelevance nor a tool with which to humiliate those intellectually less astute. Her self-respect had increased to the point where it could no longer tolerate the ritual humiliations inherent in religious love.

Age	Gap to be filled	Masculine solution
25	Need for someone who was kind without being spineless, funny without shirking gravity, was respected for his work without craving only outward signs of sucess. Someone who was intelligent without being patronizing. A saint who wouldn't shout however many attempts she needed to park her car.	

DECLARATIONS

Faced with the imminent loss of the beloved, Eric came out and said it for the first time.

They were sitting in his living-room, it was lunchtime on a Saturday, she had come to 'talk things over', the smell of coffee and death was in the air.

'I won't stay long,' said Alice, 'I've got to meet some friends at two.'

'Do you want some lunch?'

'Look, there's no point dragging this out. Eric, it's over.'

Because she no longer cared for an answer, because she wasn't presenting an argument but a conclusion, her voice was full of a confidence she had never imagined possible.

'It was always me putting more effort into this than you. I'm not trying to make you feel guilty. I just hope you realize what's happening wasn't inevitable, but you made it so. The hours I spent trying to figure you out, what made you tick, what you thought of me, what you thought of us. It makes me boil with rage, and also want to cry. It was all such a bloody waste. But I've done all the crying for now. I want to put it behind me. I'd like to say we should stay friends – I just remember you saying you never stayed in touch with old girlfriends, you thought it was a waste of time. That hurt too, I don't know why, but it stuck in my mind as being needlessly cruel. Anyway, I've said enough, I'd better be going. I've put the key on the table, and there's a box in the hall with some of your stuff.'

Then it came out, a bubble which floated lightly into the middle of the room, briefly and hopefully catching the rays of the afternoon sun before exploding into a few earth-bound droplets.

'But Alice, I love you.'

'Eric, don't, please. Just don't make it worse for both of us.'

'I'm not, I mean it. I really do. Why don't you give this a chance?'

'What have I been doing from the very start, Eric? Giving you a bloody chance, and you know what you've done every time? Spat each of them back in my face.'

'Why don't we just talk about this more calmly? We could sit down and have a bite to eat, chat in a more relaxed framework.'

'Screw relaxed frameworks. I'm as calm as need be, and everything's been said.'

'I don't understand.'

'That's always been your problem.'

'But it doesn't have to be like this. If we just behaved like two adults, we could sort the matter out, because I want to make it work – because I love you, Alice.'

So many hopes surround the word, one may with confidence take love out of its packet in the midst of almost any crisis, and count on it having a miraculous effect, a complete loss of critical faculties accompanied by salival, beatific grins.

May I ask why you're currently making my life insufferble, abusing my credit card, polluting my bathroom, wrecking my kitchen and playing pin-ball with my mind? Ah, I see. It's because you love me. Oh, well now I understand, in that case, fine, go ahead, and don't forget to burn down the house and hit the other cheek before you're done.'

Alice's mother had been an enthusiastic lover. 'But, darling, you know how much I love you,' was her chosen refrain after doing something which seemed to indicate the opposite. She loved her daughter, she told the whole world that, everyone from the washroom attendant to the President knew of this awe-inspiring, selfless and unique emotion. If she took her daughter away from school for the sake of a new destination with another husband, if she did everything to break up her few true relationships, if she undermined her confidence and self-respect, then what could these possibly have been but complex though deeply genuine acts of love?

And now here was Eric saying he loved her. She would have skipped with joy at hearing such a thing even a month before, but he could now have found no greater cynic to whom to deliver such a line, the cynic defined as *the one who has hoped too much and waited too long*. Was his declaration not simply the reflex reaction of a man realizing he would be spending the night alone and would have no one on whom to pile his bad moods?

Alice's decision may have been final, but it was still confusingly painful. Tears ran down her cheeks as she hurried down the stairs, and when she reached the car at the end of the road, she broke into unrestrained sobbing. She drove home [there was no meeting with friends] and there collapsed exhausted into bed. She felt a searing loss, the memories of times with Eric paraded themselves agonizingly through her mind – everything triggered an association and an accompanying throb of pain.

And yet she could no longer believe it was really Eric

she was missing. She felt a loss while recognizing the object of love hadn't warranted it. Love had been generated by an idea of Eric which the man had never lived up to. She was in the paradoxical position of feeling nostalgia for a situation which had not in fact happened outside the bounds of wishful anticipation. She missed someone [the tears were enough to prove it], but when she trawled back through memory, she could no longer honestly ascribe her loss to Eric.

It was strange to think that the person responsible for eliciting an emotion might be unable to live up to it. Had Eric not simply been a catalyst for a desire to love which had preceded and would succeed him? Her love had taken place *with* him, but had it for that matter been *about* him? Were her feelings for him not simply promises which had never borne fruit? Eric had been too poor to answer the emotions he had incited, he had remained insufficient to the longings provoked, unable to assuage or appease her desires. He had been like a stupid person who says something very intelligent without knowing what it means, and therefore cannot be held responsible for the worth another locates therein.

The situation was akin to the optical illusion, where a triangle appears only as a result of shapes surrounding it, a mirage determined by objects extraneous to it – as Eric had been a lover's mirage projected by the hopes marshalled around him.

It was a reminder of the subtle but vital distinction between what a person allows another to think belongs to them and what actually does so – a distinction between the need they might embody and who they in fact turn out to be.

'A part of me is still so attached to him,' Alice told Suzy later that afternoon, 'but I know it isn't really him I miss. It's crazy.'

'It's love,' sighed the flatmate.

INVITATIONS

Alice approached her single state like a traveller returned home from savage lands who draws pleasure from the simplest, most everyday routines. She could now stretch herself across the bed at night, see friends she had lost touch with, attack a pile of unread books and enrol in evening classes to learn Italian. She felt so peaceful, she couldn't imagine anyone wishing to exchange such a life for the emotional turbulence of a relationship.

A few weeks after the break-up, she organized a small dinner party for a group of friends from university, and stopped off at the supermarket after work to pick up some provisions. She was wheeling her trolley down the fruit and vegetable counter when she collided with a familiar face.

'Oh, my God, Philip, how are you?'

'I'm fine, how are you?'

'What are you doing here?'

'Buying a melon, I think.'

'Why do you only think?'

'I can't tell if they're ripe. The colour looks a bit funny.'

'No, it doesn't, these are fine.'

'Are they? Don't they seem a bit pale?'

'No, they're great, just smell, you'll see.'

'I'll trust you, I'll take it,' smiled Philip. 'Anyway, it's good to see you. It's been a long time. How are things with you?'

'Oh, fine, fine. And with you?'

'Great, you know, a bit of this, a bit of that.'

They chatted aimlessly awhile [though not so aimlessly that Alice neglected to mention the end of her relationship with Eric], then parted company at the junction of the bread and cheese counters.

Philip's lack of visible rancour in the light of the embarrassing conclusion to their last evening acted as a guilty reminder of Alice's own behaviour. Things had gotten out of hand without her being able to redeem them. But nor was meeting months later in a supermarket conducive to the sort of reconciliation the situation might have required. Walking back home with her shopping, she contemplated once again the sad but irrevocable loss of a good and kind friend.

The last thing she expected was to receive a postcard from Philip a few days later, a picture of a melon on the outside, an invitation for dinner on the reverse – nor the extent to which this prospect might simultaneously delight and terrify her.

MARTYRDOM

Philip arrived at the restaurant shortly before the appointed time. He was seated at a table attractively positioned in the centre of a small Italian trattoria off Gower Street, rapidly filling up with couples dining out on a Friday evening.

The waiter [full of heterosexual presumption] at once asked if he cared for a drink *before madam arrives*, and though he might have wished for a sip or two of water, he declined the offer and merely asked to study the wine list.

Ten minutes after he'd agreed to meet Alice, he took the first glance at his watch, reflected that traffic must have been heavy and recalled that some lines on the Underground had been having signalling problems.

The same two thoughts crossed his mind ten minutes later, when Alice still hadn't arrived, and the waiters were circling somewhat more vulturously, now suggesting he might want to take a look at the full menu before madam arrived.

A further ten minutes later, explanations were harder to find: even the heaviest traffic jam or most faulty Tube would have allowed her to reach the restaurant by now. Excuses therefore grew more creative: perhaps there had been a misunderstanding over the dates. Had she thought it was next Friday, not this one? Were there one or two branches of this restaurant? Had he correctly specified dinner not lunch? London not Rome?

But such questions lay in the realm of the philosophically

unanswerable, and after chewing them over for some minutes, Philip concluded [with all the heroism entailed] that all being fair in love and war, he had been nothing less than stood up.

The waiters, who had counted on the proceeds of a hungry bill for two, looked understandably shaken by events whose import they too were now beginning to grasp. And yet despite rejection by the object of his desire, Philip's stomach stoically continued to display appetitive signs. Therefore, though he was pitifully alone at a large table with only crisp bread rolls and now a sweating pat of butter for company, and though the eyes of other couples occasionally drifted towards him to alleviate their despair with the thought, 'At least we're not like him,' Philip decided that rather than make an escape through the bathroom window, he would stay and order a meal for one.

His bravery must have earned him the admiration of the staff, for the head waiter came over to his table shortly after the arrival of the first course and struck up a conversation which lasted intermittently until the bill and centred on the tortured affairs of the heart – the man having recently endured romantic torture at the hands of a young woman in charge of relieving customers of their coats and who it seemed had wanted to relieve the head waiter of nothing whatsoever.

Only when he reached home did Philip begin to feel some of the anger that was his due.

'What a bitch,' he muttered to himself, reflecting on his fate in the restaurant, but his anger was checked when he realized there was someone waiting for him at his door.

'Listen, Philip, I'm so sorry, I really am. Were you waiting for me?'

'No, no, I always dress up like this and go out to restaurants for dinner alone.'

'I apologize, I tried to make it, but . . .'

'The Tube got held up?'

'No.'

'You thought it was the Trattoria Verde in Milan?'

'No, I didn't. I tried to leave a message.'

'I know, it's hard leaving messages, isn't it?'

'I was just really busy.'

'Of course.'

'There was another sales meeting today, so . . .'

'Are you going to cut the crap?'

'What crap? All right, I'm sorry, I wanted to come, but at the same time . . .'

Philip didn't rush in to fill the silence.

'Say something, Philip. You're angry with me. Don't just stand there, shout at me, scream at me, but do something . . .'

'I'm not going to shout at you, I just want to ask when you're going to start being honest with me.'

'About what?'

'About everything, about why you behave the way you do. What's the game, Alice?'

'There's no game, I hate playing games.'

'Sorry, I forgot. For someone who doesn't like playing games, I must say you're doing pretty well.'

'I'm sorry. I don't know myself any more. You've every right to be furious with me.'

Philip took the key from his pocket and opened the front door.

'I've got to get some sleep.'

'Look, I hate to leave things like this. Can I just come in for five minutes?'

'Why?'

'Please.'

'Why?'

'Philip, please.'

'All right, but five minutes, OK.'

In silence, they climbed the narrow stairs into the living-room.

'I'm going to make some tea. Do you want any?' he asked severely.

'No, thanks.'

She came to stand at the entrance to the kitchen, and while the water boiled, they both stared silently at the steam rising off the kettle.

It had always been a central feature of Alice's self-conception to believe she was an emotionally generous person ready to risk everything for a man she loved. While others refused commitment in the name of mature self-protection, she conceived of love as an arena for sacrifice.

It was therefore remarkable the extent to which she had limited her attachments to men wholly unsuited or unwilling to participate in genuine dialogue. She might have longed to surrender herself to another, yet her choice of partners had studiously avoided the possibility. She had protested at their emotional blindness, she had wept in front of friends and privately despaired at the enduring cruelty she encountered, but had continued to display a stubborn refusal to locate more suitable candidates. Friends had begun to suspect an underlying attachment to these objects of complaint, an attachment which mocked any attempt to suggest alternatives.

Though irritants, these unresponsive characters seemed

necessary impediments to the realization of oft-expressed but problematic desires. They embodied a classic form of compromise, allowing her to express love without encountering the risk of acceptance; they subtly spared her the joys, but more importantly, the anxieties of being understood.

Though her emotional martyrdom had in certain circles elicited much sympathy, Alice's plight might have been capable of sustaining a different and far more sceptical reading. After all, was it really so selfless to love without ever receiving anything in return? How generous was it to offer gifts to people one knew would never accept them?

Hadn't Alice been ready to give Eric everything? Hadn't she daily protested she couldn't do enough, that whatever she gave, he spurned? But had she not chosen him precisely because he allowed her the satisfaction of thinking herself someone who could give *without needing to actually do so*?

All of which made Philip a problem, for he was prone to a form of emotional honesty which had long alerted Alice to the very different tenor a relationship with him would assume. There could be no hint of the religious structure, this was a man willing to give as much as to receive, a pleasant prospect perhaps, but only for someone for whom a powerless exchange of affect presented no practical [as opposed to conceptual] difficulties.

'I really blew it,' mumbled Alice.

'What did you say?'

'Nothing.'

'You said something.'

'I didn't.'

'Yes, you did.'

'It wasn't important.'

'What was it?'

'Just that, well, you know, I blew it.'

There was another pause before Philip added [his words swallowed up by the climax of the kettle], 'We're both idiots.'

'What?'

'I said we're both idiots.'

'I'm the only idiot around here.'

The two self-deprecating idiots smiled briefly at each other.

'I'd made a resolution never to speak to you again, but I think I've already broken it,' said Philip.

'Why?'

'Do you want me to stop?'

'No, of course not. It's just I've been such a bitch to you from the start. That time in your flat, and now and everything. And the worse thing is I don't even know why.'

'So you can make absolutely sure I've no reason for liking you?'

'Maybe.'

'The strange thing is, your efforts don't really work. I can't even be angry at you. I'd planned it all very differently, and here I am talking to you like nothing happened.'

Alice had too much the face of an angel for Philip to sustain a successful sulk for long, and though aware of the potential benefits of behaving nastily, gambled on honesty. If he desired Alice, it was for the sake of communication – it rather defeated the object to have to pretend he didn't care for her.

'You know the one about the sadist and the masochist?' he asked.

'Tell me again.'

'The masochist says to the sadist, "Hit me." And the sadist answers, "No." Well I'm going to say no.'

'Ouch.'

They smiled.

'I'm wondering what you see in me,' she said.

'That you ask that kind of question.'

'Come off it.'

Alice wrapped her hand in the end of her pullover, and moved it to cover her mouth. Philip watched her for an instant, then reached up to take her arm, took out her hand and uncurled her fingers. He entered his fingers in the fold of her sleeve, and caressed her wrist, tracing the path of her veins.

She lifted up her face, looked at him, wryly, ashamedly, warmly.

'I'm just a silly neurotic idiot. You must think I'm so strange.'

Philip combed a strand of her hair back from her face.

'I don't,' he answered.

'Go on, of course you do.'

'All right, maybe I do, but it's only normal to be strange, and so much more interesting.'

'Can I kiss you?' she asked.

'Only if you'll let me do it back to you afterwards.'